A FATE OF NIGHT AND NETTLE

A BLOOD AND BLOOM NOVEL

SANTANA SAUNDERS

For the readers who embraced every imperfect soul in this story.
The ones who know that broken things can still be beautiful.

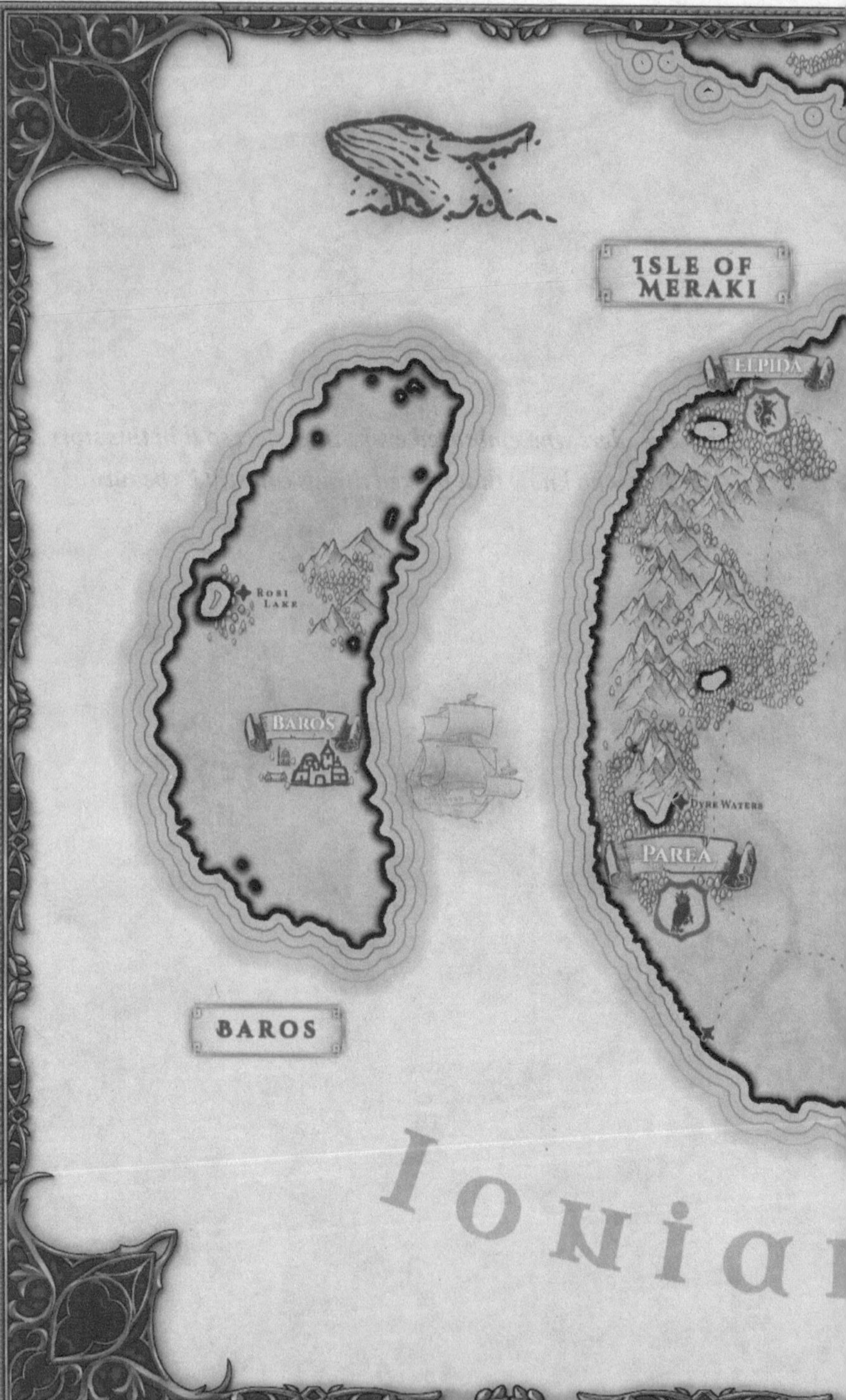

ISLE OF MERAKI
ELPIDA
ROSI LAKE
BAROS
BAROS
PAREA
DYRE WATERS
IONIA

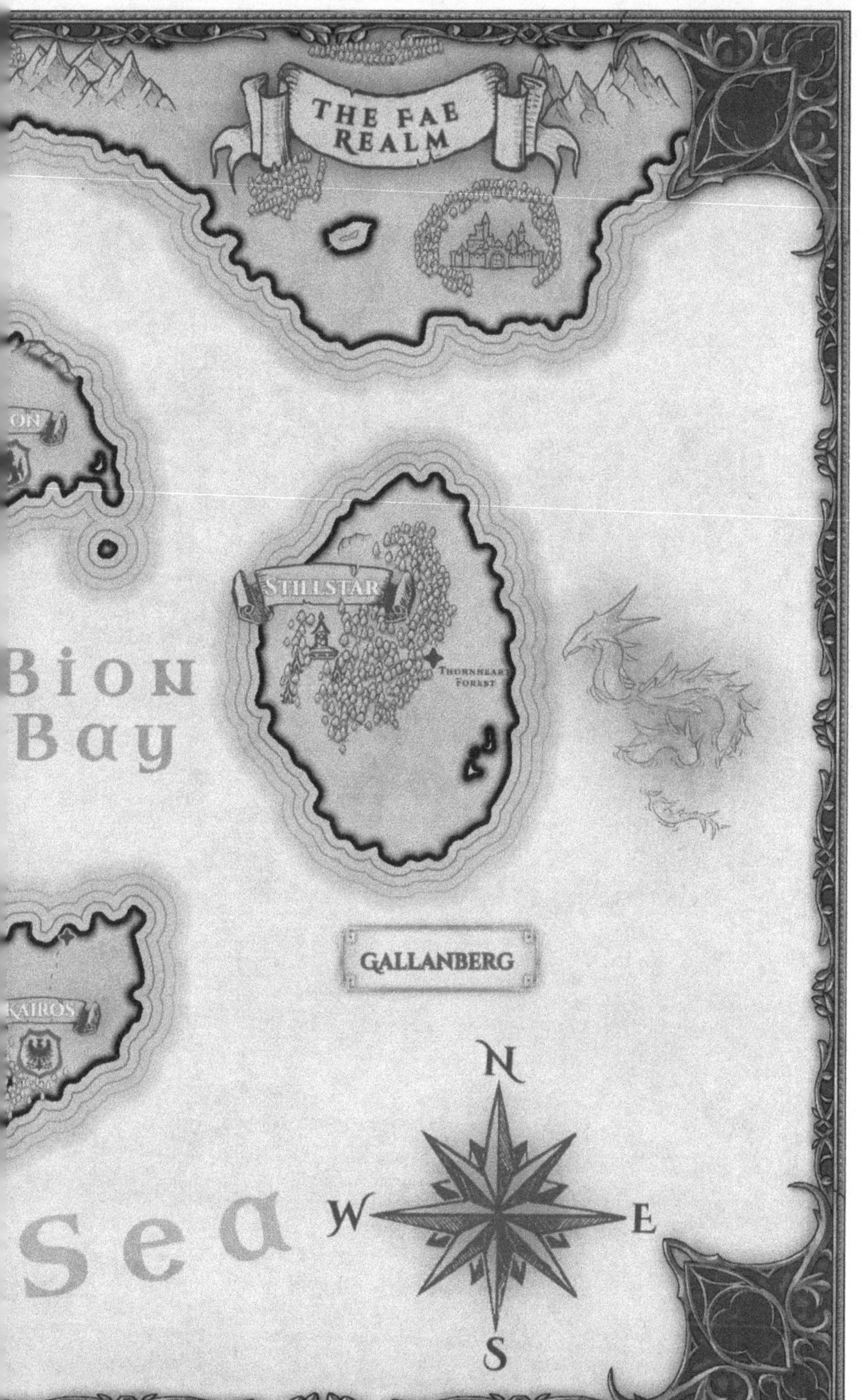

THE FAE REALM
Bion Bay
STILLSTAR
THORNHEART FOREST
GALLANBERG
KAIROS
sea
N
W
E
S

A shimmer in the path
brushes past me
a fae whisper saying,
"You've walked this moment before."
The world tilts,
time folds like wings,
and for a breath
I stand in two stories at once.

- Annonymous Fae

1

EVANTHE

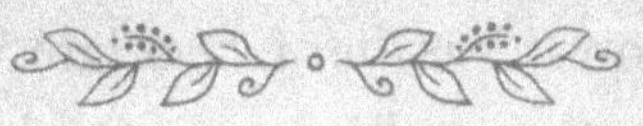

The ground beneath me is soft, but it doesn't feel safe. Moss cushions my boots, and the trees overhead sway gently in a wind that carries no warmth. The Fae Realm hums with memory, its magic ancient. The air is thick with familiarity, but something is wrong. The scent is off. Beneath the wildflowers and damp bark, there's a hint of rot. A sourness that clings to the back of my throat.

We've landed just outside the village where Liri agreed to meet us. The trees seem to lean away from the rift behind us, as if afraid of what might still come through.

I stagger forward, my body still reeling from the rift's pull. I place a hand upon a tree to brace myself. My head spins after traveling from the Human Realm to this one so quickly. It hasn't been long. Only days since I reclaimed the throne from Athena back in Meraki. But that moment feels distant now. Like it happened in another life. One where the ground didn't tremble beneath my feet and the sky didn't whisper warnings.

Aero is beside me, his hand hovering near mine, not touching but close enough to catch me if I fall. Feliks and Hera emerge from the shimmer behind us, their expressions tight. Nuala follows, her magic already pulsing faintly, sensing the wrongness in the air.

Liri rushes toward us, her face bright with relief. "You made it," she breathes, pulling me into a hug. "We weren't sure the rift would hold."

I nod, but my voice doesn't come. My chest is tight. My thoughts are tangled.

Nuala joins us, her eyes scanning the clearing, her fingers flickering with unease. "It's good to see you, Liri," she says. "But we need to move quickly. The Mortia—"

"What is this place?" I interrupt, my voice hoarse.

Liri turns to me, her expression softening. "This village, Holbek…We used to come here as children. Before the war. It was safe then. Sacred."

I glance around. The cottages are still standing, their roofs covered in moss, their windows shuttered. But the silence is too deep. The shadows too long.

"It doesn't feel sacred," I whisper.

"No," Liri agrees. "Not anymore."

I take a step back, my gaze drawn to the rift still pulsing behind us. It should've closed by now. It always does. But this one lingers, wide and shimmering, its edges fraying like torn silk.

Nuala frowns, lifting her hands. Her rifting magic

glows blue, appearing steady and strong. She closes her eyes, focusing with all her might.

Nothing.

The rift doesn't budge.

Feliks tries next, slashing at it with his sword. Then Hera. Each of us steps forward, willing it to close.

Still nothing.

I feel the bloom in my hand begin to pulse. Its petals shimmer faintly, the magic within it stirring like a heartbeat. I glance at Aero. He's watching me, his jaw tight, his eyes already knowing what I'm about to do.

"Eva," he says, stepping forward. "Don't."

But I'm already moving. I clutch the bloom tighter, its warmth grounding me. With my free hand, I reach toward the rift. The air around it is cold, sharp, like the edge of a blade. Aero grabs my wrist, but I shake him off.

"I have to see," I say.

He doesn't argue. He just watches, helpless. My fingers breach the shimmer. And the world shifts. Suddenly, I'm not in the Fae Realm. I'm in Meraki again, but it's not the Meraki I know. It's burning. The sky is black with smoke. The towers have crumbled. The streets are slick with blood. And there, at the center of it all, is Aero.

His body lies broken on the steps of the High Tower, his eyes closed, his chest still. I scream, but no sound comes. I run to him, but my feet don't move. Then a voice.

Low. Ancient.

"You were never the savior," it says. "You were the seed."

The vision shatters. I yank my hand back, gasping. The bloom trembles violently in my grip, and then—

Crack.

A single petal breaks clean off. I stare at it, horrified. The bloom has never broken. Not once. Not in all this time that I've carried it through this treachery. Its magic has been sacred. Untouchable.

Until now.

Aero is beside me in an instant, his hands on my shoulders, his eyes scanning every inch of me. "Are you hurt?" he asks, his voice sharp with panic.

I shake my head, but the fear is already coursing through me, my heart pounding in my chest. The bloom is cracked. This darkness...it's deeper than the Omen. More ancient. More personal. It knows me. It sees me. And it's coming.

I clutch the broken bloom to my chest, my breath shallow.

"We need to move," I whisper. "We need to find the Mortia. We need to end this."

Aero nods, but his eyes linger on the rift. On the shimmer that still refuses to close. And I know, deep down, that whatever came through with us...didn't stop at the border.

It followed.

It waits.

And it remembers.

The village is smaller than I expected. Stone cottages huddle beneath the canopy of ancient trees, their moss-covered roofs sloping like bowed heads. The air is thick with the scent of damp earth and something else, something sour. A rot that clings to the wind, subtle but persistent.

We take refuge in the old meeting hall, a circular structure built from woven branches and stone. The hearth is cold, but Liri lights it with a flick of her hand, the flames blooming from the wood like flowers. Diaspor stands beside me. He doesn't speak much, but his presence is grounding. He's always been that way, my mentor. When the earth tilts, he holds the line.

Liri stands near the hearth, her arms crossed, her brow furrowed. "It's worse than we thought," she says. "The Mortia...they've grown stronger. Faster than anyone expected."

"How?" Feliks asks, his voice low. "We've only been gone a few days."

"They're multiplying," Liri replies. "Feeding off the realm's instability. Off the fear. It's like they've tapped into something deeper."

Bel, the water Fae, leans against the wall, his fingers trailing through a bowl of rainwater. "They always were parasites. But this...this feels orchestrated."

Phira drops from the rafters with a flutter of wings, landing beside Hera with a smirk. "So what's the plan, fearless leader?" she says, running her fingers through her windswept hair. "We storm King Murrick's fortress? The whole lot of us?"

"We need help," Diaspor says. "An army."

"Or a spy," Nuala offers. "Someone who can get in, see what we're dealing with."

"You'd be the only one who could rift us close without detection," I say, turning to her. "But it's dangerous."

Nuala nods. "I know. But if we go in blind, we'll lose more than time."

The conversation swells around me. It's all a blur of strategies, risks, names of old allies who might still answer our call. But I'm not really listening.

The bloom trembles in my hand.

I stare at it, the single cracked petal catching the firelight like a wound. It hasn't pulsed since the vision, since the voice and the image of Aero's broken body lying in the ruins of Meraki. But now, it stirs again. Quiet. Uneasy.

I clutch it tighter, trying to focus, but the fear creeps in like smoke.

Aero moves beside me, his hand brushing mine. Through the bond, I feel his concern. His instinct to protect, to soothe. He doesn't speak, just reaches for the bloom. It takes me off guard, but I let his fingers graze its surface. And everything changes.

His body jolts, eyes wide, breath caught. I see something alarming ripple through him. And then he pulls back, fast, like he's touched fire.

I freeze.

"Aero?" I whisper.

He doesn't answer right away. His eyes flick to the bloom then to me. There's something in them I don't recognize.

Fear. I feel it through our bond. But is it fear of me? Or fear of what's coming?

"I'm fine," he says too quickly. "Just...startled."

I reach for him, but he steps back. Just a little. Just enough. The space between us feels colder than the wind outside.

"You saw it," I say. "Didn't you?"

He nods. "Meraki. Burning. You...standing over me.

2

EVANTHE

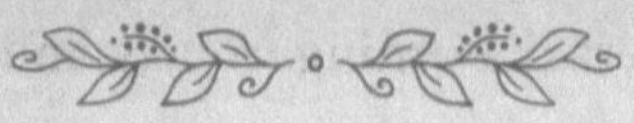

I sit alone beneath the twisted elder tree at the edge of the village, the bloom cradled in my palms like a wounded bird. Its light is faint now, barely a shimmer. The crack along its petal remains, jagged and unforgiving. I've tried everything to soothe it: whispered to it, fed it warmth from my core, even pressed it to the soil in hopes the earth would lend it strength.

But it won't respond. It's quiet. So quiet.

I close my eyes, reaching inward, searching for the pulse of my magic. It's there...but dulled. Like a song muffled by distance. I used to feel the earth's heartbeat beneath my feet, its rhythm syncing with mine. Now, it's like I'm standing on foreign land. Like the soil doesn't recognize me. A chill runs through me. Then something shifts.

The ground beneath my hand stirs. A root, thin and pale, emerges from the moss, curling upward like a curious finger. At first, I think it's reaching for the bloom. But then it wraps around my wrist and tightens.

I gasp, yanking my arm back. The root resists, coiling tighter, its texture rough and cold. Panic flares in my chest. I shake my arm violently until it recoils, slithering back into the earth like a scolded serpent.

I stare at the spot, heart pounding. The earth has never turned on me. Not like this.

Footsteps crunch behind me. I turn sharply, the bloom still clutched in my hand. Princess Liri stands a few paces away, her eyes fixed on the retreating root. Her expression is unreadable, but her posture is tense.

"How long have you been standing there?" I ask, voice low.

She doesn't blink. "Long enough, it seems."

There's no point in pretending. No use in hiding what just happened.

"I don't know what's happening," I say, my voice cracking. "My magic has dulled, the bloom is quiet...and now it seems the earth itself has turned against me."

Liri walks closer, her boots silent against the moss. She kneels beside me, her gaze falling to the bloom. "You're not the only one noticing a change."

I look at her, startled. "You too?"

She nods. "The blaze in my veins...it's dimmed. I used to feel it like fire under my skin. Now it's barely a flicker. Something is suppressing it."

I swallow hard, guilt rising like bile. "Do you think it's me?"

Liri doesn't answer right away. She studies the bloom, the cracked petal, the way it trembles faintly in my grip.

"I don't know," she says finally. "Maybe there were signs before you all returned. It's possible, but no one noticed their magic weakening until now."

I want to believe her. I want to believe this started before we came back. That whatever is happening isn't my fault. But the bloom broke in my hand. The vision came to me. The root tried to bind me.

And Aero saw it too.

"Whatever it is," Liri says softly, "we seem to carry a poison."

Her words hang in the air like smoke.

"And now the land knows it too."

I clutch the bloom tighter, as if I can protect it from the truth. But the truth is already here. In the soil. In the silence. In the way the magic recoils from us.

We are not just returning to the Fae Realm. We are changing it.

And not for the better.

The soil is cool beneath my fingers, damp with last night's mist. I press my palm into it, feeling for the pulse of life beneath the surface. It's faint, but it's there, steady and stubborn. The garden clings to its rhythm even as the rest of the realm falters.

Diaspor works beside me in silence, his hands moving with practiced ease as he prunes away the brittle stalks of last season's bloomroot. He hums under his breath, a low, earthy tune that seems to coax the plants into listening. But I know well enough that this is a simple task. One that takes little to no magic. Hera kneels a few rows down, gently brushing dirt away from the base of a struggling vine. She's not here to work—not really. Her body tires easily these days, though she hasn't said why. But her presence is enough. It always is.

We tend the garden in the early light, before the village fully wakes. The air is still, the sky a pale wash of lavender and gray. The scent of rosemary and damp moss lingers, but beneath it—always beneath it—is that faint, sour rot. The reminder that something is wrong. That something is spreading.

I try not to think about the bloom in my satchel. About the crack that runs through its petal like a fault line. About the way the earth recoiled from me yesterday. I try not to think about Aero's face when he saw the vision. The way he pulled back. The dreadful feeling in my stomach.

Instead, I focus on the garden. On what still grows.

Diaspor hands me a bundle of wilted leaves. "These won't make it," he says, voice low and gravelly. "But the roots are strong. They'll try again."

I nod, tucking the bundle into the compost basket. "They always do."

He glances at me, his eyes dark and knowing. "So must we."

I don't answer. I just return to the soil, fingers brushing over the base of a young fennel stalk. It leans toward me, weak but willing. I breathe into it, offering what little magic I can still summon. A flicker of life pulses through the stem. Not much. But enough.

The townsfae pass by in small groups, their eyes downcast, their steps hurried. They used to stop. Used to bow. Used to whisper blessings and call me their Guardian. Now, they barely meet my gaze. When they do, it's not reverence I see. It's more of a pleading. They're afraid.

Their magic is fading, and they don't know why—or maybe they do. Maybe they've begun to suspect what Liri said aloud...that we brought something back with us. That we carry a poison. That the land knows it.

I can't bear to look at them too long.

I glance over at Hera, who's sitting back on her heels now, wiping her hands on her skirt. Her cheeks are flushed, her hair damp with sweat. She catches me watching and raises an eyebrow.

"What?" she says.

I shake my head. "Nothing. Just...wondering."

"About?"

I hesitate. Then I ask, "Do you regret it? Getting wrapped up in all this?"

She blinks. "All this?"

"The Bloom. The Mortia. The rifts. The ancient vampyr horde. You could've stayed in Meraki, found a quiet place to wait it out."

She snorts. "In a city crawling with bloodthirsty corpses? Sounds like a dream."

I smile, but it doesn't quite reach my eyes. "I mean it, Hera. You had a choice."

She stands slowly, brushing off her knees. "So did Feliks. And he wasn't going to hang back. You know him; he'd follow you and Aero into the void if you asked."

"I didn't ask."

"No," she says, walking over to me. "But he didn't need you to. And I wasn't about to let some flirty shefae swoop in and steal him while he was off playing hero without me."

I laugh, startled. "Is that what this is about?"

She grins. "Partly. I've seen the way they look at him. All that charm. Please. I had to stake my claim."

I shake my head, the tension in my chest easing just a little. "You're ridiculous."

"I'm right," she says, nudging me with her elbow. "And you're not alone in this, Evanthe. You never were."

I look down at the soil, at the tiny green shoots pushing their way toward the light. They don't know what's coming. They just grow. Because that's what they were made to do.

Maybe that's what we're doing too. Trying to grow.

Even when the earth forgets our names.

3
EVANTHE

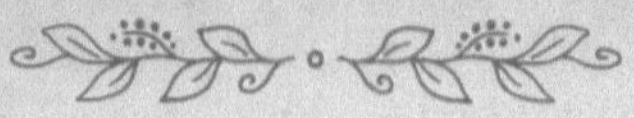

The decision to move comes quickly. Liri stands at the edge of the village, her arms crossed, her gaze fixed on the horizon. "We need to go," she says. "There's a sacred glade not far from here. The land there is older than the kingdoms. If anything can help us reset, it's that place. We will honor it with a rite."

No one argues. Not even Diaspor. The village is too close to the rot now. Too close to the fear.

Nuala steps forward, her jaw set. "I'll rift us there."

She lifts her hands, magic crackling faintly at her fingertips. But the shimmer doesn't come. No ripple. No pull. Just silence.

She tries again. And again.

Nothing.

Her breath catches. Her hands tremble. "I can't," she whispers. "I can't even rift myself."

Then the fury comes.

She turns on me, eyes blazing. "This is your fault."

I flinch, but I don't move.

"If we hadn't gone to the human realm," she spits, "if you hadn't dragged us through this, we wouldn't be standing here with our magic bleeding out of us."

"Nuala—" Liri starts.

"No," she snaps. "She broke the bloom. She broke the balance. And now the land is rejecting us."

Her words cut deeper than I expect. Because part of me wonders if she's right.

Feliks points to his brother. "Not Aero. It's not rejecting him. He still has his power."

Nuala narrows her eyes at him. "Only because he isn't Fae. His power isn't of this realm. The land barely recognizes him," she spits, her voice full of venom.

Liri steps between us, her voice firm. "You're too angry right now. Hang back. Cool off."

Nuala's eye twitches, and she stomps her foot. "But—"

"No. Not another word, Nuala," Liri puts her in her place.

The rifter nods. Barely. Then turns away.

We travel on foot. The path to the glade winds through twisted trees and silent hollows. The deeper we go, the stranger the land becomes. Birds avoid the branches overhead. The shadows bend in unnatural ways, stretching too long, curling like fingers. The air grows colder, heavier.

Hera pauses mid-step, her hand resting on her hilt. "Something's moving beneath the soil," she says softly.

Diaspor nods. "The land remembers. But it doesn't trust us."

I look to him for guidance. "What should we do?"

"We keep moving. We're almost there."

When we reach the glade, it's nothing like I imagined. The trees here are massive, their trunks gnarled and blackened, their leaves silver and trembling. The ground is soft but not welcoming. It feels like stepping into a memory that doesn't want to be remembered.

Diaspor kneels at the center, placing his palm flat against the earth. "This place is sacred," he says. "But it demands truth."

"What do you mean?" I ask.

"Any guards we've had up must come down. We greet the land with full transparency," he replies.

I step forward, but Aero reaches for me, his worry reaching out through our bond. "It's okay," I assure him. I carry the bloom in my hands. Its cracked petal glints in the fading light, a wound that won't heal. Diaspor pats the ground beside him, urging me to come. I kneel beside him, pressing the bloom into the soil.

It doesn't resist. But it doesn't welcome me either.

Diaspor begins the rite, his voice low and steady, speaking in the old tongue. The others form a loose circle around us, silent, watching. I feel the weight of their eyes. Of their hope. Of their doubt.

I take the blade from Diaspor's hand. It's small but sharp enough. I press it to my palm and draw a line.

The blood wells quickly, warm and red, and I let it drip onto the earth. The soil drinks it in, dark and quiet. Then I speak my truth.

"I'm afraid," I say, my voice barely above a whisper. "I'm afraid that I'm not strong enough to defeat the

Mortia. That fate was a fool for leaving the realms in my hands."

The wind stirs, sending a shiver down my spine.

"I don't want to win this war to wear a crown," I continue. "I want to save what's left of us."

The bloom pulses once then goes still. I lie beside it, my cheek pressed to the soil, the blood still dripping from my hand. The earth is cold. But it doesn't push me away.

I stay there through the night. Aero by my side.

Listening.

Waiting.

Hoping the land will remember me. Not as a queen... but as someone who tried.

The morning light is thin and gray, filtering through the canopy like a half-formed thought. I wake slowly, my cheek pressed to the cold soil, the bloom nestled beside me where I left it. For a moment, I don't move. I just breathe. The air is still, but not peaceful. It feels like the forest is holding its breath right along with us.

I sit up, brushing dirt from my palms, and reach for the bloom.

It looks no different.

The crack along its petal remains, sharp and unforgiving. Its glow is faint, barely more than a memory. I turn it over in my hands, searching for something, anything, that might tell me the rite worked. A pulse. A shimmer. A whisper.

Nothing.

The others begin to stir around me. Diaspor first, rising with the quiet grace of someone who's lived through too many dawns. Then Hera, rubbing sleep from her eyes. Feliks stretches beside her, his gaze already scanning the glade for signs of danger. Liri and Bel move closer, crouching around me with cautious hope.

They're all waiting. Watching.

I'm not sure what they expect to see. I'm not sure what I expected either. A miracle, maybe. A sign. Something to prove that the earth still knows me. That the bloom still trusts me.

But there's nothing.

Just silence.

Just the cracked bloom in my hands.

I lower my gaze, the weight of their anticipation pressing against my chest. "I don't know," I say quietly. "I don't know if it worked."

Diaspor doesn't speak. He just nods once and steps back, giving me space. The others follow, one by one, retreating with quiet disappointment. Not blame. But something close lingers in the air. All except Aero. He stays.

He kneels beside me, his movements slow, deliberate. His hand reaches out, brushing a strand of hair from my face then cradling my cheek with a tenderness that makes my throat tighten.

"You know as well as any," he says softly, "that not all things can be seen. It's possible the rite worked. Give it time to show."

I nod, but the sadness in my chest deepens. He means well. He always does. But I know what losing feels like. I know the shape of it. And this is starting to feel like that.

This isn't a war we can afford to lose. I look down at the bloom again, willing it to change, to speak, to shine. Then I feel it.

A tremor beneath my boots.

Aero stiffens beside me.

Small, blackened sprouts begin to push through the soil, curling upward like fingers. Their stems are thin, brittle, their leaves sharp and dark. They grow fast, too fast, surrounding us in a ring of rot.

I gasp, stumbling to my feet. "No—no, no, no."

I stomp on the nearest one, crushing it beneath my heel. Another appears. Then another. I move quickly, stomping each one into the dirt, my breath coming in short, panicked bursts.

The others rush forward, weapons half-drawn, magic flaring weakly at their fingertips.

Aero grabs my arm. "Is this the Mortia? How is this possible?"

"It has to be," I say, my voice shaking. "It has to be."

Then the sprouts stop. The soil stills, but the dread doesn't leave. It rises in my chest like smoke, thick and choking. And then I hear it.

The voice.

Low. Cold. Familiar.

But it's clear no one else hears it. Only me.

"He'll leave you," it whispers. "They all will."

I freeze.

The bloom pulses once in my hand. I clutch it tighter, as if I can silence the voice by force. But it's already inside me, already echoing through my bones.

Aero is still watching me, concern etched into every line of his face. He doesn't know. He can't know, but surely he feels it.

I turn away, hiding the bloom against my chest.

The sprouts are gone, I tell myself. *But the rot remains.*

4
AERO

The glade might be still, but it's definitely not silent. The wind moves through the trees like a whistle, brushing against my skin with a chill that feels older than the forest itself. The sprouts are gone, blackened and crushed beneath Evanthe's boots, but the memory of them lingers. I can feel it in the dingy dew. In the way the birds refuse to sing. In the way the shadows stretch too long.

We're not safe here.

And we're not strong enough to pretend otherwise.

Diaspor stands at the edge of the clearing, his arms folded, his gaze fixed on the horizon. He's been quiet since the grounding rite, watching the land with the kind of patience only an earth Fae can possess. But even he looks uneasy now.

"We need help," he says finally, his voice low but firm. "We can't face the Mortia alone. Not like this."

Feliks nods, his hand resting on the hilt of his blade. "Where do we go?"

Diaspor turns to us. "There's a village not far from here. Virelay. It's old, tucked into the roots of the eastern hills. The council there still holds sway. If anyone knows what's happening to the land, it's them."

Liri steps forward, brushing a leaf from her shoulder. "If we can't find answers there, we might have to visit Elder Thorne."

The name hangs heavy in the air like smoke, but I'm not sure why.

"He is an elder," she continues. "All elders are respected here, but he might be less so than others. His methods are a bit more...unconventional than most."

Evanthe nods, her expression unreadable. "Unconventional might be what we need."

I watch her as she speaks, the way she holds herself despite the weight pressing down on her. The bloom is cracked. The land is turning. The voice, whatever it is, has begun to whisper to her in ways I can't seem to reach. And still, she stands. Still, she leads.

I don't know how she does it.

The others begin to prepare, gathering what little supplies we have, checking weapons, whispering well wishes that barely spark. I stay beside Eva, watching the way her fingers twitch against the satchel, the way her eyes flick toward the soil as if expecting it to betray her again.

She's afraid. I feel it through the bond. And I'm afraid too.

The vision we shared of Meraki in ruins, her standing over me as I burned inside it all...it couldn't be real. It had to be the Mortia, trying to frighten us, trying to fracture us. But it felt real. Too real. A darkness like that doesn't need truth to wound. It only needs the slightest bit of doubt. And the doubt is growing.

I think of her family back in Meraki. Her aunts. The people who still fight beneath the High Tower, clinging to hope as the vampyr continue their assault. We have no way to contact them now that we've crossed into the Fae Realm. I haven't brought it up. Not yet. But I know, beneath her strong front, it burdens her. I'm the only one she can't hide her fears from. No matter how badly she might want to.

And then there's Baros.

I haven't spoken of it since we arrived. Haven't told Eva that I'm afraid to face the king I once thought was my father. That I'm afraid of what I'll find if we return. Famine. Despair. A people faded to skin and bones. I carry that fear quietly, tucked behind the bond, behind the smile I wear when she looks at me.

But right now, we need help, and I'm certainly not above asking for it.

I reach for her hand, curling my fingers around hers. She looks at me, her eyes tired but still burning.

"We'll find them," I say. "The ones who can help."

She nods, and together, we move out on foot.

The forest parts slowly, the path winding through roots and shadows. The others follow behind, their steps quiet, their magic dim. The air grows colder as we walk, the trees leaning in like eavesdroppers. Birds avoid the branches. The wind carries no song.

Eva walks beside me, her grip firm, her gaze forward.

I want to tell her that I believe in her. That I trust her. That no vision, no whisper, no cracked bloom could ever change that. But the words are sticky, trapped in my throat. Because I saw it too.

I saw her standing over me.

And I don't know what it means.

We reach the edge of the glade, the hills rising ahead, the path to Virelay stretching into the mist. Diaspor leads, his steps sure, his presence grounding. Liri and Bel flank him, their eyes scanning the trees. Feliks and Hera walk behind us, her hand resting on her hip, his arm always close.

We are a strange, broken group, but we are still moving. Maybe that's enough for now.

The path to Virelay isn't long, but the weight we carry makes every step feel heavier than the last. We've been walking for hours, weaving through the forest's thinning edges, the trees growing sparse and brittle. The land here is quieter than it should be. No birdsong. No rustle of small creatures. Just the wind and the occasional groan of old branches shifting overhead.

When Diaspor calls for a rest, the others settle quickly. Feliks passes out dried fruit and strips of smoked meat. Hera leans against a moss-covered stone, her hand resting on her belly, her eyes closed. Liri and Bel sit nearby, whispering about the terrain ahead. Even Diaspor, ever the sentinel, takes a moment to kneel and press his palm to the soil, listening.

But I can't sit. I can't be still. The tension in my chest is too tight, the thoughts too loud. So I train.

I move to a clearing just off the path, where the ground is flat and the trees give me space. I draw my blade and begin the forms. Slow at first, then faster. My feet slide across the earth, my arms slicing through the air with practiced precision. The rhythm helps. It always has. It's the one thing that's never lied to me.

But today, even the rhythm feels off.

I can feel the unease through the bond. Eva's magic is quiet, but her emotions aren't. They pulse beneath my skin like a second heartbeat. She's trying to stay strong. For all of us. But something dark has been awoken, and it's clawing at her from the inside.

I pivot, blade flashing, and nearly miss the sound of footsteps behind me. A hand touches my shoulder. I jump, spinning instinctively, blade half-raised. Eva stands there, her eyes wide, her hand still hovering.

"Sorry," she says quickly. "I didn't mean to startle you. You seemed to have gone somewhere else there for a moment."

I lower the blade, breathing hard. "I did."

She steps closer, her gaze searching mine. I turn away, grabbing my canteen and splashing water onto my face. The cold helps. A little.

"What worries you?" she asks.

I hesitate. Then I say it.

"It won't be long before the first wave of ships from Baros arrives in Meraki."

The words hang between us, heavy and sharp.

I regret them immediately. Not because they're untrue. But because I didn't want to add to her burden. She already carries too much. Her broken bloom, the fading magic, and, probably worst of all, the whispers in the soil. This is a problem for another day. Another war.

She doesn't speak right away. Just watches me.

I sit down on a fallen log, blade resting across my knees. "I didn't mean to drop that on you."

"You didn't drop anything," she says. "You shared it."

I nod, but the guilt doesn't ease.

"I feel helpless," I admit. "Like we're at a standstill even though we're moving. We're praised now, accepted by the Fae. But I feel it through the bond. The unease. The fear. Something dark has been plaguing you."

She sits beside me, close enough that our shoulders touch.

"The rift didn't seal cleanly," I say. "I know it. I felt it. Something came through with us. Or something stayed behind that shouldn't have."

She doesn't argue. Because she knows it too.

I glance at her, at the way her fingers curl around the edge of her cloak, at the way her eyes flick toward the horizon, like she's trying to see what's coming before it arrives.

"I saw you," I say quietly. "In the vision. Standing over me. Watching me burn."

She flinches.

"I know it wasn't real," I add quickly. "I know it was the Mortia trying to frighten us. But it felt real. And that kind of darkness...it has ways around the brightest of souls."

She turns to me, her eyes shining. "You're not afraid of me, are you?"

"No," I say. "I'm afraid of losing you."

She takes my hand, and I hold it tightly. We walk to the edge of a small stream, the water clear and cold, winding through the rocks like a silver thread. It reflects the starlight with quiet grace, each ripple catching the light and tossing it back.

We stand there, hand in hand, watching the shimmer. Neither of us speaks. Because we both know our time here is running out.

I glance at her, the way her hair catches the moonlight, the way her shoulders rise and fall with each breath. She's so strong. So impossibly strong. And yet I feel the tremor in her fingers, the weight she carries behind her eyes. The bloom is cracked. The land is turning. The whispers are growing louder.

I want her to feel something else. Something that matters when all of this is behind us.

I turn to face her fully, lifting her hand to my lips. She looks up at me, startled at first, then softened. Her eyes search mine, and I let her see everything—my fear, my devotion, my quiet desperation.

"I need you to know," I say, voice low, "that whatever

happens...whatever darkness tries to claim you...I won't leave."

She doesn't answer with words. She steps closer until I can feel her nose brush mine. And then she kisses me.

It's not gentle. There is no hesitation.

It's the kind of kiss that unravels everything. That pulls the breath from my lungs and replaces it with hers. Her hands slide into my hair, anchoring me, and I wrap my arms around her waist, drawing her in like I've been waiting my whole life to do it.

We melt into each other. Every unspoken word seeming to find its place. Our very touch being a sorcery of its own. This world that desperately tries to tear us apart falls away.

There's only the press of her lips, the heat of her skin, the way her magic hums faintly against mine through the bond. It's quiet now, but it's still there. Still alive. Still reaching.

I deepen the kiss, letting her feel how deep this truly runs. How far I'd go. How much of me belongs to her, even in the face of ruin. I want her to know that even if fate was cruel enough to mark her for darkness, I would walk into it with her. I would burn beside her before I'd ever let her stand alone.

She pulls back just enough to rest her forehead against mine, her breath mingling with mine, her eyes closed.

"I'm scared," she whispers. "How do you know that, despite the bond, you won't feel differently if your family decides to attempt overthrowing the throne of Meraki?"

"Nothing—not family, not death itself—could change how I feel about you, Eva."

We stay like that for a long moment, the stars dancing over the stream, the forest holding its breath around us. The others don't call for us. They know better. They know this moment is ours.

I press a kiss to her temple, then her cheek, then her lips again. Softer this time, slower. She sighs into me, her body relaxing, her fingers curling against my chest.

"I love you," I say.

She opens her eyes, and they shine like starlight.

"I love you too."

We stand there, wrapped in each other, watching the light ripple across the water. And even though the darkness waits, even though the rift still pulses somewhere behind us, even though the Mortia is growing stronger, for this moment, we are whole.

EVANTHE

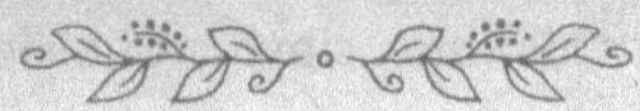

Virelay is not what I expected. The sanctuary is old, yes—its stone arches crumbled, its pathways overtaken by moss and roots—but it is not dead. The land here breathes. The trees sway with a rhythm that feels familiar, like a lullaby half-remembered. The air hums with quiet magic, and the light filtering through the canopy is soft, golden, almost reverent.

We step into the clearing slowly, taking it all in. No one speaks. Even Phira, who always has something clever to say, is silent. The weight of this place presses against our chests, not with dread but with promise.

I move ahead of the others, my boots brushing against wildflowers that bloom in defiance of the decay. I scan the edges of the sanctuary, searching for signs of blackened fauna, anything that might have been touched by the Mortia. But everything here is lush. Vibrant. Nearly as radiant as the first day we arrived in the realm.

Hope stirs in me. It's fragile, but it's there.

I kneel at the center of the sanctuary, where the old altar still stands, cracked but intact. I reach into my satchel and pull out the bloom. The crystal relic glints in the light, its cracked petal dull and lifeless. I stare down at it, willing it to respond, to tug at me with warmth or cold, as it once did. To pulse. To speak. But it doesn't. I feel nothing.

The others gather behind me, forming a quiet circle. I don't look at them. I can't. I just keep my eyes on the bloom, whispering to it in my mind, begging it to wake.

Then the ground trembles.

It's subtle, just a ripple beneath my knees, but enough to still every breath in the clearing. A vine stretches out from the soil, slow and deliberate, curling toward the bloom like a question. No one moves.

"It's green with life, so that's good, right?" Feliks asks.

"I think so," I reply, looking to Diaspor for answers.

Unsure, the commander shrugs, his eyes never leaving the plant. All our hopes hang on this little vine. I hold my breath, watching it reach, watching it shimmer faintly with green. And then—

It withers.

Black creeps along its edges, curling inward, and in seconds, it crumbles to ash. I gasp, the sound sharp and broken. The bloom remains still. I crumble with it.

My knees hit the earth, my fingers clutching the bloom as if I can protect it from the truth. Tears sting my eyes, but I don't let them fall. I just bow my head, the weight of failure pressing down like stone.

Through the bond, I know Aero feels it—every ounce

of my disappointment, every crack in my resolve. He moves toward me, slow and careful, his presence steady. I feel his hand reach for me, and then the air splits.

A shriek tears through the clearing, high and jagged, like metal scraping bone.

The creature emerges from the shadows behind the altar, its form twisted and wrong. Limbs too long, eyes too many, its skin a patchwork of bark and rot. It moves like smoke and thunder, its mouth stretching wide in a soundless scream.

The bloom pulses once in my hand. A dim pulse.

I scramble back, heart pounding, the others drawing weapons, magic flaring weakly at their fingertips.

Aero steps in front of me, blade raised in one hand, an orb of angry water hovering above the other.

The creature doesn't attack. It watches. And I realize... it's not here for all of us.

Hades, it's here for me.

The creature doesn't move. It stands half-shrouded in shadow, its limbs twitching with unnatural grace, its many eyes fixed on me. The rot clings to it like armor. Patches of bark, sinew, and something darker, something that pulses faintly with a sickly green glow. Its mouth opens, but no sound comes. Just the suggestion of a scream, like it's waiting for permission to release it.

I can't breathe.

Aero steps in front of me, his blade raised, his stance protective and sure. I feel the heat of him through the bond, the surge of adrenaline, the instinct to shield me from whatever this thing is. But I know, deep in my bones, that this creature isn't here for him.

It's here for me.

The bloom pulses again in my hand. Not with light. Not with warmth. But with something cold and ancient. It trembles against my skin, and I clutch it tighter, as if I can keep it from answering whatever call this creature has made.

Diaspor moves to Aero's side, his hands glowing faintly with earthlight. Liri and Bel flank the clearing, their magic sparking weakly, ready but uncertain. Phira hovers above, wings outstretched, her eyes narrowed.

Still, no one speaks. No one dares.

Then the creature takes a step forward.

I rise slowly, my knees shaking, the bloom still clutched in my hand. I don't know what I'm doing. I don't know what it wants. But I know I can't hide behind Aero forever.

I step beside him. The creature tilts its head, its many eyes blinking in slow succession. It raises one long, gnarled arm and points directly at the bloom. I glance down. The cracked petal glows faintly now, a dull shimmer like dying starlight.

"What does it want?" Hera whispers behind me.

"I think it's drawn to the bloom," I say, my voice barely audible.

"Then give it what it wants," Phira snaps. "Let it take the cursed thing and be done with it."

"No," Aero says sharply. "We don't know what it'll do."

The creature takes another step. The ground trembles

beneath its feet, and the vines around the sanctuary recoil, curling inward like frightened animals. The magic here, what little remains, shudders. I feel it through the bond—Aero's fear—knowing he feels mine as well, along with the weight of every choice I've made.

I step forward again, just one pace, and the creature stops. It lowers its arm. Its mouth closes. I lift the bloom. It pulses once. Then again. And then the creature shrieks.

The sound is deafening, a psychic scream that rips through the clearing and sends us all to our knees. My vision blurs. My ears ring. The bloom glows violently in my hand, the cracked petal splitting farther, a jagged line racing toward its core.

Aero grabs me, pulling me back, shielding me with his body as the creature lunges.

Diaspor slams his palms into the earth, and a wall of stone erupts between us and the creature. It crashes into it, shrieking, clawing, tearing at the barrier with unnatural fury.

"Run!" Liri shouts.

But I can't move. The bloom is burning in my hand now, the heat searing through my skin, through my veins. I feel it reaching, calling to something I don't understand. Hera locks eyes with me, recognizing the paralyzing fear behind mine.

"We have to move," she urges.

Aero lifts me, cradling me against his chest, and bolts toward the edge of the sanctuary. The others follow, magic flaring, weapons drawn, the creature shrieking behind us.

We break through the trees, the sanctuary falling away behind us, the stars overhead spinning wildly.

I clutch the bloom to my chest, tears streaming down my face.

It's awake.

But it's not the same.

And whatever it's become...it's calling out to something I don't understand.

We don't speak for a long time. The forest around us is still, save for the occasional rustle of leaves and the distant call of a bird brave enough to sing. We've put distance between ourselves and the sanctuary, but the memory of the creature's shriek still rings in my ears. My legs ache. My chest feels hollow. And the bloom, once pulsing with something dark and alive, is quiet again.

I sit on a fallen log, the bloom cradled in my hands. Its cracked petal catches the light, but there's no shimmer. No warmth. No cold. No tug.

Just silence.

"I swear it was alive again back there," I say, my voice barely above a whisper. "But it felt...different."

Bel crouches nearby, his fingers trailing through a shallow stream. He glances up, brow furrowed. "I don't love the sound of that. If it isn't guiding you again, is it safe to say it's not healed?"

I shake my head, unsure. "I don't know. It responded to something. But it wasn't like before."

The others gather around, their faces drawn, their magic dim. Feliks leans against a tree, arms crossed, his eyes scanning the woods. Hera sits beside him, quiet, her hand resting protectively over her belly. Diaspor stands with his back to us, watching the horizon.

Then Liri speaks.

"I didn't want it to come to this," she says, stepping into the center of the group. "And I don't know if he can give us answers, but we must visit Elder Thorne."

The name drops like a stone into the clearing.

Feliks straightens. "What do you mean, 'come to this'? And how far is this journey going to be?" His tone is sharp, edged with frustration. I know that sound. It's the voice of someone who's starting to feel like we're running in circles.

Bel moves to his side, arms folded. "All due respect, Princess, he raises valid questions."

Liri doesn't flinch. "Thorne is...difficult. He's been known to barter. Sometimes in ways that aren't easy to predict. I can't be certain how that will unfold."

I glance at Aero, who's been silent until now. His jaw is tight, his eyes fixed on the bloom in my hands.

"It's just north of here," Liri continues. "A quiet part of the forest. Most don't have a reason to travel through those parts. We could return for Nuala after and rest before making the journey to Murick's hold."

Aero raises his hand, his voice firm. "No. We are not returning for Nuala. She tried to attack Eva."

The words hang in the air, sharp and final.

Liri meets his gaze. "And she was most definitely out

of line in doing so. But she is our only rifter, and I've known her most of my life. If there's any chance her magic will return, we need her with us."

I don't speak.

Because I don't know what to say.

I understand Aero's anger. I felt Nuala's fury like a blade. But I also know what it's like to lose your magic, to feel it slipping through your fingers like water. If there's a chance she can recover, we shouldn't leave her behind.

Feliks sighs. "So we visit this Thorne. And hope he doesn't ask for something we can't give."

"Exactly," Liri says.

Reluctantly, we agree.

There's no other option. Marching into King Murick's territory blind would be suicide. We need a plan. We need answers. And if Thorne is the only one who might have them, then we go.

The group begins to shift, preparing to move again. Aero stays beside me, his hand resting lightly on my back. I feel his concern through the bond, quiet and steady. He hasn't said much since the sanctuary, but I know he's watching me...waiting.

I reach down, touching the bloom with trembling fingers.

"Please wake up," I whisper.

It doesn't respond, but I keep holding it anyway.

Because hope, even when it's cracked, is still worth carrying.

6

EVANTHE

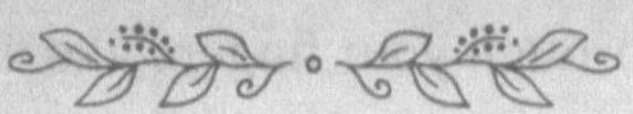

The forest changes as we move deeper. The trees here are unlike any I've seen. They're tall and silver-veined, their bark smooth as glass, their leaves whispering in languages I don't recognize. The air thickens with nostalgia. Not just mine, but something older. Something collective. Every step feels like walking through someone else's dream.

We've entered the forgotten part of the realm. A graveyard of fallen stars.

The ground glows faintly beneath our boots, scattered with fragments of light, crystals, bones, and petals that shimmer like constellations. The trees don't just grow. They remember. Their bark is etched with scenes: battles, births, farewells. Faces I almost recognize. Names I've never spoken.

No one talks. We're all too exhausted from the journey and fully in awe of the sight before us.

Even Phira is quiet, her wings folded tight, her usual

sass swallowed by the weight of the place. Hera walks close to Feliks, her hand resting on her belly, her eyes scanning the trees like she expects them to speak. Aero stays beside me, his hand brushing mine every few steps, grounding me. We're not alone here. We feel it before we see him.

The elder waits in a clearing where the trees bend inward, forming a dome of branches and light. He sits on a throne carved from a fallen meteor, his robes woven from threads of dusk and moss. His eyes are pale and endless, like he's seen too much and forgotten nothing.

"Elder Thorne," Liri says, bowing low.

He doesn't speak at first, just watches us, his gaze lingering on the bloom in my hand. I feel it pulse faintly, a flicker of recognition. Then silence again.

"You've come seeking answers," he says finally, his voice like wind through hollow reeds.

"We need to defeat the Mortia," I say. "We need to understand what they are."

He nods slowly. "Then you must understand what they were long before they destroyed so many precious relics." He looks off in the distance. "Our Sunstone that once kept the glade in perpetual light has now gone dark."

We wait, willing him to tell us more.

He stands, moving with the grace of someone who's never rushed a day in his life. He walks to one of the memory trees and places his hand against the bark. The tree responds, glowing softly, revealing an image: two Fae, radiant and wild, standing beneath a sky torn open by stars.

"Gossom and Hale," he says. "They were Fae once. Like some of you." He glances at Aero, Feliks, and Hera knowingly. "Like me."

The image shifts: Gossom's eyes darkening, Hale's hands reaching toward a dying star.

"They became obsessed," Thorne continues. "With death. With cosmic control. They defied nature. Tried to bend it. Tried to own it."

The tree shows them being cast out, banished, their wings torn. Their names stripped.

"We thought they vanished into the void," Thorne says. "But they didn't. They took root in what is now the Underrealm, over ages becoming the Mortia."

The image fades.

"They are not just a force," he says. "They are two souls. Shattered. Spread across the rift between realms."

I clutch the bloom tighter. "How do we defeat something so widespread?"

"To defeat the Mortia," Thorne says, turning to me, "you must make it remember who it once was."

Hera steps forward, her voice uncertain. "How are we supposed to do that?"

Thorne smiles, but it's not a kind smile. It's the smile of someone who knows the answer is going to hurt.

"You do not need an army," he says. "Fewer feet stir less dirt."

He walks back to his throne, settling into it like the stone remembers him.

"Go to the Sylvariaen Grove," he says, "and let the voice that rides on the wind inform you."

Silence.

The words hang in the air like mist.

Feliks leans toward Diaspor. "Do we know where that is?"

The commander nods, assuring him.

Liri steps forward, her voice soft but steady. "Thank you, Elder Thorne, for your guidance. We know what you've shared with us is no small thing."

The old Fae inclines his head, his pale eyes unreadable. "Wisdom is meant to be given, not hoarded."

"But still," Liri presses gently, "what do we owe you for this? What will it cost us?"

For a moment, Thorne says nothing. He gazes past us, toward the memory trees, their bark still glowing faintly with the images he summoned. Then he looks down at his hands, weathered, veined with starlight, and sighs.

"You can repay me by restoring the realms," he says. "And by returning."

Liri tilts her head. "Returning?"

"Once a year," Thorne says. "Come back, all of you. Sit with me. Share what you've learned. Let me remember you while you still live."

There's a pause. A long, aching silence.

"I am often forgotten here," he continues, his voice quieter now. "Others do not visit unless they need help. They come with questions, with desperation, with war at their heels. But never with stories. Never with peace."

His gaze lifts to meet mine, and I feel the weight of centuries behind it.

"I have wisdom to share beyond these crises," he says. "But no one asks for it."

My throat tightens.

Liri bows her head. "Then we will return. I swear it." She hesitates, lifting her gaze to him. "I never knew you had carried that loneliness all these years. I'm sorry we left you to it."

Thorne nods once, slowly. "No need for apologies. Just follow through on your promise. And go now. The grove awaits."

The group begins to shift, preparing to move again. No one speaks. There's a reverence in the air now, a quiet understanding that we've been given more than just direction. We've been given trust.

Aero stays beside me, his hand resting lightly on my back. I feel his concern through the bond, quiet and steady. He hasn't said much since the sanctuary, but I know he's there, waiting to see how all of this unfolds.

Before we leave, I kneel for a moment, cradling the bloom in my palms, and whisper, "Please don't forsake me."

The wind shifts—just slightly. And I swear I hear a voice. Not loud...not clear.

But there.

Waiting.

———

We return to Holbek with the faintest flicker of hope in our chests.

The forest behind us still hums with the memory of Elder Thorne's words, and though his guidance was cryptic, it felt like something real, something we could hold onto. The Sylvariaen Grove awaits, and with it, perhaps, the answers we need.

But the moment we step into the village, that flicker is snuffed out. The air is different. The Fae who once greeted us with reverence now turn away. Their eyes are cold, their mouths tight. Some whisper behind their hands. Others simply stare, their expressions unreadable but far from welcoming.

Everyone feels it immediately. The shift. The disappointment. Distrusting side-eyes passing by.

Liri slows beside me, her brow furrowing. "Something's wrong," she murmurs.

Diaspor nods, his gaze sweeping the village square. "They're angry."

Feliks mutters, "That's an understatement."

We stop near the well, where a few townsfae linger, casting glances our way. Liri steps forward, her voice calm but commanding. "What's happened here? Why are you looking at us like that?"

One of the Fae, a young woman with moss-colored hair and trembling hands, hesitates. She knows who Liri is. I can see it in her eyes. But she doesn't speak.

"Please," Liri says gently. "You know me. Tell me."

The Fae swallows hard. "We...we were told. About Evanthe."

Her eyes shift to me. My heart stutters.

"Told what?" Liri asks.

"That she returned to the human realm...before coming here."

The words land like stones. I feel the weight of them settle into my chest, heavy and sharp.

Liri's face tightens. "Who told you such things?"

The Fae looks down, her fingers twisting in her tunic. She doesn't answer.

But Liri already knows. I see it in her eyes, the realization blooming like a bruise that could only be caused by someone you love.

"Nuala?" she whispers.

The Fae nods, barely. I don't speak. I can't. The silence inside me is louder than the whispers around us. They all must hate me now. The selfish halfling who would rather chase a human throne than save the realm she was born to protect. The Guardian who abandoned them when they needed her most.

"How could she do such a thing?" I ask, my voice cracking. "She was upset, yes. Her magic was fading. But this...this could put everything at risk."

Aero steps closer, his hand brushing mine, but I barely feel it.

Liri's face is pale, her jaw clenched. She looks like someone who's been betrayed by blood.

"Where can I find her?" she asks the villager.

The Fae hesitates. "Last I saw her...she was staying in the cottage next to the tavern."

We don't wait. The group moves as one, silent and swift, down the winding path toward the tavern. The cottage is small, its door slightly ajar, the scent of stale wine drifting into the midday air. Liri knocks once then pushes the door open.

Nuala is curled on a cot, tangled in blankets, her hair a mess of curls and twigs. She squints at the light pouring in behind us, groaning as she shields her eyes.

"What...what time is it?" she mumbles.

"Midday," Liri says coldly.

Nuala blinks then sits up slowly, her movements sluggish. "Oh. Right."

Liri doesn't waste time. "Why did you tell the villagers about Eva's return to the human realm?"

Nuala drops her head into her hands.

"I—" she starts then groans. "I had too much wine. Too many carafes. I was just... I was so distraught. I couldn't rift. I felt useless. It just came pouring out of me."

She looks up, eyes glassy. "I didn't mean to hurt anyone. I swear."

But neither Liri nor I can forgive her so easily.

"You didn't mean to," I say, my voice low. "But you did."

Nuala flinches.

"You've made me look like a traitor," I continue. "Like I abandoned this realm for power. For a crown. Do you know what that means? What that could cost us?"

"I know," she whispers. "I know. I'm sorry."

Liri steps forward, her voice sharp. "You will stay here. You will keep your mouth shut. No more wine. No more stories. If your magic returns, we'll decide what to do then. But for now, you've done enough."

Nuala nods, tears slipping down her cheeks, her regret

lingering in the air. She deserves all of Liri's anger and mine, but the smallest part of me does pity her. I know the sadness that comes with feeling alone in the world. The feeling that comes with losing a best friend.

We leave her there, in the dim light of the cottage, the door closing behind us with a finality that feels like a sentence. Outside, the village is still watching.

And I wonder how long it will take for them to see me again—not as a traitor, but as the Guardian they all trusted once.

7

AERO

The cliffside is quiet. I sit with my back against a crooked stone, legs stretched out, watching the pale light stretch across the slightly familiar sky. It's a bit like Meraki's sky, but no golden haze, no familiar constellations. Here, the stars pulse faintly, like they're breathing. Below, the forest glows in patches, magic flickering in the trees like fireflies. It's beautiful. And it's wrong.

I spot Eva in the distance, sitting beneath a twisted elder tree. The bloom lies cracked and dormant beside her, catching the light but giving none back. She's still. Too still. I feel her through the bond. Her heart is heavy. She hasn't spoken much since we left Nuala behind. I don't blame her.

I lean forward, elbows on my knees, and exhale slowly. The wind carries the scent of moss and something older. A dusty old breeze. Footsteps crunch behind me.

Feliks appears, carrying a flask that looks like it's been

stitched together from bark and bone. He plops down beside me with a groan, uncorks the flask, and offers it with a grin.

"Either it's honeywine or a liquid curse," he says. "Either way, it'll drown my worries away."

I take it, sniff cautiously, and hand it back. "Smells like regret."

"Perfect," he says, taking a swig. He winces. "Definitely not honeywine."

We sit in silence for a moment, watching the horizon.

Then he nudges me with his elbow. "You know, brooding on a cliff like this? Very dramatic. Very you."

I smirk. "It's part of my title at this point."

"Prince of Shadows and Sulking, is it now?"

"Something like that."

He laughs, but it's thin. Underneath the jokes, I can see it...he's worried. Not just about the battle ahead. About me.

He leans back, staring up at the sky. "I'm just a man," he says quietly. "I bleed easily. I don't have a god for a father or a crown for my head. And yet, I'm standing at the edge of something meant for legends like you."

I glance at him. "You're not just a man."

He shrugs. "I am. And I'm fine with that. But you... you're starting to sound like a hero in one of those awful epics we grew up reading."

I raise an eyebrow. "Awful?"

"You know the ones. Tragic backstory. Impossible odds. A love that defies fate. And then—boom. Dead before the last page."

I chuckle, but it fades quickly.

"I'm not planning on dying anytime soon," I say.

"Good," he replies. "Because I'm not planning on watching you."

I nod, the weight of his words settling into my chest. "Then I'll rewrite the ending."

"How long do deities—or, in your case, partial deities—live?" he asks.

The question gives me pause. I've been so distracted by the constant state of war since I found out about my lineage that I haven't really given it thought. Surely longer than a human, but longer than a Fae? If so, does that mean I'll live far beyond Eva? I recall the descriptions of how it feels to lose a bonded. The excruciating pain of it. I release the breath I've been holding unknowingly. "I'm not sure, Feliks."

Shrugging, he lifts his flask. "To surviving impossible odds."

I lift an imaginary glass. "To seeing it through. Together, my brother."

We clink the flask against my hand, and he takes another swig, coughing dramatically.

"Definitely a curse," he mutters.

We sit in silence again, watching the stars shift overhead. The wind picks up, rustling the trees below. I glance back at Eva. She hasn't moved.

"She's scared," I say.

Feliks follows my gaze. "She should be."

"She's trying to carry all of it. The bloom. The realms. Us."

"She's not alone."

"I know," I say. "But I don't think she believes it yet."

Feliks sighs. "Then make her believe it."

I nod, standing slowly. "I will."

He stays behind, watching the sky, flask in hand. I walk down the slope toward Eva, the wind tugging at my cloak, the stars watching like silent witnesses.

Whatever comes next, we'll face it. Together.

———

The borrowed quarters are modest, the stone walls softened by woven tapestries, a hearth that flickers with a low flame, and a single window that lets in the pale light of the moon. It's quiet here, tucked away from the whispers of the village and the weight of the world pressing in from all sides.

Evanthe sits curled in the corner, her knees drawn to her chest, the bloom resting beside her like a broken promise. She hasn't spoken much since we returned. Not since Nuala's betrayal. Not since the villagers looked at her like a stranger.

I watch her from across the room, my heart aching with the quiet grief that pulses through our bond. She's trying to be strong. She always is. But I know the toll it's taking. I feel it in the way her magic flickers, in the way her shoulders slump, in the way she avoids my eyes. She's unraveling. I can't let her do it alone.

It took more effort than I expected, but I managed to barter for a wooden tub from a traveling merchant—one of the few who still pass through Holbek with wares and stories. I filled it with hot water, steeped with herbs Diaspor recommended for grounding. Steam curls into the air, fragrant and warm.

"Eva," I say gently, crossing the room. "Come. Let me take care of you."

She looks up, her starburst amber eyes tired, lips parted like she wants to protest. But she doesn't. She nods slowly and lets me help her to her feet.

I guide her to the tub, easing her in with care. The water laps at her skin, and she exhales, the tension in her shoulders loosening just a little. I kneel beside her, dipping a sponge into the water then running it down her arms, her back, her collarbone.

Her wild mahogany hair spills over the edge of the tub, damp and tangled. I gather it gently, working my fingers through the knots, then pour warm water over it, watching the strands darken and shimmer. I lather the herbal soap into her scalp, massaging slowly, letting her lean into the rhythm of my hands.

She closes her eyes.

"I'm sorry," she whispers.

I pause. "For what?"

"For believing the Mortia's lies. For letting them get into my head. For doubting myself. For doubting you."

I set the sponge aside and cup her face in my hands. "Eva. You are allowed to feel fear. You are allowed to break. But you are not alone. You will never be alone."

She opens her eyes, and I see the storm in them. The

doubt. The pain. The longing for all of this to finally be behind us.

"My family will arrive in Meraki soon," I say. "There will be questions. There will be chaos. But none of it changes this."

I press my forehead to hers.

"You are my family now."

Her breath catches.

I kiss her softly, slowly, like I'm reminding her of every promise I've ever made. She responds with a quiet urgency, her fingers curling into my shirt, her body leaning into mine.

The bond between us hums, alive and electric. Desire pulses through it, but more than that, devotion. Trust. The need to be seen. To be held.

I help her out of the tub, wrapping her in a towel then guiding her to the bed. I dry her hair with slow, careful strokes, brushing it back from her face, letting my fingers linger at her temples, her jaw, her throat.

She watches me, eyes wide, lips parted.

"I need you to feel it," I whisper. "How much you mean to me. How deeply this runs."

She nods, and I hold her close, letting the warmth of our bodies chase away the cold that's settled in her bones. I kiss her again, deeper this time, and she melts into me, the tension draining from her limbs, her breath growing steady.

Her fingers find mine, tracing the lines of my palm and down over the black markings of our bond like she's memorizing them. I brush her hair back, letting my hand linger at her cheek, her jaw, the curve of her neck. She leans into my touch, her eyes searching mine for reassurance. For something real.

"I'm here," I whisper. "Always."

She pulls me closer, and our lips meet again…slow, tender, then urgent. The bond between us thrums beneath my skin, warm and insistent. Her hands slide beneath my shirt, and I let it fall away, the fabric forgotten as our skin meets.

We move together with quiet reverence, each touch a promise, each breath a vow. I take my time, letting her feel how deeply this runs. How much of me belongs to her. She responds with soft gasps, her body arching into mine, her fingers gripping the scars along my shoulders like she's anchoring herself to the moment.

There's no rush. No fear. Just us.

The rhythm we find is gentle, grounding. A dance of devotion. Her eyes never leave mine, and I see everything in them. Her pain, hope, love, the weight of what's ahead. I kiss her again and again, until the tension melts from her body and she sighs against me, her breath warm at my throat.

We lie together in the quiet, wrapped in each other, the bloom resting nearby like a sleeping ember.

Outside, the village is still for now.

8

EVANTHE

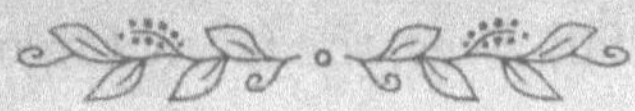

The borrowed cottage feels smaller today. It isn't the walls closing in. They're the same rough stone, patched with moss and softened by woven tapestries. It isn't the hearth, though its flame sputters low, casting more shadow than warmth. It's the air. Heavy. Close. As if the village itself presses in, its judgment seeping through the cracks.

The males have gone to barter for supplies—weapons, food, whatever they can gather—before we move toward the Sylvariaen Grove. Their absence leaves the cottage hushed, save for the crackle of the fire and the faint rustle of Hera's trousers as she settles into the chair across from me.

She studies me for a moment, her hand resting on her belly, her expression caught between sympathy and disbelief. "I still can't believe she did it," Hera says finally. "Nuala. Of all people."

I close my eyes, the words cutting deeper than I

expect. "She told them," I whisper. "She told the villagers about our journey back to the human realm. About me."

Hera leans forward, her voice sharp. "And she knew what that would mean. She knew how they'd see you—the Guardian who abandoned them for a throne."

I flinch. Because it's true. That's what they think now. That's what they whisper when I pass. Selfish halfling. Pretender. Traitor.

"She was drunk," I say weakly. "She said it just came pouring out."

Hera snorts. "Wine loosens the tongue, yes. But it doesn't invent lies. She wanted to wound you. And she did."

I look down at my hands, clenched tight in my lap. "I don't know how to forgive her."

"Maybe you don't," Hera says simply. "Not yet."

Silence stretches between us, heavy and brittle. Outside, I hear faint voices, the villagers moving about their day. I don't want to face them. Not now. Not with their eyes sharp and their whispers louder than ever.

I stand abruptly. "I need my clothes. They're drying behind the cottage."

Hera raises an eyebrow. "And you plan to stroll through the square, let them glare at you while you collect your laundry?"

I shake my head. "No. I'll sneak around the back."

She smirks. "Now that sounds like a plan."

We slip out the back door, moving quietly along the narrow path that winds behind the cottage. The air is cool, the scent of damp earth rising from the ground. My clothes hang from a low branch, swaying gently in the breeze. The garments are simple, patched but clean. I reach for them quickly, my heart pounding as if the villagers might appear at any moment.

Hera watches me, her lips twitching. "Look at you," she says. "Guardian of realms, sneaking around like a thief to collect her laundry."

I roll my eyes. "I'd rather be a thief than a spectacle."

She chuckles. "Fair enough. Though, I must say, it's not the most regal image. Perhaps I should start calling you Queen of Clotheslines."

I laugh despite myself, the sound breaking through the heaviness in my chest. "You're insufferable."

"And you're too serious," she retorts. "If you can't laugh at yourself, Eva, you'll drown in all this."

I fold the garments quickly, tucking them under my arm. "I don't have the luxury of laughter."

"Maybe not," Hera says, her tone softening. "But you do have the right to believe in yourself—and in the choices you've made."

I glance at her, uncertain. "You think I made the right choice? Taking the throne from Athena instead of staying focused on defeating the Mortia?"

Her eyes harden. "Absolutely. None of the Fae here can understand what that woman would have done if left as monarch of Meraki for another term. They see only the disruption. The change. But I saw her hunger. Her cruelty. You saved them from that."

I swallow, the weight of her words settling into me. "Then why does it feel like I've doomed us all?"

"Because you care," Hera says simply. "And caring always feels heavier than indifference."

We slip back into the cottage, closing the door quietly behind us. I set the clothes aside, my hands trembling. Hera moves to the hearth, stoking the fire, her movements deliberate.

Then comes the knock. Firm. Steady.

I freeze.

Hera straightens, her chin lifting. "Princess," she murmurs.

I move to the door, hesitating before opening it.

Liri stands there, her posture regal, her expression stoic. She looks less defeated than she did yesterday, though the weight of betrayal still lingers in her eyes. Her cloak is drawn tight, her hair braided neatly, her gaze unwavering.

"I wanted to assure you," she says, her voice calm but firm, "that Nuala will never sabotage our duty as she did again."

The words hit me like a blade. My throat tightens, a lump rising that I can't swallow. For a moment, I wonder did she end it? Did she end her long-time friend for her wrongdoing?

Hera steps forward, her chest out, her voice sharp with false confidence. "How can we be so sure of that?"

Liri's gaze doesn't waver. "She has made a vow to me. And I make this vow to you now. That, and I will not be letting her out of my sight until the Mortia ceases to exist."

I exhale slowly, the tension in my chest loosening just

a fraction. Liri's word has always meant something. Her vows are not given lightly. If she says Nuala will not betray us again, then I must believe it. But belief doesn't erase anger.

Despite pitying Nuala, I am still furious. I don't know how I'll make the journey without strangling her for such a transgression. She endangered everything. She endangered me. Yet Liri's vow means something. It always has.

I nod slowly. "Then we move forward."

Liri inclines her head. "Together."

She turns, her cloak sweeping behind her, and disappears into the night.

The cottage is quiet again.

Hera sinks into her chair, sighing. "Well...that's settled, I suppose."

I sit beside her, my hands trembling. "Is it? I don't know if I can forgive her."

"You don't have to," Hera says. "Not yet. Forgiveness isn't a gift you owe. It's a choice you make when you're ready."

I stare at the bloom resting on the table, its cracked petal catching the firelight. It remains silent. Dormant. But I feel it watching, waiting for the right time to wake.

"We'll need her," Hera says softly. "Even if you hate her. Even if you never forgive her. We'll need her."

I close my eyes, the weight of it pressing down. She's right. We'll need Nuala. And I'll need to find a way to walk beside her without letting my fury consume me. I sigh.

"The journey will come early tomorrow."

She takes in a deep breath and exhales. "You got that right. Don't worry, I'll be ready."

The fire crackles. The village hums outside. And inside, I sit with Hera, the bloom silent between us, wondering how many vows it will take to hold us together until the end.

The Sylvariaen Grove is unlike any place I've ever seen. After two days of travel on foot, the sight is welcome. My feet are aching but we made it. The moment we cross its threshold, the air changes. It thickens, humming with a resonance that feels alive, as though the forest itself is breathing. The trees are vast, their trunks pale and luminous, their leaves shimmering with faint light. The ground beneath our boots glows faintly, veins of silver running through the soil like rivers of memory. Elder Thorne's words echo in my mind: "Go to the Sylvariaen Grove, and let the voice that rides on the wind inform you."

We walk slowly, reverently. No one speaks. Even Feliks, who always has something sharp to say, is silent. The grove demands it. Every step feels like trespassing into something sacred.

I clutch the bloom in my hands, its cracked petal dull against the brilliance around us. It remains silent, but I feel it watching. Waiting. Perhaps here, in this place of memory, it will stir.

The wind shifts, carrying whispers.

At first, they are faint, like the rustle of leaves, the sigh of branches. But as we move deeper, the whispers grow stronger, weaving together into something more boisterous. They form visions, shimmering in the air, alive and theatrical.

I stop, my breath catching.

Hale appears before me.

Not as the corrupted shadow I've come to fear, but radiant. His wings gleam with starlight, his eyes bright with wonder. He stands tall, proud, a Fae of light and promise. For a moment, I see him as he once was before the Mortia, before the corruption.

Then the vision shifts. Hale turns his back.

His brother, Gossom, reaches for him, desperation in his eyes. But Hale walks away, his form darkening, the light fading from his wings. Around him, the ground cracks, the air thickens, and the Underrealm takes shape twisting, writhing, birthing itself from his betrayal. A place of rot and shadow, born from defiance.

I stumble back, clutching the bloom with one hand, my mother's dagger with the other. The vision fades, but its weight lingers.

The whispers rise again, swirling around me, pulling me deeper. I see myself now—not as I am but cradling something in my arms. A soul? A child? It's unclear. Its form shifts, flickering between light and shadow, fragile and infinite. I hold it close, protectively, though I don't understand what it is. The vision dissolves before I can grasp it.

I turn to the others, my voice trembling. "Did you see it?"

They nod, their faces pale, their eyes wide. The grove has shown them too. Pieces of the past. Pieces of what's to come.

Then the air splits.

A shriek tears through the grove, high and jagged, like metal scraping bone. Shadows ripple across the ground, rising, twisting, forming into a wraith. Its body is smoke and rot, its eyes hollow, its mouth a void. It moves like hunger, like despair.

It lunges for me.

I feel it immediately. The pull. It tries to siphon my fear, my regret, drawing them out like threads. My failures, my doubts. They surge to the surface, raw and sharp. I see flashes: Nuala's betrayal, the villagers' glares, the bloom's silence. The wraith feeds on them, growing stronger.

I cry out, clutching the bloom, fighting to hold myself together. Then I see it turning to the others.

Diaspor staggers, his hands trembling as the wraith pulls at his guilt. Feliks drops to his knees, his eyes wide with memories of battles lost. Hera clutches her belly, her face twisted with fear. Liri stands rigid, her jaw clenched, but I see the pain in her eyes. The wraith is feeding on all of us.

Aero roars.

He summons every drop of water he can, pulling it from the air, from the soil, from the very breath of the grove. Spears of liquid form in his hands, sharp and deadly. He hurls them at the wraith, each strike slicing through shadow, dispersing its form. But it reforms, shrieking, lunging again.

I summon my earth magic, pressing my palms to the ground. Vines erupt, twisting upward, lashing at the wraith. They wrap around its limbs, pulling, tearing. But the vines are laced with black thorns, sharp and cruel. They cut into my skin as they grow, searing pain through my veins. I grit my teeth, forcing them forward, binding the wraith.

It shrieks, thrashing, its form unraveling.

Together, Aero and I strike. Water and earth, light and shadow. The wraith shudders, collapses, and dissolves into smoke. The grove falls silent.

Unnaturally silent.

We stand frozen, our breaths ragged, our nerves pulsing in our bones. The air is heavy, still. No whispers. No visions. Just silence.

I clutch the bloom, my hands bleeding from the thorns. It remains quiet, cracked, lifeless. But I feel something faint and distant. A thread reminding me of the open rift. Aero draws near. "What is it?"

I shake my head. "If the rift is truly still open, is it possible that other Mortia-possessed creatures like this are finding their way into the mortal realm? Into Meraki?"

Taking a seat on a large fallen log, he draws in a deep breath. "I hope not."

Feliks grumbles. "They can barely handle the hordes of vampyr. Monsters like this would wipe them out completely in their weakened state."

Hera scoffs, welling up with tears. "They would have no chance."

Liri steps forward. "There's no use pondering such things. Worry doesn't slay such monsters."

The others gather, their faces pale, their bodies trembling. No one else speaks. We stand guard, waiting, listening for what may come next. But nothing comes, so we move.

We leave the grove, our steps slow, our hearts rattled. The visions linger, the wraith's shriek echoing in our ears. We know now...we are close. Too close. The Mortia feels us. Watches us. Sends its shadows to strike.

We are getting close.

And the cost is rising.

9
EVANTHE

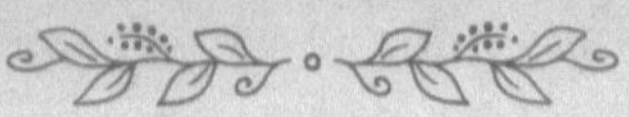

The morning begins with debate. We gather in a small clearing at the edge of the Sylvariaen Grove, the memory of the wraith still heavy in our bones. The air is damp, the ground soft beneath our boots, and the trees loom tall, their branches whispering faintly as if they've not yet forgotten what they showed us. Everyone looks tired. Everyone looks wary. But we know we cannot linger here. King Murick's territory lies ahead, and with it, the answers we need—or the doom we fear.

Diaspor kneels, tracing lines in the dirt with a stick, sketching paths and markers. "There are three ways forward," he says. "The northern ridge, steep but direct. The river path, longer but smoother. Or the western trail, winding through the marshlands."

Feliks groans. "Marshlands? No, thank you. I've had enough mud in my boots to last a lifetime."

Hera rubs her eyes, her face pale. "The river path

might be easier for us. But longer means more time exposed."

Liri folds her arms, her expression stoic. "The ridge is dangerous. Slopes that can break a leg. But it gets us closer to Murick faster."

Aero looks at me, his eyes steady. "What do you think?"

I clutch the bloom in my hands, its cracked petal dull against the morning light. It remains silent, but I feel its weight, its presence. "We don't have time to waste," I say quietly. "The ridge. We take the ridge."

Diaspor nods, though his brow furrows. "Then we must be careful."

The decision made, we set out.

The ridge is worse than I imagined. The slopes rise steeply, jagged rocks jutting out like teeth. The terrain is thick, tangled with roots and brambles that catch at our clothes. Every step is a battle—against the earth, against our exhaustion, against the weight of what lies ahead. The air grows colder as we climb, the wind sharper, carrying whispers that feel too much like the Mortia's laughter.

We move slowly, carefully. Diaspor leads, his earth magic dull but steadying the path where he can. Aero stays close to me, his hand brushing mine when the ground shifts beneath us. Feliks mutters curses under his breath, his humor dimmed but not extinguished. Hera struggles, her steps slower, but Liri supports her, her presence firm and unwavering.

Hours pass. The sun dips lower, its light filtered through the canopy. Our breaths grow ragged, our bodies weary. The battle in the grove lingers in our muscles, in our nerves. Every shadow feels like a threat. Every rustle feels like a warning.

Finally, Diaspor stops. "We rest here," he says, his voice firm. "The forest is thick enough to hide us. We need it."

No one argues.

We settle in a small hollow, the trees dense around us, their branches forming a canopy that shields us from the sky. The ground is soft with moss, the air damp but still. It feels safe enough. Safe enough to breathe.

I sink to the ground, the bloom resting beside me. My hands tremble as I set it down, the memory of the wraith's pull still sharp. Aero sits beside me, his arm wrapping around my shoulders, his presence steady. I lean into him, my head heavy against his chest, his heartbeat grounding me.

The silence is heavy. Then Feliks clears his throat.

"Well," he says, his voice light, "if we're going to sit here and brood, we might as well do it with style."

He stands, brushing dirt from his trousers, and raises his hands dramatically. "Ladies, gentlemen, and Fae of questionable taste, I present to you...a song."

Hera groans. "Feliks..."

"No instruments," he says quickly. "I'm not trying to draw attention. Just my voice. And my clever lyrics."

Diaspor sighs. "Do we have a choice?"

Feliks grins. "Not really."

He begins to sing. His voice is clear, strong, carrying through the hollow without echo.

"Oh, the mountain mocked our footsteps
With its steep and stubborn spine,
And the roots reached up to trip us
Like they'd sworn it was divine.

We've got mud inside our bootprints,
  We've got brambles in our hair.
  But we climb because we're foolish,
  And we climb because we care.

There's our Aero, ever brooding,
  Storm-cloud eyes and silent pride.
  If a pebble dared offend him,
  He'd glare it off the mountainside.

And there's Liri, carved from granite,
  Never blinking, never swayed.
  If the wind itself grew louder,
  She would hush it with a blade.

Hera's tongue is sharp as winter,
  Cuts you clean and leaves you warm.
  She'll scold you for your choices
  While she shields you from the storm.

· · ·

And old Diaspor keeps walking,
*   Never rushing, never slow.*
*   If the world collapsed behind him,*
*   He would nod and simply go.*

And our monarch, stars above her,
*   Wild-haired, fierce-hearted, brave.*
*   Clutching tight a cracked and glowing bloom*
*   She swears the realm can save.*

If the sky began to crumble,
*   If the night forgot to shine,*
*   She would stitch the dark together*
*   With her stubborn, steady spine."*

The lyrics are clever, playful, weaving humor into our weariness. We laugh. Despite ourselves, we laugh. Smiles break through the exhaustion, the fear. Hera chuckles, shaking her head. Liri hides a smile behind her hand. Diaspor's lips twitch. Even Aero lets out a quiet laugh, his arm tightening around me.

I rest my head against his chest, my body relaxing for the first time in days. His fingers run through my wild hair, slow and gentle, soothing. The bond hums between us, alive and steady. I close my eyes, listening to Feliks's song, feeling Aero's heartbeat, the warmth of his touch.

This is the good stuff. The things worth living for.

The laughter of friends. The warmth of love. The song of a brother who refuses to let despair win. These are the moments that matter. The moments that remind me why we fight. Why we endure. Why we cannot let the Mortia win.

Because the day the Mortia wins is the day the stars go dark. The day every song ever sung turns to ash.

I clutch the bloom, whispering silently to it. Please. Wake up. Please. It remains silent, but for now, it doesn't matter. For now, we have each other.

As the night deepens, Feliks's song fades. Replaced by quiet conversation, by laughter, by the crackle of the small fire Princess Liri conjures with care. We sit together, weary but grounded, our nerves soothed by the moment. The forest hums around us, alive but not threatening. For the first time in days, I feel peace.

Feliks stretches his legs toward the fire. "If we survive this, I'm never climbing another hill again. Ever. I'll build a house on flat land and refuse to leave it."

Liri snorts. "You? Stay in one place? You'd last a day before you started climbing the walls."

"I'll climb the walls," Feliks says, "but not a single gods-forsaken mountain."

Hera shifts, rubbing her lower back. "I'd settle for a bed that isn't made of roots and regret."

Diaspor chuckles softly. "Regret is softer than most beds I've known."

"That's because you've slept on battlefields," Feliks says. "Your standards are questionable."

I smile into the firelight. "You all complain as if you weren't the ones insisting we keep moving."

Feliks points at me. "We insisted because you would have marched us through the night if we didn't."

Liri nods. "She's right. You forget to stop."

"I don't forget," I protest, though the warmth in my chest betrays me. "I just...don't like wasting time."

Diaspor tilts his head. "Rest is not waste."

Hera hums in agreement. "Especially now."

Feliks leans back on his elbows, looking at me with a lazy grin. "Besides, if we didn't stop, when would I have the chance to serenade you all with my unmatched talent?"

Aero throws a twig at him. "Unmatched is one word for it."

"Jealousy doesn't suit you, brother."

"Neither does your singing," he fires back.

Their bickering is soft, harmless, almost comforting. The kind of teasing that only exists when people trust each other enough to be tired together.

I let out a slow breath, the tension easing from my shoulders. "I needed this," I admit quietly.

Hera looks over, her expression gentle. "We all did."

Feliks lifts an imaginary cup. "To surviving another day."

Liri raises her hand in mock salute. "And to not dying tomorrow."

Diaspor smiles faintly. "A worthy goal."

Aero leans down, his lips brushing my hair. "Rest," he whispers. "I'll keep watch."

I nod, my body sinking into his warmth. I close my eyes for a moment, letting their voices wash over me, letting the fire warm the places the cold had settled too deeply. The day the Mortia wins is the day all of it dies. And I will not let that day come.

The forest is still when I wake. It is not yet light, though the faintest suggestion of dawn lingers somewhere beyond the canopy. The air is cool, damp with dew, and the silence is heavy, broken only by the occasional rustle of leaves. I sit up slowly, careful not to disturb the others. I take one step, and my breath catches. Laying beside me, the bloom is cracked but faintly glowing. Not guiding me as it once did, but seemingly alive.

I lift it in my hands, the faint warmth seeping into my skin. My heart races. For days it has been silent, dormant, lifeless. And now it trembles, a vision flashing before my eyes. I watch it all unfold until I'm left with tears nearly springing from my eyes.

Aero stirs beside me, rubbing his eyes, his chestnut hair tousled from sleep. He blinks at me then at the bloom. His gaze sharpens instantly, the bond between us humming with instinct. He sits up, his voice low. "Eva?"

I grin, unable to help myself. "I was asleep when I felt the bloom tremble at my side. It didn't show me the Mortia. It showed me...the part of me that he could use against me."

I feel the way my words trigger his instinct to protect

me, the bond surging with his concern. It makes me smile, even through the weight of what I've seen.

"I'm not going to lie," he says, his voice tight, "it's slightly disturbing that such a statement brings you joy. But I suppose it's good to know his strategy. What part exactly does he speak of?"

I rise quietly, motioning for him to follow. We move through the darkness, careful not to wake the others, until we reach a small pool of water nestled among the roots of an ancient tree. The surface glimmers faintly, reflecting the faint glow of the bloom.

"I fell asleep praying to the Great Divine for answers," I say softly. "And the next thing I know, I woke up next to the bloom. Immediately, a memory I had buried long ago resurfaced."

I hesitate, my fingers tightening around the bloom. The memory is sharp and painful. Heat prickles at the back of my neck as I search for the right place to begin. I stare at the ground, tracing circles in the dirt with my boot. Aero's presence steadies me. He urges me on, his eyes locked on mine, his hand brushing mine in silent encouragement.

"I was young," I begin. "Maybe eight years old. I was standing at the table, holding a sad-looking cup so large and uneven my small hands could hardly keep it upright. My mother, father, and some of the other townspeople were there. She was radiant, my mother, captivating them all with her stories. I tried to get her attention, over and over, but I kept going unheard."

The memory unfolds vividly, as if the grove itself whispers it back to me.

"I said, 'I made this for you,' holding out the cup. No one looked. I tried again, louder this time. Mother! Look, I put a handle on it like you like!"

I swallow hard, the ache rising in my chest. "She just gave me a quick glance then smiled tightly. 'Not now, girl. Go play.'"

My face burns with the memory—the humiliation stings even now. "My face flushed as one of the other women chuckled softly. A few of the others had started to stare. So I laughed too. Too loud, too forced. Then I dropped the cup on the table."

I close my eyes, the knot in my stomach twisting. "'I didn't really make it for you anyway,' I muttered, backing away. My stomach twisted in knots. She didn't even notice me walking away."

The silence that follows is heavy. Aero's jaw clenches, his eyes dark with anger. He doesn't speak at first, but the bond hums with his fury, his protectiveness, his grief for me.

Then he reaches for my hand—gently, reverently—like he is holding something sacred and breakable. His voice is soft, steady. "She didn't see you. But I do. Every bit of you."

Tears slip down my cheeks, but an uncontrollable grin breaks through them. He wipes one away with the pad of his thumb, his touch tender, grounding. I breathe deeply, gathering my composure, the warmth of his presence steadying me.

"It was in that moment," I say, my voice trembling, "that something shifted. I didn't expect the bloom to react at all. Certainly not to that memory. I've spent years pretending it didn't matter, that I'd grown past it. But when it surfaced, when I felt that old sting of being small and unseen...the bloom answered, as if it had been waiting for me to stop pretending I was untouched by it."

I draw a breath, surprised all over again by the truth of it.

"I thought strength meant leaving those pieces behind. But the bloom doesn't want the polished parts of me. It wants the ones I've tried hardest to forget."

Aero's gaze is unwavering, his voice low but fierce. "I've watched you fight the dark—not just around you, but within. And I feared it might take you, might change you into someone I'd no longer recognize. But I see now... you didn't vanish. You expanded. If the Mortia feeds on the buried, then let nothing in you be hidden. Not from it. Not from me. I want even the parts you once tried to forget —the ache, the rage, the guilt. I want all of it."

His words pierce me. I've spent all these years searching for a purpose, a belonging, thinking it was the throne. But here I am. Far from it. But I don't feel homesick at all. I glance back down at the bloom. It warms against my skin. Not glowing or guiding, but healing. The cracks seem softer, less jagged, as if the memory itself has stitched something back together.

I exhale, the weight in my chest loosening. "Then that's how we fight him," I whisper. "Not by hiding. Not by pretending. But by embracing everything. Even the parts that hurt."

Aero nods, his hand tightening around mine. "Then we'll do it together."

The dawn breaks slowly, light spilling through the canopy, painting the forest in hues of gold and green. The others stir, their faces weary but determined. I tuck the bloom close, its warmth steady against my skin. For the first time in days, I feel hope. Not fragile or fleeting, but real hope.

We return to the clearing, the group gathering around the small fire Diaspor rekindles. Feliks stretches, groaning dramatically. "Another day, another chance to die horribly," he mutters, earning a sharp look from Liri.

But even his humor cannot dampen the shift I feel. The bloom is healing. My soul is healing. And with it, perhaps, the realm itself.

I glance at Aero, his eyes meeting mine, the bond humming with steady strength. He smiles faintly, and I know we are ready. Whatever lies ahead, whatever the Mortia throws at us, we will face it. Together.

10
AERO

The forest is quiet when we break away from the others. Eva and Hera remain near the campfire, their voices low, while Liri keeps watch with Nuala. I can feel the tension between them even from here. Feliks hums softly to himself, sharpening a blade, trying to keep spirits high. But Bel, Diaspor, and I move deeper into the trees, away from the group, away from the weight of their eyes. Sometimes, it's easier to carry the burden when no one else is watching.

The air is damp, heavy with the scent of moss and rain. The canopy above filters the light into pale threads, weaving shadows across the ground. I kneel by a small stream, pressing my hands to the water. It responds instantly, rising in shimmering arcs, filling the canteens lined before me. The magic hums through me, steady and familiar, though it costs more than it once did. Every drop feels heavier now, my energy stores low after the journey. Still, I force it, filling each vessel until they brim.

Bel crouches beside me, pretending to help. He dips his hands into the stream, but I can see the strain in his face, the way his magic flickers weakly. He masks it with a grin, tossing me a wink. "See? I'm useful."

I don't call him out. He doesn't need the reminder of his weakness. Not now. Actually, I can relate. I may still have my power, but that doesn't exactly clarify how I'm supposed to help Eva defeat the Mortia as their prophecy reads. Why couldn't their prophets have included a little instruction?

Diaspor stands a few paces away, his eyes scanning the forest. His posture is rigid, his hand resting on the hilt of his blade. Always the commander. Always the sentinel. I'm well aware that we both share a strong need to keep Eva safe. His desire comes from a paternal place. I'm glad that she has him. Her relationship with her father may have been strained, but I know how she misses the good parts of him through our bond. Diaspor gives some of that back to her, and I'm grateful for it. He doesn't speak, but I know his mind is racing, calculating, preparing for what lies ahead.

We are so close to getting everything we have fought so hard for. If history has taught me anything, it's how easily that can be taken away, especially when hopes are high. Fate has a strange way of doing that. It creeps in, like a night taking hold of broad daylight when you least expect it. I try to focus on the bloom's awakening, on the faint glow Eva showed me this morning. It should bring hope. It should be enough to steady me. But the thoughts keep creeping in, intrusive, relentless.

"I keep dreaming of Baros," I say suddenly, my voice low. Bel looks up, curious, while Diaspor turns slightly, his gaze sharp. "Except, it's all wrong. The sky is red. The rivers...they run backward. My family's palace rotting from the inside. My mother sitting upon an abandoned throne, something grim wearing her voice, saying, 'You abandoned us, son.'"

I shake my head, the words catching in my throat. "I try to tell myself it's just this realm playing games with my head, but..."

I don't finish. I don't need to. The silence says enough.

Bel draws in a deep, knowing breath. His eyes soften, his voice heavy with memory. "I know all too well those nightmares. I had many while trapped in Stillstar, while my realm here was being burnt to the ground. While innocent Fae were tortured and murdered if they didn't join King Murick. But mine were real. You, on the other hand, can still hold on to hope that yours are only dreams, nothing more. Hold on to that for dear life."

I want to believe him. I want to cling to the idea that these visions are nothing but shadows, tricks of the Mortia. But the dread lingers, sharp and heavy. And I know Eva feels it too, through the bond. The last thing I want is to weigh her down. She carries enough already. But I would rather be prepared than blind.

The people of Baros are starving. The famine has spread, gnawing at their bones, hollowing their faces. Eva could restore the land with her magic, yes. She could bring life back to the soil, and I could bring water back to the rivers. But how long would it last? And her people in

Meraki...they don't know about her magic. They don't know about her lineage to the Fae. She doesn't seem eager to share it, not with their history, not with the way they've treated her kind. And I can't blame her.

I have to protect her. And I have to protect my brother. Or none of this will matter.

I look to Diaspor, my voice steady but heavy. "Why do you think I'm plagued by such nightmares?"

He hesitates. I can see it in his eyes. The reluctance, the weight of truth he doesn't want to share. But out of respect, he answers. "I think the rift between our realms is still open. Though narrow, its shadow-touched energy could be leaking into Baros and Meraki as well. Logic would tell us that the longer it remains unsealed, the faster the Mortia can unravel the realms from within. But it's all speculation at the end of the day. There's no point in making guesses."

A prickly sensation runs down the nape of my neck. The words settle like stones in my chest. The tension thickens in the air around us, heavy and suffocating.

Bel shrugs, forcing a grin. "Don't listen to him. He's just grumpy right now. We're all a bit out of sorts, given the state of things. Nothing a good night's rest can't fix."

Diaspor scoffs, his voice sharp. "I'll feel better when King Murick and the ghoul inside him are no longer among us."

The silence that follows is heavy, broken only by the rustle of leaves. I stare at the water, watching it ripple, watching the reflections twist. If we don't do something soon, our people may be lost forever.

We move deeper into the forest, the canteens filled, the weight of our conversation lingering. Bel hums softly, trying to lighten the mood, but his eyes betray his worry. Diaspor remains silent, his gaze sharp, his posture rigid. I walk between them, my thoughts heavy, my heart torn.

The path is rough, the terrain thick. Roots twist across the ground, slopes rise steeply, branches claw at our clothes. Every step is a battle, every breath heavy. The forest feels alive, watching, waiting. Shadows linger at the edges, whispering, reminding us of the Mortia's reach.

I try to focus on the bloom, on the faint warmth it carries. Eva's words echo in my mind: *To heal the shade, I have to embrace all of me.* She's right. She always is. But the thought of her pain, of the memories she carries, gnaws at me. I want to shield her from it. I want to carry it for her. But I know I can't. Not this time.

Bel breaks the silence, his voice low. "Do you ever wonder what it would be like if none of this had happened? If the Mortia had never risen? If Murick had never taken the throne?"

Diaspor snorts. "Pointless wondering."

But I answer, "Yes. Every day."

Bel nods, his eyes distant. "I think about Stillstar. About the way the rivers used to shine, the way the trees used to sing. I think about the children who laughed in the streets, the families who gathered at the fire. And I wonder if I'll ever see it again."

Diaspor's jaw tightens. "You won't. Not as it was. But maybe as it could be."

Bel sighs, his shoulders slumping. "Maybe."

I glance at him, my voice steady. "We'll make it right. Somehow."

He looks at me, his eyes searching, his voice soft. "You really believe that?"

I nod. "I have to."

The day stretches long, the forest thick and unforgiving. We move slowly, carefully, our bodies weary, our spirits heavy. But we keep going. We have no choice.

As the sun dips low, we return to the group, the canteens filled, the path scouted. Eva looks up as we approach, her eyes meeting mine, the bond humming with quiet strength. I feel her hope, her determination, her love. I want to scoop her up in my arms and take her to another realm none of us knows. A new, safe beginning. But I know we can't run away from this. Not until the Mortia is gone. Not until the realms we know are safe.

But the nightmares linger.

The visions of Baros, twisted and broken. The palace rotting, the rivers running backward, my mother's voice warped by shadow. I try to tell myself they're only dreams. Only tricks. But the dread remains, sharp and heavy.

And I know we're running out of time.

11

EVANTHE

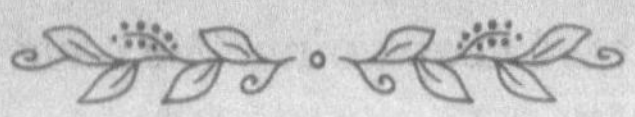

The morning air is crisp, carrying with it the scent of pine and damp earth. The forest hums faintly, alive but subdued, as though it knows what lies ahead. I rise before the others, the bloom clutched in my hands. It glows faintly, warm against my skin, alive and steady. For days it was silent, cracked, lifeless. Now it hums with purpose, pulling me forward, guiding me. My heart races with the certainty of it. This is my fate. My confidence surges, stronger than it has ever been.

I glance around the camp. Aero is still asleep, his arm draped protectively across his chest, his face softened in rest. Feliks snores lightly, muttering something incoherent. Diaspor sits half-awake, his eyes scanning the trees even in his weariness. Hera and Liri are speaking quietly near the fire, their voices low.

I move toward them, the bloom glowing faintly in my hands. "I need to speak with you," I say softly.

They look up, their eyes sharp with curiosity. I motion

for them to follow me a few steps away, into the shadow of the trees.

The words spill out of me, urgent and alive. "The bloom wasn't broken. It's awake. I feel it pulling me in the same direction we've been going."

Liri's eyes widen, her breath catching. "Toward Murick's fortress," she says, her voice trembling with relief.

Hera's lips part, her eyes glistening. For a moment, her hard exterior cracks, and a tear slips down her cheek. She wipes it away quickly, her voice sharp but unsteady. "I never doubted it would wake for you. For all of us."

I stare at her, surprised. Hera has always been sharp-tongued, sarcastic, armored in wit and defiance. But beneath it, I see her now—her fear, her humanity. She has carried more than she lets on.

With a smile, I lift my hands to her. "We wouldn't have made it here without you."

She scoffs, choking on a bit of phlegm. "Nope. None of that. Enough warm-and-fuzzy talk."

I laugh softly, the tension easing. For a moment, we are not warriors, not Guardians, not rulers. We are simply people, bound together by fate and choice.

Liri steps forward, her face alight with joy. "This changes everything," she says. "We have direction. We have purpose. And we have hope."

Her voice grows stronger, her posture regal. She looks at us, her eyes fierce. "Listen to me. This is more than a battle. This is our kingdom. Our realm. With so many of our rulers lost, I may be the one left to lead when the dust settles. This victory means everything—not just to me, but to all of us. To every Fae, every soul who still believes in this place."

Her words hang in the air, heavy with truth.

I feel the weight of it. The responsibility. But I also feel the strength in our group. The bloom hums in my hands, alive and steady. Aero's bond pulses faintly in my chest, grounding me. Hera's sharp wit keeps me on my toes. Liri's stoic resolve unable to mask her big heart. We are all pieces of this fight, all threads in the tapestry of what must be done.

Liri continues, her voice steady. "Murick's fortress lies ahead. It will not be easy. His forces are strong, his corruption deep. But we have something he does not. We have unity. We have the bloom. And we have each other."

Hera snorts softly. "And sarcasm. Don't forget sarcasm."

Liri smiles faintly, shaking her head. "Even that."

I clutch the bloom tighter, its warmth steady against my skin. "Then we march," I say firmly. "No more hesitation. No more doubt. This is our path."

The group gathers soon after, the camp dismantled, the fire extinguished. The air hums with anticipation, with fear, with hope. Aero stands beside me, his hand brushing mine, his eyes steady. Feliks hums a tune, his humor dim but present. Diaspor checks his blade, his posture rigid. Hera rolls her eyes but smiles faintly. Liri stands tall, her presence commanding.

We march.

The way ahead turns unforgiving, the land choked

with undergrowth. Steep rises force our steps higher, roots writhe across the earth like traps, and low branches snag at our clothes as if trying to hold us back. The forest feels alive, watching, waiting. Shadows linger at the edges, whispering faintly. But the bloom pulls me forward, steady and sure.

Hours pass. Our bodies grow weary, our breaths ragged. But we keep going. The fortress lies ahead. The Mortia waits.

As the sun dips low, we stop to rest. The forest is thick, the canopy shielding us from the sky. We settle in a small hollow, the ground soft with moss, the air damp but still. It feels safe enough.

If the Mortia were to triumph, it would not just claim land or thrones. It would silence this. The glow in our laughter, the fragile courage in our songs, the pulse of hope that keeps us moving. That is what would vanish. That is what I cannot allow.

I draw the bloom close, its faint warmth steady against my palm. Stay with me, I whisper inside, not as a plea but as a promise. Lead me, and I will follow.

The cracks no longer look like wounds. They look like lines of strength, scars that prove survival. And as its pulse steadies with mine, I feel less doubt.

The night deepens. The fire crackles softly, the forest hums faintly. We sit together, weary but grounded, our nerves soothed by the moment. Liri speaks quietly, her voice steady. "Tomorrow, we reach the fortress. Tomorrow, we face Murick. Tomorrow, we fight for everything."

Her words settle into us, heavy but steady.

I glance at her, at Hera, at Aero, at all of them. And I know we are not alone. We are bound together by an undeniable fate. This is a choice for every one of us. And we were all meant for this.

The bloom hums in my hands, alive and steady.

And I whisper to the stars, to the Great Divine, "This is our fate. This is our fight. And we will not fall."

The canopy above us is the thickest I've ever seen. Layer upon layer of leaves knit together so tightly that not even the most radiant of stars can pierce through. It feels like we've stepped into another world, one hidden from the heavens, cloaked in shadow. The air is damp, heavy with the scent of moss and water.

We stop beside a stream, its surface clear and smooth, winding through the forest like a silver ribbon. My stomach growls, and I realize I'm not the only one. Hera scans the area with a grimace, Feliks mutters something about "dying of starvation before the Mortia even gets us," and even Diaspor looks weary.

Then I notice them.

Tiny insects flutter from the surface of the water to the tips of the grass, glowing faintly like drifting embers. Their light is soft but steady, illuminating the stream just enough for Aero to crouch beside it. He leans forward, his eyes narrowing. "Look," he murmurs.

"Lunakai," Liri whispers, her mouth watering.

I peer closer. Beneath the surface, silvery fish dart

gracefully, their scales catching the glow of the insects. They shimmer like fragments of moonlight, their movements fluid and mesmerizing.

Bel steps forward, his voice low and reverent. "Silvery moonfish," he says. "Believed to grant dreams when eaten. Old tales say they carry fragments of the night sky within them."

Feliks grins. "Dreams, eh? Better than empty stomachs."

Our bellies rumble in agreement. Aero straightens, his expression firm. With a flick of his wrist, the water ripples, and the lunakai leap from the stream, arcing through the air before landing neatly into an empty satchel placed along the pebbled shore.

"Show-off," I tease.

Aero smirks. "Hungry show-off."

We gather around a small fire, the flames crackling softly, casting warm light against the shadows. The lunakai cook quickly, their silvery scales turning pale and crisp. The scent is rich, filling the hollow with promise.

We feast together, laughter mingling with the crackle of the fire. Feliks makes exaggerated faces as he chews, claiming the fish tastes like "hope seasoned with despair," which earns him a sharp jab from Hera. Bel tells us stories of Stillstar, of nights when the rivers glowed with moonfish.

His voice takes on a softer timbre as the firelight flickers across his face. He leans forward, elbows resting on his knees, and begins to weave a memory that feels older than the stones beneath us.

"In Stillstar," he says, "the rivers used to glow at night. Not faintly, not like these lunakai we've caught, but with a brilliance that made the whole valley shimmer. The moonfish would rise to the surface in great schools, their scales catching the light until it seemed as though the river itself had become a ribbon of silver fire. The elders would say something about being trapped on that island making our magic shine brighter. I believe them now."

His eyes glimmer as he speaks, and for a moment, I can almost see it—the water alive with light, the night sky mirrored in its depths.

"The children," Bel continues, "would chase them with nets woven from reeds. Simple things, fragile, but enough to scoop up a few of the glowing creatures. They'd laugh as they ran along the banks, their feet splashing in the shallows, their voices carrying across the valley. And when they caught one, they'd hold it up like treasure, its scales dripping light onto their hands."

Feliks chuckles. "Sounds like a festival. I'd have been the one falling face-first into the river."

Bel smiles faintly. "It was a kind of festival, though no one declared it so. Just joy, pure and unplanned. Families would gather along the banks, watching their children play, listening to the songs of the river. Some believed the moonfish carried dreams in their scales—that if you ate one, you'd dream of the stars themselves."

He pauses, his gaze distant. "I remember my sister catching one once. She held it so carefully, afraid it might break apart in her hands. That night, she dreamed of flying, of wings made of starlight, carrying her across the valley. She woke laughing, convinced the fish had given her the dream."

The fire crackles, and silence settles for a moment.

Liri listens quietly, her posture regal but her eyes far away. I see the faint smile tugging at her lips, subtle but real. It softens her, makes her look less like the princess burdened with duty and more like a girl remembering something precious.

Bel notices, his voice gentling. "You remember nights like that too, don't you, Princess? Before the wars. Before the Mortia."

Liri exhales slowly, her gaze fixed on the flames. "I do. A long time ago, before Stillstar. In Sylvaria, we had fireflies that lit the meadows. My sisters and I would chase them until our feet were raw. My mother used to say they were fragments of the stars, fallen to earth to remind us that light always returns."

Her voice falters, but the smile remains. "I haven't thought of that in years."

Hera nudges her with a crooked grin. "And here I thought you were born serious. Imagine that...little Liri chasing fireflies."

Liri rolls her eyes, but the smile lingers. "Even princesses were children once."

The moment hangs between us, fragile and luminous. Bel's story has done more than fill our bellies with dreams; it has reminded us of what we fight for. Not just survival, not just victory, but the chance for children to laugh along rivers again. For sisters to chase fireflies in meadows. For families to gather without fear.

I watch Liri's face, the way her smile flickers like the firelight. And I realize how much this means to her. This realm is her kingdom, her inheritance, her burden. But it is also her memory, her joy, her future.

And in that moment, I see her not just as a princess, not just as a leader, but as someone who longs for the same simple things we all do.

As I eat, I feel something shift inside me. Despite the dire circumstances, despite the looming shadow of Murick's fortress, I know I will miss moments like this. The laughter. The warmth. The simple act of sharing a meal in the forest.

My time with the Fae has taught me to soften my heart, to see that every life has a purpose, every soul a story worth hearing.

And Hera...how strange it feels to think of her now as a friend. Once, we were pitted against one another, ready to kill for the throne. I hated her. She hated me. And yet, here we are, sitting side by side, sharing food, sharing laughter. She has given me faith in humanity, proof that even the deepest wounds can heal, that enemies can become allies, even sisters.

Then there is Aero. If anyone had told me we would be where we are today, I would have laughed in their face. The way I would lay down my life for him...it still astonishes me. He is proof that hope can be born from the unlikeliest places, that even the most guarded hearts can learn to trust again.

I glance around the circle, my chest tight with

emotion. I can hardly believe I am worthy of all their affection.

Feliks finishes a song, his voice fading into the night. The silence that follows is soft, almost sacred. I realize I've been quiet, lost in thought. Aero notices, his eyes sharp, his voice gentle. "Eva," he says. "What's going through your mind?"

I swallow, my throat tight. "I want you all to know how grateful I am. For each of you."

My gaze pans the circle. "Bel, always steady and eager. Hera, I'll always be grateful for your loyalty. Liri, I'm convinced no one has ever been as regal and fierce. Feliks, your lighthearted songs get us through even the worst despair. Diaspor, my mentor. Your vigilance is unmatched. And Aero, my anchor, my bond."

Then my eyes pause upon Nuala.

The rifter's gaze meets mine, her eyes widening. For a moment, I see the hope flicker there...the desperate need to be included, to be forgiven.

I hesitate.

But then I nod, just slightly.

Her breath catches, her shoulders loosening. The silence lingers. Maybe I should have sung the smallest bit of her praises. She is the only reason we made it back on time for Noonsnight. But the betrayal still stings. The fire crackles, the stream hums softly, the insects glow faintly above the water. We are weary and battered, but I can't let more doubt creep in.

The night deepens, the canopy above holding back the stars. The fire burns low, casting faint shadows across our faces. I lie back, resting my head on Aero's lap. His fingers do their best to run through my tangled mess of hair. It soothes me.

I clutch the bloom, its warmth steady against my skin. It hums faintly, alive and well. I look up at Aero. "I can still hear my father's voice, his last words to me. 'You need to go find the box under Blackstone. It is for you to carry.'"

"And you carry it well," he replies.

I don't say it out loud, but I also remember the way his eyes fell closed. How his lifeless body became heavy in my arms. I look down at the bloom and whisper, "The day I found you was the day I lost him."

12

EVANTHE

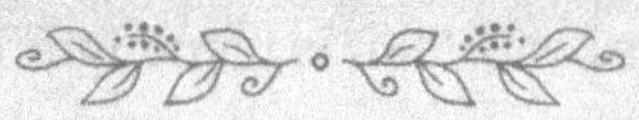

The morning begins with unease. I feel it through the bond before Aero even speaks. The quiet tension. The weight pressing against his chest. His eyes are steady, but his silence is louder than words. We walk side by side, the bloom warm against my palm, guiding us forward. Finally, I stop, turning to him.

"What is it?" I ask softly. "You're holding something back."

He exhales, rubbing the back of his neck. "I don't want to snuff out your determination, Eva. You've found your strength again, and it's carrying all of us. But…" His voice falters, his jaw tightening. "I keep questioning what my role is in all of this. The fables said you were meant to bond with a deity to restore the realms. That's our fate. But how exactly do I play a part in defeating the Mortia? I'll do anything to protect you, but it's eating me up inside not knowing what I'm supposed to do. I'm here, constantly moving forward, but blindly."

I reach for his hand, squeezing it firmly. "Aero, you've already helped keep us safe. You're the only one in our group whose power hasn't been muted by the Mortia. Without you, we wouldn't have made it this far. You've fought off sea serpents, vampyr, and every other creature the Mortia has thrown our way. You protected us when the rest of us faltered. That's not nothing."

He shakes his head. "But is it enough?"

I step closer, my voice steady. "It will be. I'm certain you'll know what to do when the time comes. I have faith in you."

His eyes soften, the bond humming with quiet relief. He nods, though the doubt lingers faintly. "Then I'll hold onto that faith. Yours, if not my own."

We walk onward, the group gathering behind us, the path leading deeper into the jungle. The Verdant Wrangle greets us like a living labyrinth. Great Divine, can we just catch a break?

The air is thick with humidity, clinging to our skin, heavy in our lungs. Bioluminescent vines coil around towering trees, pulsing faintly with light. Oversized leaves drip with nectar, their edges curling like tongues. The ground is soft, tangled with roots that shift beneath our feet.

Hera flinches at the movement. "What the Hades?"

Vines react to our movement, releasing faint clouds of pheromones that disorient, making the air shimmer, our senses blur. Pools of iridescent nectar glisten between the roots, their surfaces rippling with colors too vivid, too unreal. Liri warns us, "Do not touch them. Hallucinations await those who touch them."

Insects buzz with unnatural rhythms, their wings beating like drums. Flowers whisper fragments of lost stories, their voices faint but haunting. I catch some familiar words, but nothing connecting into thoughts I understand.

We move carefully, Diaspor leading, his blade cutting through the thick undergrowth. Feliks mutters curses under his breath, swatting at glowing insects. Bel steadies Hera when the roots shift beneath her feet. Liri walks tall, her eyes sharp, though I see the tension in her jaw.

Then the air changes.

A strange coolness radiates from the heart of the jungle, unnatural in this steamy place. Ash-colored butterflies swarm briefly, their wings shimmering with frost, before vanishing. Frost-kissed petals remain in their wake, fragile and glistening. I gaze up at them. "They're beautiful."

Diaspor halts, his hand raised. "Something's wrong."

Bel reaches for a tree trunk, his fingers brushing against a chilled scale embedded in the bark. He jerks back, shaking his hand vigorously. His breath catches. "It's cold," he mutters. "Too cold."

Then the warmth begins to leach away from us. Any spark of joy or anger all fade subtly, leaving emptiness. A shimmering mist rolls across the jungle floor, chilling vibrant leaves until they shatter like glass.

Then it emerges.

The frost viper coils from beneath a mossy root

system, absurdly elegant amid the jungle's heat. Its scales shimmer with frostfire, steam billowing as its body makes contact with the humid air. A halo of swirling fog surrounds it, its eyes glowing with a pale, haunting light.

Its voice slithers through the canopy, bringing all those jumbled words into form. "You do not belong here. You will be undone."

"Did the snake just speak?" Feliks mutters, backing away.

The viper lashes out, frost-coated fangs striking. Trees freeze instantly, their trunks warping, cracking. The terrain shifts, brittle and fragile. Its venom spreads through the air, slowing thought, disrupting magical memory. Any tactics vanish from my mind.

Diaspor curses, his blade trembling. "It's disrupting us so we can't think clearly."

The viper coils tighter, its body shimmering with frostfire. It strikes again, the ground freezing beneath its weight.

I summon my earth magic, vines erupting from the soil. But they falter, brittle, shattering against the frost. My breath catches, panic rising.

Then Diaspor's eyes widen. He points to a cluster of strange fruit hanging from a nearby tree, their skins shimmering faintly. "That fruit," he says urgently. "Hallucinogenic. When consumed, it lets warriors reexperience lost awareness. It can resist frost effects. Eat it!"

Nuala chimes in, "He's right. I've heard the same."

We hesitate only briefly before reaching for the fruit. Its taste is sharp, bitter, but warmth floods through me instantly. Memories surge...my mother's voice, my father's laughter, the first time I touched the bloom. They anchor me, steady me, resisting the viper's frost.

The others eat as well, their eyes widening as memories flood back. Feliks laughs suddenly, his voice strong. "I remember my first sword. That rusted, crooked old friend."

Hera exhales sharply. "I remember the day I swore I'd never bow to anyone again."

Liri's eyes glisten. "I remember my sisters chasing fireflies in the meadows."

Aero's voice is steady. "I remember the moment I knew I'd protect you, Eva. Always."

The memories seem to strengthen us, resisting the viper's venom. We fight with every bit of magic we have.

Diaspor commands the vines, twisting them around the viper's body. Feliks hurls stones, each one spinning rapidly with his regained fervor. Hera strikes with her blade, cutting through frostfire scales. Liri summons fire, her flames burning against the fog. Each Fae gives all they have, our magic still dulled but strong enough. Aero summons water, spears of liquid striking true.

I press my hands to the ground, summoning vines once more. This time, they hold, strong and steady, wrapping around the viper, pulling it down.

The jungle itself begins to resist. Trees shudder, their branches striking. Flowers ignite in rage, their petals burning. The ground trembles, roots twisting, lashing out. The land has not forsaken us. The dark plague upon it has not possessed all the earth.

The viper shrieks, its body unraveling. Frostfire smoke billows, swirling, dissipating. Its form disintegrates, leaving behind only what appears to be a gem, its form lying there, pulsing faintly.

I reach for it, my fingers brushing against its surface. It is cold, unnaturally still. A gem of stillness. Something so tiny for what it once was. My heart stills, slow to recognize the threat is gone. I clutch it tightly, my breath steady. "We did it," I whisper.

The others gather, their faces still pale. Aero's hand finds mine, his eyes steady. "We did."

The jungle quiets, and the mist fades. Aero runs his hand along his arm. "I feel the warmth returning." The bloom hums faintly against my palm, alive and steady.

"I feel it coming back too," Phira says.

I wasn't sure before, but I know now. They can dull our magic and play with our heads. It doesn't matter. We are ready. We move onward, toward Murick's fortress.

13
AERO

The cavern breathes around us, its walls humming faintly with a glow, veins of luminescence running like rivers through the stone. The air is cool, damp, carrying the scent of moss and mineral. Whispering stones line the walls. The smooth, pale rocks hum softly, echoing the faintest vibrations of thought and sound. They don't speak in words, but they carry nerves louder than any voice. Every heartbeat and flicker of doubt reverberates through the chamber.

We've set up temporary camp here, deep in the Unforgiving Woodlands. The journey has worn us thin, but the cavern offers shelter, a place to breathe. Eva rests near the fire, the bloom glowing faintly in her hands. Liri sits beside her, speaking quietly.

"You should sleep while you can," Liri murmurs. "Your magic won't thank you for stubbornness."

Eva huffs a tired laugh. "My magic never thanks me for anything."

Diaspor sharpens his blade nearby, each stroke deliberate. "Magic rarely appreciates its wielder," he says without looking up. "Steel is simpler."

Bel sits cross-legged against the cavern wall, humming under his breath. His eyes stay closed, head tilted as if the stones themselves whisper to him.

Feliks paces in a tight line, boots scuffing the dirt. "If we stay here too long, something's going to find us," he mutters. "This place feels...wrong."

"It feels like a forest," Hera snaps from her place near the entrance, arms crossed. "Not everything is a threat."

Feliks stops pacing long enough to glare at her. "In these woods? Everything is a threat."

Hera lifts a brow. "Then sit down and conserve your energy instead of wearing a trench into the floor."

Feliks throws his hands up. "I'm conserving my sanity."

Eva glances up from the bloom, a faint smile tugging at her mouth. "Good luck with that."

Their voices settle into the cavern's dimness, a fragile warmth against the cold stone. I take perimeter duty, moving along the edges of the cavern, checking the wards Liri and Diaspor set. Threads of magic shimmer faintly, woven into the stone, pulsing with protective energy. I trace them with my fingers, reinforcing them where they falter. My power hums steady, stronger than it has been in days. For the first time, I feel confident in my place on this journey. Eva's faith in me has anchored something inside. I know I can protect them. I know I can protect her.

But then I hear more voices.

Raised. Sharp.

I pause, half-hidden behind a curtain of shimmerleaf vines that hang from the cavern wall. The leaves glow faintly, their edges shimmering like glass. I duck behind them, listening. Feliks and Hera have found a nook farther into the cavern.

His voice carries first. "It's not just your strength, Hera. It's...the possibility. You could be carrying our child."

My breath catches. No, it can't be. I must not have heard him right.

Hera's response is icy fire, her tone cutting through the cavern like a blade. "And that makes me fragile now?"

I wince. I know that tone. I've heard it from Eva in battle, when someone questioned her resolve, her power. It's the sound of pride being tested, of strength being challenged.

Feliks stammers, his voice faltering. "No. I didn't mean it like that. I just...I worry. I can't help it."

Hera's laugh is sharp, bitter. "Worry all you want, but don't mistake me for something breakable. I've fought harder battles than this, Feliks. I've bled more than you can imagine. And if I am carrying a child, then that only makes me stronger, not weaker."

Feliks tries again, his voice softer. "I know. I know you're strong. Stronger than anyone I've ever known. But strength doesn't mean you have to carry everything alone. Let me carry some of it with you."

Silence follows, heavy and brittle.

I duck away before they notice me, my heart pounding. I don't want to intrude. Their words are theirs, their battle private. But the echo of it lingers in me, reverberating through the whispering stones.

I move back toward the perimeter, my thoughts heavy.

Eva's faith in me has steadied my place, but Feliks's words remind me of the weight we all carry. Hera's pride, her defiance...it mirrors Eva's—mirrors mine, if I'm honest with myself. We are all fighting not just the Mortia, but the doubts that gnaw at us, the fears that threaten to unravel us.

I glance back at the group. Eva looks up, her eyes meeting mine, the bond humming faintly. She doesn't speak, but I feel her presence, her strength. I give my best closed-mouth grin, but I know she senses the unease in me, the result of what I overheard.

I take a deep breath, steadying myself.

This journey is more than battles and wards. It's about trust and carrying each other when the weight becomes too much. Feliks sees that, even if his words stumble. Hera resists it, even if her pride roars. And me...I suppose I must learn it too.

But as I walk back toward the fire, another thought gnaws at me. What if it were Eva in Hera's shoes? What if she were here, in this dangerous place, carrying our child? The idea alone makes my chest tighten. I can picture it. The bloom in her hands, her determination unshaken, insisting she fight beside us. And me, standing there, knowing every strike, or every venomous fang, could take not just her, but something more.

Would I bite my tongue and let her go on fighting? Could I? Or would I lose my mind trying to shield her from every blow, every risk? The thought drives me half mad, even in imagining. I know her pride, her determination. She would never accept being treated as a fragile thing to be doted over. And yet, the instinct in me would burn against it, demanding I protect her at all costs.

I return to the fire, sitting beside her. She leans against me, the bloom glowing faintly in one hand, her mother's dagger in the other. The whispering stones hum softly, a song in the background of all this turmoil.

For the first time, I don't flinch at the sound. I let it settle into me, hoping it will steady me, but with the quiet knowledge that if fate ever placed Eva in Hera's place, I would be tested in ways I can barely imagine.

And I pray I'll have the strength to trust her, even then.

***

The morning is hushed, the kind of silence that feels heavier than night. The Fae-glow cavern has dimmed, its veins of light fading as dawn creeps through cracks in the stone. I step outside, the air cool against my skin, and follow the faint sound of pebbles striking water.

Feliks sits alone at the edge of a creek, his shoulders hunched, his expression shadowed. The water glows faintly, shimmering with an unnatural light. But it doesn't reflect faces. It reflects fears. Shapes ripple across its surface. They're shadows of doubt, fragments of dread. I see them flicker in the glow. Hera's silhouette, fragile and strong all at once, and Feliks himself, reaching but never quite holding on.

He tosses another pebble, watching the ripples distort the visions. His jaw tightens, his voice low. "I hate this place," he growls.

"It's just the Mortia trying to mess with your head—with all our heads," I remind him.

"I'm scared, Aero. What if she is pregnant? What if something happens in this gods-cursed place?"

I pause, standing a few steps away. I hadn't been sure if he knew I'd overheard them last night, but it's clear now. He knows. And he's carrying it like a stone in his chest.

I move closer, lowering myself to sit beside him. For a moment, I say nothing. The creek hums softly, its glow catching on the edges of our boots. Finally, I speak. "You think calling her 'fragile' helps keep her safe? Hera isn't one to break, brother. And she certainly isn't one to insinuate such things."

Feliks groans, dragging a hand down his face. "I said the worst possible thing, didn't I?"

I smirk, nodding. "Top five, at least."

He lets out a humorless laugh, tossing another pebble into the creek. The water ripples, showing a vision of Hera standing tall, her eyes blazing, her hand clenched around a blade. She looks unyielding, unstoppable. Feliks stares at it, his expression torn.

"You're trying to shield someone whose whole life has been war," I continue. "Maybe this child, if they exist, will grow up knowing two people who protect each other—not one trying to keep the other out of harm's way."

Feliks looks up, surprised. His eyes search mine, as if

he's not sure whether to believe me. "You're...weirdly wise sometimes."

I shrug. "Don't get used to it."

He laughs again, softer this time. The tension in his shoulders eases, just slightly. He tosses another pebble, watching the ripples fade. "I'll apologize," he says finally. "Not for caring, but for thinking she needs me to keep her whole. She doesn't. She's already whole."

I nod. "Good choice. These Merakian women are built differently."

The bond hums faintly in my chest. Eva's presence is steady, even from a distance. She's resting back at camp, the bloom glowing faintly in her hands. She doesn't know what I'm hearing now, but she'll feel it soon enough.

Feliks sighs, leaning back on his hands. "Keep this between us, alright?"

I raise an eyebrow. "You're asking me to keep secrets now?"

He smirks, but his eyes are serious. "You're going to tell Eva, though, aren't you?"

I exhale, shaking my head. "She's going to know I'm hiding something through the bond. I can't keep it from her."

Feliks groans again, burying his face in his hands. "Of course she will."

I watch him stand, his steps hesitant, unsure. The Fae moonlight catches on his figure, painting him in silver. He walks toward Hera, his shoulders squared but his stride uneven. He looks like a man stepping into battle—a battle against his own instinct to protect her.

I remain by the creek, staring into its glow. The water ripples, showing fragments of my own fears. Eva, standing alone, and the bloom shattered at her side. My mother's voice, twisted by shadow, calling me a traitor. My brother, hunched over with his head in between his hands. His laughter gone.

The creek reflects what I try to bury.

It's clear to me now: love isn't armor. It doesn't shield us from pain or loss. It's the fire and the forge. It burns deeply, and it reshapes us in ways nothing else can. It makes us vulnerable, but it also makes us unbreakable.

I think of Eva. If she were in Hera's place, there would be war inside me too. The thought alone makes my chest ache. Could I bite my tongue and let her fight? Could I stand back and trust her strength, even when every instinct in me screams to protect her?

I don't know.

But I know she wouldn't let me shield her. She would fight, because that's who she is. And maybe that's what love is...not keeping someone safe from the world, but standing beside them as they face it.

The creek glows brighter, the visions shifting. I see Eva, her hair wild, her eyes fierce, the bloom glowing in her hands. She looks at me, steady and unyielding. And I know I have to trust her, even if it breaks me.

Feliks's voice carries faintly from across the cavern, speaking to Hera. I can't hear the words from this distance, but I see the way she turns to him, her eyes sharp, her posture rigid. Then, slowly, her expression soft-ens. She listens. And for the first time, I see Feliks as grown. No longer the younger brother who jokes too much, but as a man willing to bare his heart, even when it terrifies him.

I smile faintly, turning back to the creek. The water ripples, the fears fading. I rise, brushing dirt from my hands, and move back toward camp. Eva looks up as I approach, her eyes steady, the bloom glowing faintly in her hands. She smiles, and the bond hums with warmth.

I sit beside her, the weight of the creek's visions still heavy in my chest. But for the first time, I don't flinch at them. I let them settle into me, steady and strong.

14
EVANTHE

Aero clears his throat subtly. "Eva," he murmurs, low enough the wind almost swallows it, "Feliks told me something—not meant for your ears yet."

Eva arches a brow. "Then why tell me?"

"Because you notice things. Hera's sharper than all of us, but she'll see it in your face if you're not prepared." He hesitates. "He thinks Hera might be pregnant."

Aero's words linger long after he falls silent. Pregnant. Hera. A child in the midst of this ugly war. The thought presses against my chest like weighted fog, heavy and suffocating. I keep walking, but my mind races, replaying every battle, every moment Hera and I stood side by side... or against each other. There was a ferocity that once made us enemies, a grudging respect that grew into something resembling friendship. And now, this possibility, fragile and dangerous, could be threading itself into the heart of our journey whether we are ready or not.

I exhale through my nose, forcing steel into my voice. "You'd better hope I'm a better actor than Feliks is a secret keeper."

Aero narrows his eyes, doubt flickering there. "We both know this secret is not for long in your hands. I doubt you make it to our next camp."

I shrug, unwilling to challenge him. He's probably right. Secrets have a way of unraveling when I'm involved. My face has always betrayed me, even when my words did not. He smirks at my conceding defeat. "You know I'm right."

"Just this once. Don't get a big head over it," I spit, unable to keep the smile from my face.

We keep moving, the path narrowing beneath the canopy. The air is thick, heavy with the scent of damp earth and vines. Hera strides ahead, strong as ever, her blade cutting through the undergrowth with deadly grace. But now, every motion of hers weighs differently in my mind. Every stumble on uneven ground, every hand brushing near her stomach. It all feels magnified, suspicious. Is she softer than before? Or am I imagining it, betraying her strength with my doubt?

I hate it. The wondering feels like betrayal. Hera has never been fragile. She has never asked for protection. To even think of her as vulnerable feels like stripping her of the very spark that defines her.

Still, a memory flickers. Hera binding Feliks's arm after a skirmish, her hands lingering longer than necessary. The way their eyes met, unspoken words passing between them. I had known they were together. It wasn't a secret.

But I assumed she took maidenroot tonic, as most of us did, to prevent conception. In the chaos of this war, though, I can see how easily one might forget. Aero had made sure to gather tonic for me before our bonding ceremony. Had he not, who knows if I wouldn't find myself in the same condition now?

The thought unsettles me, not because of the possibility itself, but because of what it would mean here, in this dreadful place. A child born into shadow. A child carried through battle. The risk is unbearable.

The path tightens further, vines creeping across the ground, pulsing faintly with light. I quicken my pace, moving to Hera's side. A vine trap coils ahead, its tendrils twitching, waiting to ensnare. I step forward, shielding her, slicing through the vines before they can strike.

Hera smirks, her voice sharp. "You trying to mother me now, Evanthe?"

I don't flinch. "No. Just clearing the path. Some people might think you're...fragile."

Her snort is pure fire. She slices through the remaining vines with deadly precision, her blade flashing. "Let them think it. The delicate human making her way through the Fae Realm."

I don't look back at Feliks. I don't need to. I know he heard. His silence is louder than words, his guilt heavy in the air. He wants to protect her, but Hera will never accept being treated as breakable. And I, caught between knowing and doubting, don't really know which side of the line I should stand on.

We march on, the jungle pressing close around us. The

canopy thickens, blocking out the sun, casting us in shadow. The air hums with strange energy, vines whispering, flowers sighing. Every step feels heavier, every breath thicker. The fortress lies ahead, but the path is treacherous.

Aero walks beside me, his presence steady, the bond humming faintly. He doesn't speak, but I feel his thoughts pressing against mine. He knows the weight of what he's told me. He knows the conflict it stirs. And he knows I will not keep it hidden for long.

Hera strides ahead, unrelenting. Feliks lingers behind her, his eyes fixed on her back, his expression torn. Liri walks tall, her gaze sharp, though I know she's wearing the weight of her kingdom. Diaspor leads, his blade cutting through the undergrowth, his posture rigid. Bel hums softly, his voice carrying faintly, steadying the air.

I watch Hera move fiercely through the terrain. And I wonder, if she is carrying a child, what does that mean for us? For her? For this war? Can she fight as she always has? Will she let anyone protect her?

The doubt gnaws at me. But beneath it, something else stirs. Respect. Hera has always been unyielding. Despite her lack of Fae magic, she refuses to bend. She endures like no other. She survives. It's what made her such a fierce competitor of mine. Where others falter, she pushes forward, carving her place in a world that has tried again and again to break her. I owe her my faith.

The path twists, leading us deeper into shadow. The vines thicken, and the air grows heavier. We stop briefly, gathering our breath. The silence is brittle, tension humming between us. Feliks shifts, his eyes flicking toward Hera then away. Hera notices, her gaze sharp, but she says nothing.

I sit, my jaw still dropped with the shock of this news. I close my eyes, breathing deeply, letting its warmth settle into me. The bond hums, Aero's presence steady, grounding me. He finds a place beside me and places a handful of whisper fern tips in my hand. The tender shoots remind me of some kind of sprout we would find in the fields outside Parea. I sift through them in my palm. "Salad? Really?"

He laughs, "It's all I could find, your highness."

Hera sits nearby, her blade resting across her knees. She looks strong, unyielding, but I see the flicker of something weighing heavily behind her eyes.

Feliks sits apart, his shoulders hunched, his gaze fixed on the ground. His silence is heavy, his guilt palpable. He wants to protect her, but he doesn't know how. He wants to shield her, but she will never let him. And I, caught between knowing and doubting, don't know how to help either of them. I wouldn't know the first thing about a baby. I certainly know nothing about how to care for one whilst it's still inside you.

The silence stretches, brittle and sharp. Finally, Hera speaks, her voice low but steady. "We keep moving. The fortress is close. No more delays."

Feliks sighs but rises to his feet as we all do. Gathering our things, the path narrows once more. The vines coil, the air thickens, the shadows press close. We march on, the fortress looming ahead, the weight of secrets heavy in the air.

I walk beside Hera, my blade ready, my eyes sharp. She strides forward, fierce and unrelenting. Whatever the truth is, whatever the secret holds, she will not break. She will fight for her life and the one growing inside her.

And I will stand beside her as her sister.

The jungle hums, and the path twists. The secret lingers, and that's alright for now. Despite the impossible odds, something about it makes me giddy.

Our little family is having a baby.

We cautiously enter the Hollow. The canopy above glows faintly, threads of light weaving through the branches like veins of some ancient heart. The air smells of sweet clover and something older, like promises made long ago but never fulfilled. Moss-covered stones ripple with pulses of light, soft and steady, as though the land itself is sighing.

We move carefully through the narrow pass, the trail winding beneath the canopy's glow. Ahead, the path diverges—one trail leading deeper into Mortia-shadowed lands, the other curling back toward Fae refuge. The cross-roads hum with tension, as though it knows the weight of the choice before us.

I lead, the bloom warm in my hand, its faint glow guiding me forward. Aero walks close, his presence steady. Hera strides behind, her posture rigid, on the lookout for possible danger ahead. Feliks hovers near her, his eyes narrow, his worry palpable. Diaspor scouts ahead, his blade ready, his gaze scanning the shadows. Liri and Bel flank the group, their eyes wary, their silence heavy.

Then we see them.

A band of Fae travelers, moving urgently in the opposite direction. Their steps are quick, their weapons drawn but not raised. Both parties halt abruptly, the air thickening with tension. Subtly, I reach for my mother's dagger. The Hollow hums louder, as though listening.

Hera stiffens, her hand brushing her stomach. She exchanges quiet glances with Aero and Feliks. One Fae traveler eyes her warily, his gaze lingering. He whispers, his voice low but clear. "You carry a gift within. You should not walk into the dark."

The words hang heavy in the air. Hera's jaw tightens, her eyes narrowing. Feliks shifts closer, his hand brushing hers. Aero's gaze flicks to me. He nods, urging me to take the lead through our bond.

I step forward, my heart beating wildly, but my voice carrying the old weight of the Guardian's bloodline. "I am the Guardian of this realm," I say, my voice steady. "We journey to confront King Murick and destroy the Mortia."

Shock ripples through the Fae group. Their eyes widen, and their posture shifts. Some bow their heads in respect, their voices murmuring faintly. The Hollow hums louder, its light pulsing.

One Fae steps forward, his voice urgent. "Murick's fortress lies less than two night's march from here. You'll be seen before you speak."

The words strike like a blade. The fortress is close. Too close.

Hera instinctively reaches for her weapon, her hand tightening on the hilt. Feliks notices and moves closer beside her, murmuring, "You shouldn't—"

Her glare silences him instantly. He bites his tongue, his jaw tight.

Then, a Fae child steps forward. Her brown-and-yellow eyes are wide, her hands trembling. She holds out a pink folded flower, its petals glowing faintly. She offers it to me, her voice soft. "Trust."

I take it gently, my heart tightening. The bloom hums faintly in my hand, its warmth steady. The group relaxes slightly, the tension easing. The female next to her addresses the group. "Murick's power grows unstable. Mortia spirits now hunt in daylight. The land itself trembles beneath his shadow."

Another Fae steps forward, his eyes sharp. "There is a route known only to dream-menders. Hidden. Dangerous. But possibly undetected. It may lead you closer without being seen." Reaching into his satchel, he pulls out a small scroll and unrolls it before us. "This is where we are now." He runs his finger along the narrow opening through a forest. "Take this path."

The words settle into me, heavy but hopeful. A hidden path. A chance.

I incline my head, the bloom warm in my palm. "You've given us more than directions," I say quietly. "You've given us hope. For that, I thank you."

The eldest of the Fae travelers, his hair silvered like

moonlight, bows slightly. "Hope is a fragile thing in these lands. Guard it well, Guardian. It will be tested."

Another Fae, younger and sharp-eyed, adds, "We cannot walk with you, but our prayers will follow. May the Hollow's light shield your steps."

I meet his gaze, steady. "And may your refuge remain untouched by shadow. You've risked much even speaking to us."

The Fae child who had offered me the folded flower tugs at her mother's sleeve then looks up at me again. "Make the dark go away," she whispers, her voice trembling but earnest.

I crouch, taking her small hand gently. "That is why we walk forward," I tell her. "So that younglings like you will never have to fear the dark again."

Her mother's eyes glisten, and she bows her head. "Then may the Great Divine walk with you. May your bloom burn brighter than the Mortia's shadow."

Behind me, I hear Hera shift, her blade sliding back into its sheath. Feliks exhales, tension easing from his shoulders. Even Diaspor lowers his weapon, though his eyes remain sharp.

The eldest Fae straightens, his voice solemn. "Go swiftly, Guardian. Murick's eyes are everywhere. But if you take the dream-menders' path, you may yet reach him unseen. And when you do...strike true."

I nod, my voice firm. "We will."

As the groups part, one female Fae lingers. She steps close to Hera, her voice soft but clear, just loud enough for me to hear. "The child within will be born under war's breath. Let its first cry be heard in peace."

Hera's eyes widen, her hand resting low on her stomach. She watches them disappear into the Hollow, a single tear falling down her cheek. She wipes it away quickly.

I turn to Aero, my voice steady. "We knew this would come fast."

He nods, his gaze fixed on Feliks, who frets over Hera. "We just didn't know how fast."

The Hollow hums softly, its glow fading as we move forward. The path narrows, the light dimming. The fortress waits ahead, its shadow pressing closer.

We march on until the Hollow's glow fades behind us, replaced by the silence of Mortia-shadowed lands. The ground grows harder, the air colder. The bloom hums faintly in my hand, its warmth steady, guiding me forward. Diaspor and Aero scout ahead, their blades cutting through the silence. Liri and Bel flank us, their eyes sharp, their silence heavy. The path twists, leading us deeper into shadow.

I clutch the bloom tighter, the Fae's words echoing in my mind: *Murick's fortress lies less than two night's march from here. You'll be seen before you speak.*

The weight of it presses against me. But beneath it, something else burns. Faith.

We march on. I hold on tightly to the pink folded flower, its petals glowing faintly. A sign of trust. A reminder of what we fight for.

15

EVANTHE

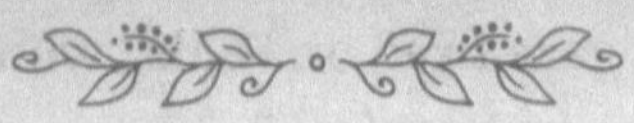

The cavern shudders like a wounded heart. Its walls pulse faintly, veins of light threading through stone as though the petrified Fae tree above still carries echoes of what it once was. Bioluminescent fungi cling to the walls, their glow dim and uneven, casting shadows that flicker like broken wings. The air is damp, metallic, heavy with the scent of roots and old blood.

I lead the party inside, my steps careful, my eyes sharp. Every crevice is a threat until proven otherwise. My mind runs through the necessities. Sleeping arrangements, food, drink, proximity to escape routes. The cavern is vine-choked, its floor uneven, and its ceiling low in places. It will serve as shelter, but only if we make it so.

Behind me, I hear Hera groan softly. It is barely audible, but I notice. My ears are tuned to her now, every sound weighted differently. I glance back, catching the way her hand brushes her abdomen as she paces. The others don't see it. They wouldn't, but I do.

Feliks hovers near her, his worry sharp but restrained. He tries not to make her feel caged, but his eyes betray him. He watches every step she takes, every breath, every flicker of discomfort. Hera lies back against the cool stone, her eyes closed, her jaw tight. Her body is still strong and unyielding, but I can't unsee the slight swell of her belly, subtle but undeniable.

The weight of knowledge presses against me. Hera is pregnant. She is still fighting. And my silence at Aero's request is becoming heavy. After what happened to Sorrow back in the human realm, I couldn't live with myself if something happened to Hera or her unborn child.

She's iron shaped by battle, I think. But even iron needs tending, or it will crack.

I walk deeper into the cavern, away from the others. The walls flicker with shadows that move like bloodied wings, mirroring my unease. The cavern feels alive, listening, as my thoughts churn. Am I being a poor leader by hiding the truth? Or a good friend by protecting her wishes to keep this hidden? The line is too blurry. The Guardian must carry everyone's burdens. But who carries mine?

I stop near a cluster of fungi, their glow faint, and their shadows stretching long. My breath catches, the weight pressing harder. Aero joins me quietly, his knowing gaze surely finding this amusing. He doesn't speak at first, just stands beside me, his eyes scanning the cavern. Finally, his voice is low. "You okay?"

I exhale, my voice sharp but weary. "We're all walking on daggers. Some of us more than others."

He nods, his gaze steady. "When this ends…you need rest. We all do."

I glance back at Hera, her figure outlined faintly by the fungi's glow. "She won't break, you know."

"No," Aero says, his voice firm. "But someone's going to need to be there if she does."

The words settle into me. He's right. Hera is strong, but even strength like hers has limits. And when it falters, someone must be there to catch her.

Diaspor moves to the cavern's entrance, his blade steadied. Using what little magic he has, he inscribes a protective sigil into the stone, his movements precise. The magic glows pale green, pulsing faintly, weaving protection into the walls. The cavern hums softly, the sigil anchoring its breath.

The group settles slowly, their weariness heavy. Feliks sits near Hera, more relaxed but still keeping an eye out. Liri and Bel rest near the fungi, their eyes closing. Diaspor remains near the entrance, his vigilance unyielding. Aero stays close to me, making sure I don't overexert myself. I know he means well, but at some point, he will have to recognize I've been taking care of myself my whole life. He can't always be there to dote on me.

I stand watch, my eyes scanning the shifting shadows. The cavern flickers, its walls breathing, its fungi glowing faintly. I search for Mortia's scouts, for whispers in the dark. Sometimes a shadow moves too quickly, startling us both.

My mind drifts to Sorrow back in the mortal realm, of the loss that still burns there. Surely feeling the ache in my chest through our bond, Aero turns toward me and cups my face with his palms, pulling me to him. "Close your eyes, Eva."

I fidget with the hem of my tunic.

"Just do it, please," he pleads.

I'm far from thrilled by the notion, but I do as he asks.

"Place a hand over your chest."

Reluctantly, I place my right palm over my heart.

"Good girl," he murmurs, making my shoulders shake with amusement. "Now, take in a deep breath." I let the air fill my lungs to the brim. "And let it out," he says.

I exhale, my chest shrinking back down to size. My eyes well up with tears. He lifts a thumb, catching the droplets that fall to my face, and gently wipes them away.

"You know why they follow you?" he asks.

"Why?" I ask, sniffling.

"Because you can't fail. You were destined for this. It's already done."

I roll my eyes.

"No, don't diminish it. There is power in your words. Say it with me: It's already done."

I try to make light of it again, but his gaze is sharp, serious. I might actually believe him. His mouth parts again, and this time, I say the words with him.

"It's already done."

Just for a moment, I let myself feel everything. The weight of Hera's secret. The burden of leadership. The fear of failure. The hope of victory. It's already done.

16
AERO

The cave murmurs like a sleeping beast. Each exhale of damp air sends goosebumps down my arms; the sensation disgusts me. I cannot wait to be out in the open again, no longer hiding in this miserable Hades hole.

I roll onto my side, eyes tracking the lazy drift of bioluminescent spores above. Hera rests across the chamber, her breathing steady, hand curled instinctively over her belly. Feliks lies beside her, his arm draped over her side. Every few minutes, he stirs, like dreams won't leave him alone.

I don't sleep. Apparently, gods don't sleep the night before a reckoning.

I shift my gaze toward Eva. She stands sentry near the mouth of the cave, her silhouette tense against the pale-green glow of her sigils. She hasn't spoken to me since our little breathing exercise, but her thoughts feel loud. Some days, I can read her posture better than words.

A part of me wants to rise and walk to her, to ease the weight gathering on both our shoulders. But tonight isn't for comfort. It is for readiness. Behind me, a stone cracks with a soft pop as an ember from the fire between us goes flying toward Hera. It happens so quickly no one notices until she jolts up, repelling the smoldering chunk of wood away. Her eyes are wild with fear. Startled by the commotion, Feliks leaps up, his fists clenched, ready for a brawl. "What's wrong? What is it?" he asks frantically.

Everyone is awake now and goes to Hera's aid. Eva searches her for any sign of injury. I try to tell Diaspor it was just the fire, but he still goes on to search the cave for signs of an enemy. Hera, still catching her breath, lifts a finger. "It was just an ember from the fire. I'm fine."

A sigh of relief washes over the group. I hand Eva a drink of water. "She's okay." She lowers the canteen from her lips. "I know, but it feels like a bad omen."

Nodding, I remove my cloak and wrap it around her. "Get some rest."

She lies down beside me. The others also find their way back to their beds. I, on the other hand, remain awake, staring into the dark, listening. We are close now. I can feel it. The thinning of the air, the way silence presses harder. It's as if the entire realm is bracing for war.

I reach for my blade, holding the hilt like it can answer all the questions I can't ask.

Tomorrow, we will walk toward King Murick's fortress.

Tonight, we breathe like it might be our last.

I lie still, eyes open. The walls hum low, seeming to respond to the tension they're filled with. They've been pulsing steadily all night. Every bit of fear written in moss and mineral.

Once she realized sleep wasn't going to find her either, Eva took position near the entrance. She's more shadow than flesh, leaning against the petrified arch with her arms folded and her thoughts locked deep. I used to think I understood the way her mind worked. Now I realize I only understood the parts she and our bond let me see. Liri joins her, pointing out into the vast forest ahead. Eva seems to agree with whatever path the princess has informed her of.

Dawn creeps into the cave like a cautious animal.

Light doesn't reach us directly, but the spores shift their hue, pale golden now, like the realm itself is holding its breath.

Eva straightens. Without a word, she walks past each of us. The sigil they etched by the cave's mouth pulses once. Green, then blue, then fades into dust. That means it's broken now. Time's up.

"Wake up," she says quietly. One touch to Hera's shoulder. A nudge to Feliks's boot. No urgency, just certainty.

Feliks groans. Hera opens her eyes and instantly sits up. Feliks shoots her a look, maybe worried she moved too fast, and she shoots one right back, daring him to say something. Wisely, he doesn't dare.

I rise, stretching the stiffness from my limbs. Eva meets my eyes for a beat longer than usual.

"We're close," she says. Her voice is calm but stripped of mercy. "The fortress lies beyond the ridge. If we cut through the scorched grove by midday, we'll be in range by dusk tomorrow...so long as nothing slows us down."

Feliks rubs his face. "So...we're skipping breakfast and heading straight into hell?"

"No," Eva says. "We're bringing hell with us."

That earns a small grin from Hera. Even Feliks seems steadier.

Eva turns to me last. "Watch the northern trail. If the Mortia rise early, we need a fifteen-second warning. No less."

I nod.

And just like that, the quiet ends. The cave exhales again. But this time, the breath carries steel.

17

EVANTHE

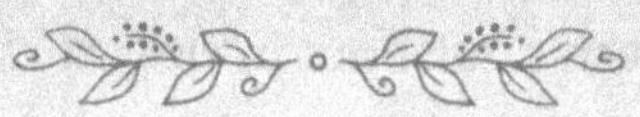

Twisted trees rise around us like skeletal sentries, their branches clawing at the sky. The ground beneath my boots is cracked, veins of dormant magic running through it like scars. Every step feels like walking across a battlefield that has been waiting centuries to wake again.

The air hums with tension, buzzing like static before a storm. We are too close now. King Murick's fortress lies ahead, hidden in the folds of shadow and stone, and every heartbeat feels like a countdown.

The group prepares in silence, each of us caught in our own rituals. Diaspor sharpens his blade with steady precision, the scrape of steel against stone echoing faintly. Bel murmurs a prayer under his breath, his arms swinging back and forth. Liri checks her bowstring, tightening it ever so slightly for perfect precision. Feliks paces, restless energy spilling from him, his eyes flicking constantly toward Hera. The concern he has for her is sweet. I hope Hera has patience with him.

Aero stands near me, his hands clenching then releasing on repeat, the bond between us humming faintly against my chest. I know he and Feliks are not brothers by blood, but beneath his hard exterior, Aero is a lot like him —at his core. He just wants what's best for the people he loves. He just doesn't go about in sing-song.

Hera checks her blades. Her jaw is set, her gaze hardened, but her posture is tighter than usual. Protective. Measured. She slices through a thornvine with practiced ease, her movements sharp but deliberate. She is strong, unyielding, but beneath it all, I can see the subtle shift, the quiet weight she carries. I let myself watch her for a moment, my chest tightening. Then I move.

Leaving the others to their preparations, I approach her quietly. My steps are steady, my eyes sharp. She notices me, of course, but she doesn't pause to look up. Her blade flashes, slicing through another vine, her movements fluid.

I lean casually against a ruined obelisk, its stone cracked and weathered, its surface etched with faint runes long since faded. I smirk, my voice sharp but playful. "So, you're planning to charge into a death trap with a whole second heartbeat tagging along? Bold."

Her eyes flick to me, cautious. "Feliks did tell you. That rat. I knew it."

I shrug, my smirk widening. "He told Aero. Aero told me. The chain of secrets in this group is about as sturdy as Feliks's nerve."

She sighs, her blade flashing again, slicing through another vine. "Are you here to lecture me?"

I step closer, my voice softening. "No. I'm here to remind you who you are. You're not just carrying life; you've grown through every fight, every choice. You're a force, Hera. Pregnant or not, you burn through the dark."

Her blade stills. For a moment, her posture cracks just slightly. She sets the weapon down, her shoulders tightening. Her voice is steady but fragile. "I'm scared," she admits. "Not of the fight, but of what happens after."

I place a hand on her shoulder, my grip firm, grounding. "Then we make sure there is an after."

Her lips twitch, almost a smile. "And if I falter?"

My grin is wicked and warm. "Then I drag your stubborn, radiant ass out of the fire myself. Sisterhood is exhausting, but I'm committed."

She nods, quiet. Strong again. Her shoulders straighten. "Let's finish this."

I watch her walk toward the others, her hand brushing lightly across her stomach. I don't say it aloud, but I think it: *If anyone can fight while carrying the future...it's you, Hera.*

Ashen Hollow stretches before us like a wound in the world. Once, it was said to be a luminous clearing lit by eternal twilight, a place where Fae gathered to sing beneath the stars. Now it is charred, quaking with lingering heat.

Cracks in the ground pulse with emberlight, expelling

bursts of heat that sting the skin. The air smells of ash and scorched moss. Around the edges of the clearing, silhouettes of Fae statues stand frozen mid-scream, their bodies blackened, their faces twisted in agony. They look like mourners, locked forever in grief. I peer over to find Princess Liri blinking away tears forming in her violet eyes. These may not have been Fae of her kingdom, but each soul meant something to someone.

We move cautiously, the bloom warm in my hand, its faint glow steady against the Hollow's oppressive heat. Diaspor kneels near a tree trunk, his fingers brushing against burnt bark. Symbols are etched there, ancient and jagged. He frowns, his voice low. "Old Fae script. Warnings."

I step closer, reading the faint lines. *Let no heart speak where shadows listen.*

The words chill me, even here in the heat. Silence as protection. Silence as survival.

Before I can speak, a rumble rolls through the Hollow. The ground trembles, cracks widening. I jump at a bursting flare of emberlight as a wave of heat surges, warping the air, singeing foliage. Wildlife scatters. The birds shriek, wings beating frantically, small creatures darting into the shadows.

Then it emerges.

Its silhouette blazes against the Hollow's charred backdrop. Antlers burn like living pyres, flames licking upward. Its eyes are molten gold, glowing with fury and sorrow. Each breath scorches the moss, sending waves of heat across the clearing.

"What in the wilding winds is that?" Phira whispers.

"Some kind of cursed ember elk," Liri replies, bracing herself.

We freeze, weapons shifting, tension coiling. The elk lowers its head, antlers blazing brighter. Then it charges.

It moves in zigzag patterns, impossibly fast for its size. Trails of fire ignite in its wake, corralling us into vulnerable positions. The heat aura presses against us, forcing our bodies to resist or falter. My lungs burn, and my skin prickles, sweat pouring down my back. Every breath feels like swallowing a flame.

Diaspor shouts, his blade flashing. "Stay spread! Don't let it corner us!"

But the elk is cunning. Its trails of fire twist, cutting off escape routes, forcing us into pockets of heat. Feliks curses, his bowstring snapping taut, arrows flying. But they burn to ash before reaching the beast.

Aero surges forward, his hands glowing with water magic. He douses flames as quickly as they rise, torrents of water clashing against fire. Steam billows, thick and choking, clouding the battlefield.

The elk roars, its voice a furnace. It slams into a fallen tree trunk, the wood infused with what I can only imagine is frost magic. The impact explodes, shards of ice and fire scattering. The blast knocks Bel to the ground, his prayer cut short. Liri stumbles, her bow clattering against stone.

I raise my blade, vines erupting from the cracked earth, twisting toward the elk. They catch its legs, but the heat sears them instantly, turning them to ash. My breath catches, my heart hammering in my chest.

The elk charges again, its antlers blazing. It slams into Diaspor, sending him sprawling, his blade skittering across the ground. Feliks shouts, firing another arrow, but the flames consume it mid-flight.

The heat presses harder, exhausting us, draining stamina and hope. My vision blurs, sweat stinging my eyes. My chest tightens, each breath a battle.

Then, a pause.

The ember elk halts, its molten gaze fixed on Liri. She stands tall, her face pale, her eyes glistening with sorrow. For a moment, the battlefield stills. The elk hesitates, its flames dimming, its form shifting.

Then I see it...its original self. Radiant, majestic. A creature of twilight, not fire. Its antlers glow softly, its eyes mournful, its body shimmering with light.

Liri's voice trembles, but it carries. "You were once a noble. I see it. I feel it."

The elk's flames flicker, its body trembling. For a heartbeat, hope sparks.

But the pause is short-lived.

The flames surge again, molten fury returning. The elk turns, its gaze locking on me now.

Then it charges.

I raise my blade, vines erupting again, twisting desperately. Aero shouts, torrents of water surging, dousing flames, but the elk barrels through. Its antlers blaze, and its breath scorches, its body a furnace.

It slams toward me, the ground cracking beneath its weight. I dodge, barely, the heat searing my skin. My blade flashes, striking its flank, but the fire consumes the steel, melting it. My hand burns, pain shooting up my arm.

The elk roars, its antlers sweeping. I stumble, the heat pressing harder, my lungs burning. My vision blurs, and my strength falters.

Aero shouts, his water surging, dousing flames around me. "Eva!"

I fight, desperate, my blade flashing, vines twisting, but the elk is relentless. Its antlers ignite the dusk, its breath hissing with heat, its frame blazing as though a furnace roars beneath its hide. My strength wanes; my resolve falters.

Hope flickers, fading.

Then—

Nuala. She leaps from the shadows, her blade flashing, her body a blur. She strikes the elk's flank, her blade piercing deep. The beast roars, flames surging, but Nuala is relentless. She moves with fury, her strikes precise, her blows unyielding.

The elk stumbles, its flames dimming, its body trembling. Nuala strikes again, her blade piercing its heart. The beast roars, flames surging one last time, throwing all its rage at her. Then it fades.

Its body shimmers, its form shifting. For a moment, I see its radiant, majestic form once more. Then it collapses, its flames extinguished, its body dissolving into ash and emberlight. Nuala collapses beside it. Liri runs to her.

The Hollow stills, the battle over but uncertainty clinging to the air. We stand, each of us trembling, exhausted. I also collapse, pain shooting through me. My skin burns, seared by the elk's flames. My breath catches, and my vision blurs. Aero rushes to me, his hands glowing with water, dousing the burns, cooling the pain. His voice trembles, "Eva, stay with me."

I gasp, every inch of my scorched skin crying out. The bloom hums faintly in my hand, its warmth steady, but it does nothing to ease the pain.

Diaspor stands over the elk's ashes, over Nuala's body, his blade still in hand, as if his body hasn't yet caught up with his mind. She saved me. She saved us.

The Hollow exhales, emberlight fading, silence settling.

I lie on the cracked ground, pain burning, breath shallow as my eyes roll shut.

18

EVANTHE

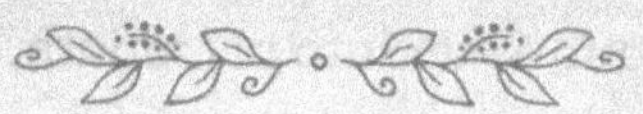

Ashen Hollow is quiet now, but it is not peace. The charred earth steams around us, the shallow glade warped by fire and grief. Aero's power has cooled patches of scorched moss, leaving damp streaks across the blackened soil, but the air still tastes of ash. The ember elk's corpse smolders nearby, its antlers shattered like glass, its eyes dulled remnants of ancient fire. Once radiant...now only ruin.

I lie on my side, skin blistered, armor cracked, lips parched. My breath hitches in my throat, shallow and uneven, each inhale scraping like sandpaper. The heat lingers in me, as though I am still burning. My body feels heavy, pinned beneath invisible weight.

Memories twist in the haze. Earlier times with Nuala, her voice bright against the stone. Hera's blades flashing, sharp arcs of steel. The sound of someone sobbing—was that...Liri? I feel like I'm floating beneath a thick wave of heat, unable to rise, unable to breathe. My mind clings to one thought: Did anyone survive?

A shadow falls over me. Aero kneels beside me, his hands frantic, his power faltering. His face is streaked with soot and saltwater, his gray-blue eyes wide with fear. "C'mon, Eva. Please. Don't do this." His voice cracks, raw and desperate.

He tries to pour water into my mouth, but my throat is scorched, the liquid searing instead of soothing. His veins pulse, his arms trembling as his power strains to soothe the burns. Coolness spreads across my skin in patches, but the pain is relentless. His magic flickers, his strength waning, but he refuses to stop.

Behind him, Liri stands. Her hands are clasped, blood staining her sleeve. Her voice is low and hollow. "She's fighting. Evanthe wouldn't let go. Not like this."

But her eyes are empty, staring past me to where Nuala had stood only moments before. Her mourning is silent, regal, suffocating. She does not weep, does not wail. Her sorrow is quiet, restrained, but inside, she is bursting at the seams. She stands like a statue, her grief carved into her frame.

I force my eyes open briefly. Aero's face looms above me, warped with fear, his jaw tight, his breath ragged. Liri stands behind him, whispering an ancient Fae prayer I don't understand. I try to speak, my lips cracked, my throat raw. Only fragments emerge. "Am I dead or...did someone finally love me enough to cry?"

Aero lets out a strangled laugh. It's half relief, half despair. "If you crack jokes while charbroiled, you're not dying yet." His laugh steadies me faintly, but the heat drags me down again, pulling me into darkness.

My last sensation is Liri kneeling beside me, her hand gentle as she brushes burnt hair away from my face. Her whisper is soft, trembling. "Nuala would want you to heal. I know your short history with her was strained, but she never gave up on you."

Steam rises gently around me. Aero's hands tremble as he draws water from the scorched moss, cooling my burns with desperate precision. His fear is ferociously running through our bond. He doesn't know if his efforts are enough. Neither do I.

The Hollow exhales, the emberlight fading. The elk's corpse smolders, its antlers shattered, its eyes dulled. Nuala's body is lying only steps away but is now surrounded by a wreath of half-burnt wildflowers and tall grass. The glade steams, cooled by Aero's power, scarred by fire and grief.

I drift in and out, caught between pain and memory. Nuala's leap flashes again in my mind. The moment she struck the elk, her blade piercing deep, her body a blur of fury and grace. She saved me. She saved us. And now she is gone. Her sacrifice burns sharper than the wounds across my skin. I feel it in my chest, heavy and cruel. She gave everything, and I lived. The weight of it presses harder than the fire.

Aero's fear pulls me back to the present. His hands are steady, but his breath is ragged, his eyes wild. He pours water across my burns, cooling them, soothing them, but his power falters, his strength wanes. He is terrified—

more than I have ever seen him. The ferocity of it cuts through me. He cannot lose me. Not now. Not ever.

Liri's grief shadows the moment. She does not speak again, but her silence is louder than any scream. She lost Nuala, and the absence of her voice is suffocating. This victory feels heavy, cruel. The elk is dead, but the cost is unbearable.

Hera kneels beside me, her hand gentle, brushing burnt hair away. Her voice trembles, "You can't give up. What was it that you and Sorrow always said when times were tough?" There is a pause as she waits, hoping I will find it in me to say it out loud. I clear the smoke from my throat—

"Let the sky fall,
I will not tremble,
I am the stone,
The moon who claims them,
For I carry the fallen."

I hear Sorrow's soft, high voice as I say the mantra. It's bittersweet. I try to lift my hand to Hera, but my arm weighs more than a ton of stones. She reaches for me, but then the world all goes black.

———

Inside the healing tent, the world is reduced to shadows and damp cloth. Cloaks and tree limbs have been lashed together to form a fragile shelter, its seams dripping with Aero's water magic, the air heavy with moisture. The smell is thick, like moss, salt, and scorched skin mingling into something that clings to the lungs. Soft light seeps through the patchwork fabric, fractured beams that dance across my blurred vision like ghosts.

I wake slowly, as if dragged upward through layers of ash. My body is heat and static, every nerve raw, every breath a reminder of flame. My skin stings as though it still remembers the elk's fire, blistered and cracked, refusing to mend.

Murmurs drift around me, voices blurred by pain. Aero's voice cracks through panic, words tumbling too fast, too desperate. "What if she never wakes up? She has to wake up."

"She will rise. She has to."

Liri's quiet pleas thread through his, steady but hollow. Somewhere nearby, someone is crying, the sound muffled but sharp enough to pierce the haze.

My throat aches. I try to speak, my lips parting, but only smoke-shaped silence escapes. My chest tightens, frustration burning hotter than the wounds.

Through the haze, I see Liri's silhouette bathed in gray light. Her eyes are red-rimmed, grief carved into her face, but her posture remains composed, regal even in sorrow. She kneels in silence, her head bowed in prayer.

Aero's hands hover above me, trembling. His brow is slick with sweat, his breath ragged. He whispers apologies to a body barely listening, words spilling like water, desperate and unending. His fingers twitch, his power faltering.

The tent flaps ripple gently, stirred by a faint wind. In

the whisper of fabric, I swear I hear Nuala's name. The sound cuts through me, sharp and cruel.

I know I survived—but barely. The fire lingers in me, heavy and unyielding. And though I barely knew her, I feel Nuala's absence like a phantom limb. Her sacrifice burns sharper than the wounds across my skin. She gave me her last breath, and I cannot even stand.

Inside, grief thrashes against survival instinct. The thought claws at me, bitter and raw. She gave me her last breath...and I can't even stand.

Aero notices my eyes open. Relief chokes him, his breath catching. He cups my cheek with salt-drenched fingers, his touch trembling. His eyes are wild, his fear unmasked.

I rasp, my voice broken, my throat raw. "I was supposed to save her. I'm supposed to save all of them. That was the deal."

Liri kneels beside me, her voice distant. "She made her choice to fight. For you. For us." Her words are heavy, but her eyes remain hollow, staring past me, still lost in grief.

I close my eyes again, bitterness spilling from me in a whisper. "Sisterhood is a reckless thing."

The pain pulses again, sharp and unrelenting. Darkness drags me down, heavy and cruel. But this time, grief follows me in. I do not dream. I burn. I'm not sure how much time has passed. It could be hours, could be days. No, it can't be days. We don't have days.

The tent hums softly, dampened by Aero's magic. The air is thick with grief. My body lies broken, blistered. I almost forget where I am, what has happened, but then I hear Liri's voice. A soft crying in the distance reminding me of our loss.

I let my eyes close, but before darkness takes me, I whisper a prayer to the Great Divine. My voice is cracked, faint, but it carries. "Great Divine, hear me. Liri stands strong, but her heart is breaking. Do not let her grief rot inside her as mine did after my mother's death. Give her the courage to weep, to mourn, to let sorrow flow instead of fester. Let her know it is not weakness to grieve. It is the proof of love."

The words tremble from me, half-breath, half-plea. I know she hears, even if she pretends not to. Her shoulders stiffen, her eyes glistening, but she remains composed, regal in her silence. Still, I pray she will not hold it in forever.

Steam rises gently around me. Aero's hands shake, cooling my burns with a furrowed brow. Liri's whisper lingers, heavy and sharp, but now softened by my prayer. Nuala would want you to heal. She never gave up on you.

I drift into darkness, but this time, I carry the prayer with me. An offering for Liri's heart, a hope that she will not bury her grief as I once did.

19
AERO

The grove is slick with dew, the air still trembling from the heat that Ashen Hollow left behind. Steam rises in thin ribbons from the blackened earth, curling upward into the sparse canopy like smoke from a dying fire. The burnt Fae statues loom in the distance, their twisted silhouettes frozen in agony, watching us like forgotten gods who no longer care to intervene. Every time I glance at them, I feel the weight of their silence pressing down, a reminder of what happens when heroes fail.

I kneel beside Eva, her shallow breaths rattling like a timer ticking down. Each rise and fall of her chest feels too fragile, too uncertain, as though the next one might not come. My thoughts race, colliding against each other in panic. Too many injuries. Too much loss. And no way to fix it with water alone. My power can soothe burns, cool fever, but it cannot undo death or restore what fire has already stolen.

I keep damp cloths pressed against her blistered skin, drawing moisture from the air and moss around us. The cloths steam faintly as they touch her, the heat still trapped beneath her flesh. My hands tremble, but I force them steady. "She's cracked through everything," I murmur, my voice breaking. "Even the part of me I thought was solid."

Her face is pale, lips parched, eyes twitching beneath closed lids. I want to shake her awake, demand she fight, but I know she is already fighting harder than any of us.

Across the camp, Liri sits alone. Her bloodied hands clasp a shard of Nuala's blade, the metal catching faint light from the fire. She hasn't spoken much since the elk fell. Her eyes are hollow, her body rigid, as though grief has carved her into stone. I want to go to her, to comfort her, but guilt knots in my chest, heavy and cruel. One of us died. Possibly their last rifter. Maybe the last of Liri's childhood. And Eva survived, but at a cost that might haunt us all.

I look back at Eva, remembering her strength, her stubbornness. How she never cries until everyone else is alright. How she carries burdens no one asks her to carry, simply because she refuses to let anyone else fall. I want to see her rise from this with the same fierce twinkle she had in her eyes the first day I met her back in the thicket of Parea.

I remember her laugh from three nights ago, sharp and bright, teasing Feliks for snoring so loudly that even the Hollow's birds fled. That laugh had been a spark in the dark, a reminder that joy could still exist. Now, I watch her eyes twitch beneath closed lids and wonder: *If she wakes... what will she carry with her?*

The camp hums with tension. Phira and Diaspor argue again, their voices sharp, cutting through the silence. They debate whether we should keep moving, whether staying here makes us vulnerable. Phira insists we cannot linger, that every moment wasted is another moment Murick gains ground. The commander counters, his voice tight, that Eva cannot be moved, that forcing her onward will kill her.

Their words scrape against my nerves, each syllable a blade. I rise, biting down my panic, and step toward them. My voice is quiet, but it carries. "She needs a day. Just one. If we leave now and she doesn't make it, I'll drag you both back here myself."

The silence that follows is brittle. Phira's jaw tightens, and Diaspor exhales sharply, but neither argues further. The group agrees...barely. Time is slipping through our fingers like sandwater, but for now, Eva has a reprieve. Diaspor clears his throat. "I will look for some marrowroot to muddle. Its healing properties are just what she needs."

"I'll go too," Phira says, searching the commander's face for approval.

"Alright, but you follow my lead."

Without hesitation, she follows him into the forest. I return to Eva's side, my knees sinking into the damp earth. I find a patch of cool soil and coax a tiny stream from beneath it, trickling water beneath her resting form. The stream glimmers faintly, reflecting flickers of firelight and memory. I watch the ripples dance, each one carrying fragments of the past—the elk's flames, Nuala's leap. I lean close, my voice a whisper meant only for her. "You hold the weight of the world to keep it standing. Just...let me steady it for you awhile."

The words hang in the air, fragile but true. My hands tremble as I adjust the cloths, cooling her burns, soothing her fever. Her breath hitches, shallow but steady. I cling to it, each inhale a promise, each exhale a prayer. The grove is silent, save for the crackle of fire and the hiss of steam. I feel Feliks's eyes on me.

"Worrying won't heal her any faster, brother. You need to rest. Try to eat something. What good will you be to her when she rises if you collapse mid-journey due to lack of everything?"

He lifts a leaf full of berries and nuts, urging me to eat. Reluctantly, I place one of the round red morsels in my mouth and sigh. "I have no appetite. Enjoying food or a good night's sleep while she lies here wrecked with pain...I just can't, Feliks."

It sickens me. All I can think of is taking her pain away and destroying the monster that did this to her. The vile thing that possessed such a regal creature and made it do such violent things. My brother places his hand on my shoulder.

"We will do all of that. I know we will because you never break your word. But add one more vow to that list, and promise me you'll also take care of yourself?" He locks eyes with me, more serious than I have ever seen the silly fool, so I nod. "I'll try."

Diaspor and Phira return with fists full of fauna and

victorious grins. The commander places it onto a large flat stone before us. "We found the marrowroot. Most of the forest is still burnt to a crisp, but there is a small meadow that the flames didn't reach."

He wastes no time getting to work, grinding the plants into a sticky paste. Then he leans in and inspects Eva's burns. Her eyes flutter open. "May I?" he asks, looking for permission to apply the medicine.

She nods, encouraging him to go on. Upon its contact, she winces a bit, and I want to leap from my own skin to take the pain from her, but then her furrowed brow softens. A peace flows through our bond, assuring me this is good. This is helping. "I think it's working," I whisper to Diaspor quietly, as not to tempt fate.

I can't stop the joyous tears from bursting from my eyes. The others gather at the commotion, hopeful smiles spreading like a welcome blight.

The stream trickles beneath her, glimmering faintly, catching traces of light. I watch the ripples dance, each one carrying fragments of the past. I whisper again, my voice breaking, "We've come this far...you can't give up now. I need you."

The words hang in the air, fragile but true. My hands tremble, my heart breaks, but Eva breathes. Shallow but steady.

And I kneel beside her, praying it will be enough.

Dawn breaks unevenly across the grove, fractured light filtering through the scorched canopy as though the sky itself is reluctant to return. The moss beneath the trees glistens with dew, fragile beads of water clinging to green that is only just beginning to recover. The land breathes again. Ashen Hollow smolders in the distance, its smoke curling upward in thin, stubborn ribbons, a reminder of what was lost and what still lingers. The air tastes of soot and rebirth, bitter and sweet in equal measure.

I stand near a ring of stones, their arrangement too deliberate to be chance. Once, perhaps, an earth Fae placed them here, shaping the circle as a marker of balance before darkness fell upon this place. Now they are cracked, blackened. I press my palm against one, feeling the faint warmth that clings to its surface, and I wonder if it remembers what it was meant to guard. Eva survived the night, but I did not sleep a single moment. My body feels heavy, dragged down by exhaustion, but the weight pressing hardest is worry. Every shallow breath she takes feels like a countdown, every twitch of her burned skin a reminder of how close she came to being ash herself.

The land stirs faintly beneath me, subtle vibrations that ripple through the soil. It feels as though the earth itself knows we have lost someone, that it grieves with us. I whisper into the silence, my voice rough from sleeplessness, "The land grieves too. But it doesn't stop."

I press my palm deeper into the dirt, feeling tiny particles slip through my fingers. They cling to my skin, damp and fragile, and I think of Eva's magic, lying dormant now, buried beneath pain and exhaustion, but not absent. She is tied to the land in ways none of us can fully understand. "Even if she can't move the land right now," I murmur, "she is the land." Maybe the earth will lend her its strength.

Footsteps approach, hesitant but familiar. I don't turn immediately; I know who it is. Liri joins me at the edge of the stone circle, her presence quiet but heavy. Eventually, her voice breaks the stillness, low and trembling. "I don't know how to mourn her...Nuala."

I close my eyes briefly, the name cutting through me like a blade. Nuala's sacrifice is still raw, still burning. I turn to Liri, my voice steady but soft. "Then we start by not pretending it didn't happen."

Her eyes glisten, but she doesn't cry. She holds herself firm, but I can see the fracture lines beneath her composure. She clutches the shard of Nuala's blade tighter, as though holding onto it will keep her friend from fading completely. She steps forward. "It doesn't seem fair to mourn her while Evanthe is still fighting for her life."

I can't pretend to feel as torn as she does, to have the kind of history she had with Nuala, but I understand the complexities of being a leader and also wanting a moment of release. Release of all that we keep pent up inside for the better of our people, including grief. I clear my throat. "Maybe you can let yourself do both at the same time. Send strength to Eva as she heals and sorrow into the stars for the way you will miss Nuala. Eva wouldn't mind one bit."

She lets a tear spill onto her cheek and nods. "Thank you."

The camp stirs behind us. Diaspor and Bel approach, their faces grim. Diaspor's voice is clipped, efficient. "A scout spotted movement near the Hollow. Could be survivors. Could be trouble." Bel's eyes flicker with unease, his prayer beads clutched tightly in his hand.

Already, Hera is moving, her blades flashing as she prepares for a forced march. Her movements are precise, as though control over steel can replace control over fate. Feliks watches her, his jaw tight, but his eyes flick to me. He doesn't speak, but the look he gives me is clear. He will follow my lead.

I glance back toward the makeshift bed, where Eva still lies helpless, her body broken but breathing. The sight twists my chest. I don't want to leave her here, exposed and vulnerable, but I cannot risk the Mortia creeping closer. The decision claws at me, heavy and cruel.

I step forward, my voice even, firm. "We remain here. We stay alert. The land's unstable, but so are we."

The words settle into the group like stones dropped into water. Hera's jaw tightens, but she doesn't argue. Feliks exhales, relief flickering across his face. Diaspor nods curtly, his blade steady. Bel murmurs a prayer, "By root and star, by breath and bloom. Guard us blight and bitter doom. Let light remain where shadows tread, and bind the living to the thread."

I return to Eva's side, my knees sinking into the damp earth. Her breath is shallow, fragile, but steady. I press my hand against the ground beneath her, feeling the faint thrum that pulses through the soil. It is subtle, but it is there...the land responding to her, tied to her, keeping her steady.

I lean close, my voice a whisper meant not for her, but for the earth itself. "Keep her steady. She's one of yours."

The ground hums faintly beneath my palm, a vibration I've never felt before. One that feels like acknowledgment. I close my eyes, exhaustion pressing against me, but I do not falter. I cannot falter. Eva breathes, and for now, that is enough.

The dawn light fractures through the canopy, dew glistens on recovering moss, and Ashen Hollow smolders distantly. The air tastes of soot and rebirth. The land grieves, but it does not stop. And neither can we.

20

EVANTHE

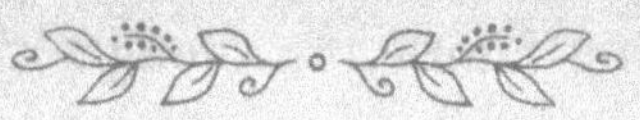

The clearing is quiet in the way only wounded land can be. Just beyond Ashen Hollow, the grove moss is slowly creeping back over scorched bark, damp roots knitting themselves into the soil again. The air no longer reeks of fire. It smells instead of wet earth, of something fresh that has been waiting to come back to life. I lie on a thick bed of leaves softened by Aero's water magic, their edges cool against my blistered skin. Around me, a small ring of stones encircles my body. Diaspor placed them there for warmth and stability. Symbolic, yes, but I feel the weight of their presence like guardians standing watch.

For the first time since the elk's fire, I wake fully. No haze, no drifting between dreams and ash. My eyes open to the fractured light filtering through the canopy, and the world is sharp again. My skin still aches, raw and tender, but beneath the pain, my magic murmurs. Low and earth-bound. It hums like a heartbeat under the surface, reminding me I am still here.

I test my fingers against the moss beneath me. The sensation is faint at first, but then it deepens. Strength flows upward, not just mine but the land's. The grove is healing, and it lends me its patience, its resilience. The bloom laying beside me warms in reaction to my waking, its petals glowing faintly, as though it, too, has been waiting for me to rise.

I turn my head and see Feliks asleep with his back against a tree, his bow resting across his lap. His face is slack, but even in sleep, his posture is tense, as though he expects danger to wake him at any moment. Hera sits nearby, sharpening her blades with deliberate precision. Her expression is composed, but I notice the way her eyes flick toward me, sharp and watchful. She is keeping guard, not just against threats beyond the clearing, but to protect me in my fragile state.

Beside me, Aero sleeps sitting up, his head tilted back, his hands damp from constant contact with the stream he has coaxed to run near my bed of leaves. His face is streaked with exhaustion, his jaw tight even in rest. I know, without a doubt, he hasn't left. Not once.

I shift upright, my body protesting but yielding. The motion jolts Aero awake. His eyes snap open, and in an instant, he is beside me, his hand hovering near my shoulder, his breath catching. "You're up," he whispers, relief and awe tangled in his voice.

I smirk weakly, my lips cracked but determined. "Well, are we marching or moping?"

His smile breaks through exhaustion, tears glistening but not quite disguised. I go on, "Whatever Diaspor smeared all over me must have worked." I grin, looking down at all the crusted remnants of the green paste on my skin. He stares at me like a ghost that's come back to life.

"Thank gods. I'd wrap my arms around you right now if it wouldn't cause you pain."

I steady myself, pressing my palm against the earth. The soil hums beneath me, lending strength. "Then let's make the ground remember us."

"Take your time, Eva. Don't rush this if you still need to heal," he pleads.

It warms my heart the way he cares for me, but we really don't have time. "People in the mortal realm could be dying right now, and you see how the Fae are struggling to survive here." Moving closer, I place my hand on his chest. "Look at my arms. That salve truly did wonders, Aero. The pain is nowhere near what it was. If there ever was a place to start believing in miracles, this is the one."

With a growl, he shakes his head. "Alright, but the very moment you feel weary—and I mean the very moment—we stop and give you rest."

I nod, looking over his shoulder at the others. "I told them we wouldn't move until you led the way," he says.

I rise, slower than usual but unshaken. Each step feels deliberate, the land steadying me, guiding me. I walk to the edge of camp, the ring of stones behind me, the bloom glowing faintly at my side.

The others gather as they notice me standing. Feliks rubs his eyes, startled, then straightens, his bow in hand.

Hera sets her blades aside, her gaze sharp but softened by something like relief. Diaspor throws his fists into the air in a small fit of celebration. "We never doubted you."

I look out toward the ridge, where King Murick's fortress looms unseen beyond the horizon. The air hums faintly, the land trembling with anticipation. My voice is steady, carrying across the clearing. "We move at my pace. But we move. The Hollow didn't bury us. It woke us."

The words settle into the grove, into the soil, into the hearts of those who stand with me. The land hums in response, roots trembling, moss glowing faintly. The clearing breathes, patient but alive.

I stand at the edge of the camp, my body still aching, my grief still heavy, but my resolve unbroken. Liri steps beside me and reaches for my hand. It's one of the few spots the elk's flames didn't touch. She doesn't mention it, but I can feel the sadness that burdens her, like a gaping cavern inside her chest that can't be filled. "I'm so sorry, Liri," I whisper, choking back tears.

She squeezes my hand a bit tighter. "As am I."

"I promise her death will mean something. Whatever it takes, her part of this story will be sung for generations."

Wiping her eyes, the princess nods. Nuala's sacrifice anchors me. Aero's devotion steadies me. The land itself lends me strength.

We move forward, not as survivors alone, but as something awakened. The Hollow tried to consume us, but it failed. We rise from its ashes, carrying grief and strength in equal measure.

The fortress waits. The land remembers. And so will we.

Just beyond the clearing, the group begins to prepare for the march. The mist clings low to the forest floor, curling around roots and stones like it doesn't want to let us go. My shoulders are tight, every step deliberate but strained, as though my body is reminding me of the burns that still haven't fully healed. I walk a few paces ahead, needing the space, needing the rhythm of movement to keep me upright. The earth beneath me hums faintly, steadying me, and I try to will myself into steadiness with each stride.

Inside, my body whispers warnings I don't want to hear. Flashes of light, the burned ground, Nuala's voice swallowed by silence. I recall the momentary hatred I felt for her. Regret sinks in. The memory presses against me, sharp and cruel, but I ignore it. I need momentum. Stillness hurts more.

I hear footsteps catching up behind me, heavier than the others. Aero. He doesn't call out, doesn't announce himself, just closes the distance until he's beside me. The others linger behind, giving us space without saying it aloud. He places a gentle hand on a less tender part of my arm, his touch grounding, his eyes searching my face. "Eva. You're bleeding again. You need to rest."

I resist the pull to stop, brushing him off with a half-smile that doesn't reach my eyes. "I'm fine. The Hollow didn't kill me, and neither will a few more steps."

His voice is low, steady, but it cuts through me. "But it cracked you."

The words strike harder than I expect, and something inside me snaps, just slightly. Cracked. Just like the bloom. The panic beneath my strength peeks through, sharp and raw. "If I stop now, I fall. I can't fall."

He doesn't argue. He doesn't push. He just stands with me, present, his hand outstretched, ready to catch me at a moment's notice. "Then let me walk beside you. You don't have to lead every step."

I slow, my breath catching, the weight of his words pressing against me. A small tremor runs through the soil underfoot, echoes of my pain rippling outward. I glance sideways at him, searching his face. His concern isn't pity; it's belief. He believes I can keep going, but he also knows I'm stubborn as a mule.

"Fine," I murmur, my voice rough but steady. "Side by side."

He nods, relief flickering across his face, but his eyes remain sharp. "I don't want to worry you, but you need to know. Bel and Diaspor spotted movement not far from here."

The words make my shoulders tense, my jaw tighten. I knew this was what laid ahead. We are at war. What happened back in the hollow woke us up, taught us a lesson of what we are truly up against. And now the enemy stirs.

We walk—not fast, but in step. The path forward is

dense, uneven, roots twisting across the soil, branches clawing at the mist. But it is no longer silent. Each step feels like a death wish, each breath whipping through the dark like a siren. "The nettle is consuming our trail. It doesn't even feel like day," Phira murmurs.

"Like marching into a night we don't want to know," Bel adds.

The princess lifts her chin, crouching down to the ground before us. Her fingers trace a symbol into the soil. Roots curled around a cresting wave. A sword driven through the middle of it. No flame. Just a vow whispered to the land. She looks back, locking eyes with me.

"Sometimes fate comes to us like nettle in the night, burning us awake so we rise sharpened rather than spared."

I meet her gaze. "Then let it burn. I've already paid the price in fire, and I'm not afraid of the dark."

21

EVANTHE

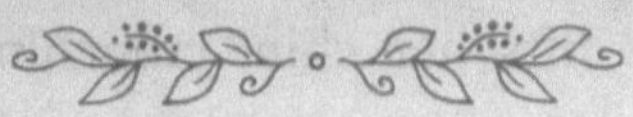

The ridge is jagged beneath my boots, stone edges biting through the thin soles as if the land itself wants to remind me where I stand. Just beyond the final Fae boundary, the world changes. The sky above is blotted with thick veils of Mortia mist. There are no stars, no sun, only swirls of shadow that coil and uncoil like serpents. The air buzzes faintly with whispered warnings, impossible to locate and impossible to forget, voices that seem to come from nowhere and everywhere at once. Each breath tastes of ash and iron, and the silence between the whispers is heavier than sound.

We crest the ridge together, the group moving as one but fractured in spirit. My pace is deliberate, strained, tension locked in my shoulders. I force myself forward, feeling the earth beneath me, trying to will myself into steadiness. But the land resists me. My magic recoils, pulling back like a wounded animal. It refuses to speak here.

Below sprawls Murick's fortress. My breath catches as the sight unfolds, a blackened palace with jutting spires like broken teeth gnashing against the horizon. Veins of voidlight pulse along its walls, reaching outward like claws, stretching into the canyon as though the fortress itself is alive and hungry. Surrounding it are toppled Fae ruins, sunken into ashen trenches, remnants of a world erased. The bones of what once was lie scattered, swallowed by shadow.

Everything is wrong. The trees twist in spirals unnaturally, their bark slick and whispering, voices that scrape against the edges of thought. Pools of shadow bubble and disperse when touched by the faint light that filters through the mist, as though the darkness itself resents illumination. Echoes bounce through the canyon, cries that might be real or might be memory...impossible to tell.

Feliks mutters under his breath, his voice sharp with unease, "This looks like the inside of a nightmare someone never woke from." His words hang in the air, brittle, and none of us argue.

Liri falters, her gaze locked on the fortress. Her lips part, her voice a whisper that trembles. "It's worse than I imagined. This place...it eats souls." Her words cut deeper than Feliks's, because I feel it too—the way the mist presses against thought, the way the whispers gnaw at recollection.

Hera narrows her eyes, her hand resting on the hilt of her blade. "We'll need to keep watch of each other's backs. Stealth feels like a fantasy here. I feel its eyes on us." Her voice is calm, but I hear the tension beneath it, the awareness that we are already exposed. I place my hand on her arm. "I need you to know that you and Feliks don't need to step a foot farther." I look down at her abdomen. "You have a new duty that far exceeds any other."

She shakes her head. "If it means that we can welcome this new life to a safer realm, I don't really see another way to move forward." Standing behind her, Feliks nods in agreement.

"Then we move without miss," I reply.

Aero reaches for me, his hand brushing my wrist briefly, grounding me. His touch steadies the tremor in my body, though it cannot quiet the lightning in my blood. "We stop here," he says, his voice low but firm. "Plan. Rest while we still remember who we are."

I feel torn, caught between the weakness in my body and the relentless drive in my chest. Nuala's sacrifice surges in my thoughts, the memory of her leap, her blade, and then her fall. Knowing that the moment we end the Mortia will be the end of Sorrow as well. My dearest childhood friend. Knowing she has been forced to live out her last days as one of the Omen eats me alive. She also fought her new dark nature to save me. She deserves better.

The land beneath my feet trembles with sadness. It mourns with me. I respond to it beneath my breath, '*If this is where the world ends, then I walk into it whole.*'

Aero hears my whisper and replies, "And you will. We will. Very soon."

In agreement, I take his hand as we slowly pull back from the ridge, each step reluctant, as though leaving the edge feels like surrender. We set up camp nearby, the mist curling around us, the whispers pressing closer. No one speaks much. The silence is heavy, but we keep moving. Liri stokes the fire, large enough to warm a small meal, but hopefully small enough not to attract the wrong kind of attention. The others arrange supplies and take inventory of what food we have left. All busy work to keep the dark thoughts at bay. And I can't fault them for it.

I remain at the ridge's edge longer than the others, staring down into the abyss. The fortress looms below like a wound in the world, pulsing with voidlight, its spires jagged against the mist. My breath is shallow, my chest tight, but I do not look away.

I press my hand against the stone beneath me, feeling its cold weight, its silent endurance. I whisper to it, my voice low, "Hold me steady. Tomorrow, we fracture the dark."

The stone hums faintly beneath my palm, the ancient part of it seeming to recognize my presence. The mist coils tighter. My body aches, my burns sting, but my resolve is unbroken. Nuala's and Sorrow's sacrifices will mean something. I'm not broken.

The ground here doesn't want us. Every root I touch with my magic pulls away, shrivels like burned parchment. So I sit with my knees drawn to my chest on a slab of stone still solid beneath me.

The air tastes like iron, making my mouth dry as if it were trying to shrivel away from the foul tang. Hera returns from her patrol, eyes sharp even beneath exhaustion. She settles beside me silently, one hand resting absently on her stomach.

I nudge her with an elbow. "You know you've lost the right to be reckless, right?"

Hera exhales through her nose, almost smiling. "Says the woman whose idea of subtlety is punching the earth until it screams."

I bump her again, harder this time. "I'm serious. You don't get to go galloping off into the void anymore. That child—" my voice falters. "That child is our future. And you...you're my anchor. If you do anything stupid, I swear I'll drag your ghost back from wherever it lands and give it a lecture so long the dead will beg for silence."

Hera's eyes glint. "You really know how to flatter a pregnant warrior."

"I'm gifted. But I mean it." I lower my voice. "You matter to me. Not just as a fighter. As you. Your stubborn, blade-wielding, terrifyingly loyal self."

Silence falls between us, but Hera reaches out and gently grips my wrist. "Then let's both live through this. For the baby. For the rage we still need to unleash."

I nod in agreement and wander quietly from the camp edge, past Liri's circle of wards and Feliks muttering rune threads under his breath. There I find Aero standing near a crumbled altar stone, twirling the shiny metal ring around his finger.

He doesn't turn when I approach, just lifts his hand behind him and touches my waist lightly, as if he already knows. I lean into him, my arms wrapping around his middle, forehead pressed between his shoulders.

His body is warm, impossibly steady.

If he dies, I will break. I've heard the stories. Bonded souls...shattered, screaming into eternity because a part of them has been ripped so violently away that it never heals.

I whisper, "I couldn't bear it. Not you."

His fingers tighten over mine.

"I know," he says quietly. "But we are not like the stories. We are stronger. We choose each other. Not because fate demands it, but because love insists."

I turn him toward me, my breath catching. His eyes reflect the edge of my fear and the vastness of his calm, and it overwhelms me.

The kiss is not quiet. It crashes through the silence, desperate and grounding and full of all the things we won't say tomorrow when blades are drawn and magic boils.

When we part, Aero presses his forehead to mine.

"We survive, Eva. No matter what darkness says, we both leave here intact."

22

AERO

The jagged crevice beneath the fortress ridge breathes like a wound in the world, veiled by shifting shadows and vines made of brittle bone. Each vine cracks faintly when brushed, as if it resents being touched, and the mist curls around us in unnatural rhythms, pulsing like a heartbeat buried underground. The main gates of Murick's fortress shimmer in the distance, warding magic rippling across them in waves of voidlight. Something inside me raises an alarm that if we tried to breach them, the entire Mortia horde would descend upon us before we took a single step inside.

I pause, narrowing my eyes, listening. There's something beneath the stone, something that doesn't belong to the fortress. The mist's rhythm is off, not just shadow but something deeper. I kneel, pressing my hand close to the rock without touching it, feeling the faint hum of moisture buried far below. Water, sealed long ago by Fae magic, twisted now by Mortia decay. It's still there, waiting, pretending to be still.

"There's movement here," I murmur, keeping my voice low. "Something buried deep, pretending not to stir."

Feliks shifts behind me, his bowstring creaking as he adjusts it. "Movement? Down there? Great. Because what we really need right now is more things hiding under rocks." His laugh is nervous, brittle, and no one joins him. The silence that follows is heavier than his words.

I trace the rhythm again, following it with my senses, my hands hovering inches above the stone. The aquifer is warped, but it hasn't been consumed. The fortress forgot it—or perhaps couldn't take it. That means it's ours to use. I focus, channeling water pressure into the cracks, parting the stone with precision. The rock groans, resisting, then yields. A hollow opens, slick with condensation, symbols carved into its walls older than memory itself. They glow faintly, Fae script etched deep, untouched by Mortia corruption.

Hera steps closer, her blade angled toward the opening, her eyes narrowing. "You sure it won't collapse?"

I glance at her, my voice steady. "I'm not holding the stone. I'm holding what's beneath it."

She exhales sharply, not quite reassured, but she doesn't argue.

We step inside, one by one, the tunnel swallowing us in damp silence. The walls drip faintly, condensation running down the carved symbols, pooling at our feet. The air is heavy, thick with moisture and shadow. As we move deeper, the Mortia reacts. Black tendrils slither from the cracks, reaching for us, whispering in voices that scrape against thought.

I raise my hands, summoning my power. Water surges outward, forming a circle around us, hissing as it touches the shadow. The tendrils recoil, shrieking quietly, but they do not vanish. The barrier holds, temporary but strong.

Eva steps forward, her hand brushing one of the tendrils. Her earth magic is muted here, but something responds beneath it. The stone trembles faintly, like a heartbeat pressed against drowning stone. She doesn't flinch, doesn't speak, just listens.

I watch her closely, my chest tightening. She's determined, flickering with anticipation inside. I lower my voice, speaking only to her. "Can you feel the land?"

Her eyes meet mine, steady despite the strain. "Yes, it's bruised...but not broken."

My grip tightens on the ward, my jaw clenched. I can't lose her. Not here. Not now. I wonder if the Mortia can feel our bond, if it knows the way our magic threads together, if that makes us vulnerable. The thought gnaws at me, but I push it aside.

The tunnel winds deeper, the symbols glowing faintly, guiding us. The air grows colder, the moisture thicker, until we reach a cracked stairwell hidden beneath Murick's west tower. The stone steps are jagged, broken, but they lead upward, toward the fortress.

The group pauses, tension thick in the air. I cup my hands, condensing droplets from the mist, testing the pressure above. The water flows freely, unsealed. That means the path is open.

"Water still flows above," I say, my voice steady. "That means there's no seal. If we move fast, we get inside before it realizes."

Eva steps closer, her hand finding mine. Her grip is firm, grounding herself through me. Her voice is hushed but stern. "We finish this together."

I nod, my chest tightening, but I don't let it show. I lead the way up the steps, each footfall damp, leaving fading footprints behind us. The shadows stir, whispering, but the ward holds.

The fortress looms ahead, seething and silent, its pinnacles knifed upward, stark and uneven against the rolling haze. I draw a deep breath, my voice carrying across the tunnel. "I am sea-born. And no fortress can drown me."

The words echo against the stone, against the mist, against the fortress itself. The shadows hiss, the tendrils recoil, but we move forward. Together.

***

Inside Murick's fortress, the air itself feels like it is pressing against my lungs, thick with decay and memory. The architecture is a grotesque parody of Fae design, arches that once soared now bent inward as if crushed by invisible hands, walls veined with hollow stone that pulse faintly with Mortia wards. Every hallway hums, like it is remembering pain, and the sound is not just in my ears but in my bones. Even the walls seem to breathe, exhaling faint drafts that smell of rot and iron.

We halt in a vault-like chamber filled with cracked crystal murals. The murals shimmer faintly, fractured depictions of Fae triumphs and rivers of light, but the cracks bleed shadow, twisting the images into something unrecognizable. I stand at the center, closing my eyes, listening. Moisture lingers in the walls. I map it in my mind, tracing the flow. Water still moves beneath the throne room, but barely. It is sluggish, strained, as though the fortress itself is choking it.

Liri's voice breaks the silence. "Thrones are never centerpieces. They're kept at height, overlooking power, not surrounded by it." Her eyes linger on the murals, her jaw tight, grief shadowing her words.

Diaspor nods, his hand resting on the hilt of his blade. "Expect a spiral ascension. And if Murick has twisted tradition, as I imagine he has, the highest spire is now the deepest wound." His voice is grim but certain.

I open my eyes, tracing the faint moisture lines again. "We can't take the main ascension. Too exposed. Too many wards. We'll need an indirect climb. The servant tunnels. They're flooded now with shadow runoff, but the foundation points are weaker. We can exploit them."

Eva steps forward, her hand brushing the cracked crystal. Her eyes narrow, her voice low. "He's weakened the foundations. I can feel it. The stone resents him. It will let us through."

Feliks mutters behind us, his voice sharp but hushed, "Dead corridors whisper louder than guards. Let's not wake ghosts if we can help it." His attempt at humor falls flat, but the truth in his words lingers.

We move, slipping through jagged staircases and smoke-veiled archways. The air thickens as we descend, shadows pressing closer, whispering in voices that scrape against thought. I summon a flowing spell, water dancing across our boots, muffling each step. The sound of our movement fades, replaced by the faint hiss of water against stone.

Hera raises her hand, motioning for silence. The air shifts, heavy and sharp. Diaspor's eyes narrow, his voice a whisper. "They patrol with silence wards. Too late to avoid them."

The shadows ripple, and soldiers emerge. Their skin is ashen, their eyes hollow, their blades humming with grief. They move without sound, their presence pressing against us like a weight.

I react instantly, summoning high-pressure bursts from the underground streams. Water surges upward, striking the soldiers, knocking them off-balance. The hiss of water against shadow fills the chamber, sharp and violent.

Eva fights beside me, her movements heavy and deliberate, like stone waking from slumber. Each strike is precise, each blow resonant, her strength unyielding. Hera and Phira shield Liri, their blades flashing with terrifying precision, cutting through shadow with relentless fury. Feliks lands a solid strike, his arrow piercing one of the soldiers, his usual jokes replaced by grim focus.

Diaspor is wounded, blood seeping from his side, but he holds up a scroll, his voice steady despite the pain. He burns the last sigil, and the wall behind us shudders, revealing a secret stairwell hidden behind a dead tapestry.

We stumble into the stairwell, breathing heavy, the air thick with shadow. I press my hand against the wall, listening. The flow beneath the stone speeds up, pulling toward a central point. The current is stronger, sharper, like a storm gathering.

"We're near," I say, my voice low but certain. "The current draws to a storm."

Eva kneels, pressing her hand against the floor. Despite the deadness, her voice is steady. "He's above us. The weight of him presses down here."

We ascend, floor by floor, the shadows thickening with each step. The air grows heavier, darker, pressing against us like a tide. Our vision dims as the wards pulse stronger, the whispers louder. Each step feels like walking deeper into a wound, the fortress itself resisting us.

Feliks mutters, his voice strained, "I swear the walls are watching us. Every time I blink, they shift."

Hera snaps, her voice sharp, "Focus. If the walls are watching, then let them see us unafraid."

Liri whispers, her voice trembling, "It's worse than I imagined. This place...it eats memory."

I glance at her, my voice steady. "Then we hold each other's memories. If it tries to take them, we remind each other who we are."

Eva's hand brushes mine briefly, grounding me. Her voice is low, resolute. "We finish this together."

The staircase ends at a threshold carved in obsidian. There is no door, only a jagged opening, the stone slick with shadow. The air hums, heavy and sharp, pressing against my chest. I feel it, like the tide before a wavebreak, the moment before the storm crashes.

"He's here," I whisper, my voice steady but heavy. "The crown's rotted through, but the power hasn't faded."

The group stands behind me, silent, their breaths heavy, their eyes sharp. The fortress looms ahead, seething and silent, its power pressing against us like a tide. I draw a deep breath, my hands trembling but steady. The water hums beneath the stone, faint but present, waiting.

We step forward, into the obsidian threshold, the storm pressing closer, the crown waiting.

23
EVANTHE

Inside the fortress's upper chamber, the air is thick enough to choke, humming with distorted magic that crawls across the walls like a living parasite. Bone-veined archways loom overhead, their curves warped into unnatural spirals, and the vaults above thrum with a resonance that feels less like architecture and more like a heartbeat. Every step we take lands on fractured stone tiles that pulse faintly beneath our boots, veins of shadowlight threading through them as though the floor itself is keeping some monstrous body alive.

There is no throne here. No seat of power, no crown resting on velvet. Instead, the chamber is dominated by a central dais tangled in black roots and hollowed Fae relics. The relics are broken, gutted of their light, their shells twisted into grotesque ornaments. The roots coil upward, feeding into the dais like veins feeding a heart. The largest of them in the center is shattered into the most pieces. Liri gasps at the sight.

"The Sunstone that Elder Thorne spoke of. He was right. This is the relic that once kept the glade in perpetual light," she mourns.

I step forward, my heart pounding with a rhythm that doesn't feel like my own. Each beat is too heavy, too sharp, as though something inside this chamber is dictating the pace. My mother's dagger feels small in my hand, laughably inadequate against the cathedral of decay that surrounds us.

Murick stands at the center. Once, he was elegant, regal, a Fae king whose presence commanded reverence. Now his body twists unnaturally, a grotesque fusion of flesh and Mortia rot. An antlered crown is fused to his skull, the bone branching outward like a parasite feeding on him. His skin is mottled, veins black and moving beneath the surface, writhing as though alive. His eyes glow amber, but the glow flickers with something ancient and wrong, a light that doesn't belong to him.

I don't just see him...I feel him. I feel the Mortia inside him, a pressure that presses against my chest, a pulling that scrapes at my magic from within. Invisible claws rake through me, trying to strip me of what I carry. My earth magic recoils, cowering, refusing to rise. Even stone knows to stay silent here.

That's not possession. That's fusion. The Mortia isn't just puppeteering him; it's feeding, restructuring, wearing Murick like a cloak of flesh.

His voice cuts through the chamber, layered and wrong. It is his voice, but beneath it are hundreds more, whispering, screaming, consumed by the Mortia. "You carry the root, Guardian. But your roots bleed in my soil."

The words scrape against me, sharp and cruel. My grip tightens on my dagger, though it feels like a child's toy in this place. Aero stiffens beside me, his water magic flaring against the unnatural heat that radiates from Murick's body. I sense him as the only source of purity here, the only thing untainted. If he falls, we all drown in this rot.

Hera shifts her stance immediately, her blades flashing as she positions herself between Liri and Feliks. Her movements are tense, maternal, lethal. Liri's eyes are wide, her breath shallow, but she doesn't falter. Feliks's bow is drawn, his jaw tight, his usual humor gone. Phira and Bel stand guard in front of him. Diaspor whispers ancient words, prayers so old they scrape against the air, and the Mortia hisses through Murick's mouth in response.

I feel sick, my stomach twisting, but I am anchored. I remember Nuala. I remember the Hollow. I remember the promise I made to the soil and to myself. Let him wear his parasite like a crown. I know how to tear it off.

Murick raises his hand, shadows erupting from his fingertips. The darkness coils outward, sharp and violent, reaching for us. I lift mine, my dagger flashing, and Aero steps forward with a surge of shimmering blue. His water collides with the shadow, hissing, steaming, the clash filling the chamber with a sound like thunder. We stand as one.

But the chamber begins to fracture. The walls pulse harder, and the tiles beneath our feet crack, veins of shadowlight bursting outward. The vaults above groan, the bone-veined archways trembling. The final confrontation stirs, the storm gathering.

Murick's voice echoes, layered and cruel. "You think roots can resist rot? You think water can cleanse what has already drowned? You are children playing in a grave."

I step forward, my voice steady despite the tremor in my chest. "You're not a king anymore. You're a husk. And husks burn."

The shadows lash out again, sharper, faster. Aero's water surges, colliding with them, forming a barrier that shimmers blue against the black. Hera moves, her blades flashing, cutting through tendrils that reach for Liri. Feliks fires, his arrows piercing shadow, each strike precise. Diaspor's prayers grow louder, the words burning against the Mortia, making Murick's body twitch.

I press my hand against the fractured tiles, forcing my earth magic to rise. It resists, cowering, but I push harder. The stone trembles, faint but present. Roots stir beneath the floor, weak but alive. They respond to me, faintly, reluctantly.

Murick snarls, his voice layered with hundreds. "You think the land will save you? The land is mine. I have eaten its memory. I have drunk its veins."

I grit my teeth, my voice sharp. "Then choke on it."

The roots surge upward, weak but defiant, wrapping around the dais. Murick's body twists, the antlered crown glowing faintly, the veins in his skin writhing. He raises both hands, shadow erupting in waves, crashing against Aero's water. The clash fills the chamber, the sound deafening, the air thick with steam and rot.

Aero's voice cuts through the chaos, sharp and steady. "Eva! The roots—anchor them! I'll flood the cracks!"

I nod, pressing harder, my magic surging through the fractured tiles. The roots respond, wrapping tighter around the dais, anchoring it. Aero's water floods the cracks, surging upward, colliding with the shadow. The chamber shakes, the vaults groaning, the archways trembling.

Murick screams, his voice layered, hundreds of voices screaming with him. His body twists, the crown glowing brighter, the veins writhing faster. His eyes flicker, amber light burning, wrong and ancient.

I step forward, my dagger flashing. "Nuala gave me her breath. The Hollow gave me its soil. You don't get to take that."

Murick raises his hand, shadow erupting, but Aero surges beside me, his water colliding with it. We stand as one, the clash filling the chamber, the storm breaking.

The chamber fractures, the final confrontation stirring. The walls pulse harder, the tiles crack deeper, the vaults groan louder. The storm gathers, pressing against us, pressing against him.

I grip my dagger tighter, my voice steady. "Let's end this."

Murick's throne chamber is a wound in the world. The walls are eroded by shadow, their surfaces slick with Mortia corruption that pulses like veins beneath rotting flesh. The air itself is alive, thick and heavy, vibrating with a rhythm that feels like a heartbeat stolen from something ancient and wrong. Above us, the jagged dome fractures slowly, each crack spreading outward as Aero's presence churns the dark. His water magic pushes against the corruption, but the dome resists, groaning like a beast unwilling to die.

The dais at the center is tangled in black roots and hollowed Fae relics, relics that once carried light but now hang, gutted, empty shells mocking what they once were. Between me and that dais, the Mortia forms a barrier—viscous, almost sentient, a wall of shadow that reacts violently to my every attempt to cross. It writhes like tar alive, whispering in tones that scrape against my bones.

I try to step forward, my dagger clenched, my heart pounding. The moment my foot touches the barrier, it repels me. Flesh burns, searing pain ripping through my skin, and my magic goes mute, silenced as though the earth itself refuses to speak here. I stumble back, gasping, the taste of ash thick in my mouth.

Aero summons tides, streams of divine water surging forward, colliding with the barrier. The water hisses, steaming, pushing against the dark, but the Mortia resists. It knows him. It knows me. It knows us too well. The parasite learned our shapes, I think, my chest tightening. It knows how to break us.

Murick grins from the dais, his face twisted, his voice syrupy with malice. "You'd die for them, Guardian? They'll forget you the moment the stars fall." His words drip like poison, layered with voices that are not his own, hundreds consumed by the Mortia, whispering through him.

I clutch the crystal bloom in my hand. Its surface is dull, lifeless, but as I hold it tighter, a faint flicker stirs. My own reflection stares back at me, faint but undeniable. It isn't just showing me; it's remembering me. The realization cuts through the haze. This was never a weapon. It's a mirror. A key. A reckoner of truth.

My grip tightens, my voice sharp. "You're going to see yourself, Murick. You can't hide from what you gave away."

I step forward slowly. The wind howls, the ground cracks beneath my feet, the chamber trembling as though it knows what is coming. Aero moves beside me, streams of divine water surging outward, shielding me, but even his power falters at the Mortia's edge. The barrier hisses, resisting, pressing back against him.

Murick's voice becomes vicious, layered with venom. "You were always weak. Chosen by dirt. You'll die faceless."

Pain surges through me with every step. My bones scream, my muscles burn, my skin feels like it is tearing. But my purpose rises above pain. My voice cuts through the chamber, sharp and steady. "Weak? I watched everything burn. I stood anyway."

I press forward, each step agony, each breath a battle. The barrier lashes against me, burning my flesh, silencing my magic, but I refuse to stop. Aero's water surges beside me, colliding with the shadow, hissing, steaming, but faltering. Hera's blades flash behind us, shielding Liri and

Feliks, her movements sharp and lethal. Diaspor's prayers echo, ancient words burning against the Mortia, making Murick's body twitch.

I reach striking distance. My hand lifts, the bloom glowing faintly. Murick stares, his grin twisted, his eyes burning amber. Confusion flickers across his face, then amusement. But then his own reflection stares back at him.

In that brief heartbeat, recognition bleeds into his face. A flicker of purity. A memory of who he was before the Mortia fed on his fears. His body falters, and his voice stutters, the layered whispers breaking.

The bloom erupts. Blinding-white light bursts outward, like dawn devouring night. The chamber shakes, the dome fractures, the walls groan. Murick screams, the shadows in his voice crying out, but the light consumes him. His veins crumble from within, his body turning to ash, the crown fused to his skull shattering.

At the same time, Aero summons an ancestral wave, a surge from the mythic deep. It roars through the chamber, a tide born of memory and purity, sweeping the ashes into oblivion. The fortress erodes, walls collapsing, shadows peeling away. The wave surges around us, protecting us in a cocoon of shimmering water.

The Mortia's heart is exposed. A jagged, pulsing orb, black and alive, thrumming with corruption. It beats like a parasite, pressing against the chamber, whispering in those voices.

I approach, bloodied but unbroken. My body aches,

my skin burns, but my steps are steady. I speak with all my soul.

"I stand before you because she fell," I say, my voice cutting through the chamber like a blade. "Nuala gave her life so the rest of us could still draw breath. She walked into the Hollow, knowing it could take her. She faced the darkness with nothing but her courage and her name."

I take another step, the pain in my body flaring, but I refuse to falter.

"You speak of power as if it is something inherited, hoarded, passed down like a crown. But Nuala taught me that true power is sacrifice. It is choosing to stand when the world begs you to kneel. It is giving everything so others may live."

My fingers tighten around the cracked bloom.

"The Hollow remembers her. The realm remembers her. And I will not let her be forgotten. Not by you. Not by anyone."

I lift my chin, meeting every gaze that dares to hold mine.

"You want to know what I carry? I carry her last breath. I carry the sorrow she left behind. I carry every wound this world tried to bury. And I will not break beneath them."

My voice rises, steady and sharp.

"I am here because she believed I would be. And I will not fail her."

The Mortia recoils from my words. It cannot consume memory that resists silence. It cannot devour what refuses to be forgotten.

I finish with one word. "No."

The heart shatters. The orb cracks, light bursting outward, shadows peeling away, the whispers silenced.

The chamber trembles then stills. The fortress erodes, collapsing, the corruption peeling away. Aero collapses beside me, alive, his breath heavy, his body trembling. Liri kneels where the Mortia fell, her hand pressed against her chest, her eyes wide, her breath shallow. Hera lowers her blades, her shoulders trembling. Feliks exhales sharply, his bow lowering. Diaspor sinks to his knees, his prayers fading.

I sink to the ground, clutching the bloom, its surface glowing faintly. My voice is low, steady, whispering, "We remember. That's how we won."

The chamber is silent.

The fortress is broken.

The Mortia is gone.

24

EVANTHE

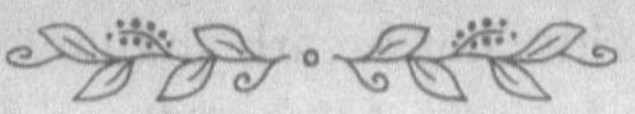

The fractured remnants of Murick's fortress lie around me like the bones of a beast finally slain. The jagged dome above, once a prison of shadow, dissolves slowly into light. The veil that had smothered the sky for generations lifts, mist rising in gentle spirals as though the land itself exhales for the first time in centuries. The air is different now. No longer heavy with Mortia corruption, but fragile, tentative, like a child learning to speak.

The stones beneath my feet no longer pulse with that sick rhythm, no longer thrum with the parasite's hunger. They feel quiet and finally willing to rest. I sink to my knees, the weight of everything pressing down at once, gripping the crystal bloom as if it anchors me to reality. My fingers tremble around its surface, and tears fall freely, unbidden. Joy and sorrow braid together in every drop, indistinguishable, inseparable.

Aero stands nearby, silent, watching me with reverence. His eyes are steady, but I know he sees what no one else can. The cost etched into me, the fractures that victory leaves behind. He doesn't speak, because he knows there are no words. They would only scatter against the enormity of this moment.

I whisper Sorrow's name, the sound fragile, breaking in my throat. My heart aches not for the soul freed from torment, but for the absence that follows. "Meraki will bloom again," I murmur, voice trembling, "but I won't see her laugh beneath its branches." The truth cuts deeper than any wound. Victory is never whole; it always takes something with it.

The air shifts, subtle but undeniable. The lingering spectral tether fades, unraveling like smoke in the wind. I turn toward the forest, and for a moment I see Skira's ghost staring back at me, the faint shimmer that had haunted me through every step of this journey. It is empty now. It will always be empty. For a moment, I smile through tears. "She's free. No chains. No echoes. Just seafoam and peace."

Around us, the land begins to stir. Grass pierces cracked stone, fragile blades pushing upward with stubborn resilience. Vines unfurl toward the light, curling along broken walls, reclaiming what was stolen. Faint birdcalls echo overhead, tentative at first, then stronger, as though the world itself is remembering how to sing.

I place my hand on the soil, pressing my palm against its surface. It hums beneath me, gentle, grateful. My earth magic stirs fully again for the first time since entering the fortress, rising like a heartbeat, steady and warm. It hums with gentle gratitude, not demanding, not desperate, but whole. "We're whole again," I whisper, my voice breaking. "Not untouched. But healed."

Liri weeps openly, her voice trembling as she sings the first free Fae verse in centuries. The sound is fragile, raw, but it carries through the ruins like light breaking through clouds. Diaspor collapses to his knees, overwhelmed, his hands pressed against the soil, his lips moving in silent prayer. Bel laughs triumphantly, his voice ringing as he watches the waters return to their true form, clear and untainted.

We form a small circle, instinctively, drawn together by something older than words. We thank our ancestors, the ones who carried us here, the ones who endured so we could stand. They thank me, and they thank Aero, their voices heavy with reverence. Diaspor bows his head first. "To those who walked before us," he murmurs, voice rough with emotion. "May they rest easier now."

Liri places her hand over her heart. "And to the ones who stood with us today. Eva... Aero... you carried more than your share."

Bel exhales shakily, eyes shining. "The realm breathes because of you both. The stones themselves feel lighter."

Feliks lets out a soft, disbelieving laugh. "I thought we were done for. Truly. But you—" He looks between us, his voice dropping. "You pulled us back from the edge."

Hera steps closer, her usual sharpness softened. "You honored every life the Mortia tried to claim. Every one." She inclines her head to me. "Thank you, Evanthe."

Then she turns to Aero. "And you...you fought like the sea itself had chosen you."

Aero shifts beside me, uncomfortable with the praise. "We fought together," he says quietly. "None of us would be standing without the others."

I draw a breath, the weight of their gratitude settling warm and heavy in my chest. "Our ancestors carried us," I say. "But so did each of you. This victory belongs to all of us."

Silence follows.

Then Diaspor lifts his gaze. "Let the realm remember this day."

Aero walks to my side, his steps steady, his presence grounding. When he touches my face, his hand is cool against my skin. Cool enough that I flinch before I can stop myself. The adrenaline that carried me through the fight drains all at once, leaving the raw sting of my burns exposed, pulsing beneath every breath. His thumb stills, his eyes flicking over me with quiet understanding, but he doesn't pull away.

"Easy," he murmurs, voice barely above a breath. "You're hurt."

"I'm alive. We're alive," I whisper back. "That's enough."

His jaw tightens. "It's not enough for me."

I swallow, the ache in my throat sharper than the burns. "Aero...we did it. The Mortia is gone."

His forehead dips toward mine, not quite touching. "You nearly went with him."

"But I didn't," my voice wavers, but I hold his gaze. "Because you were there."

He exhales, a sound that trembles at the edges. "I thought I might lose you. For a moment, I—" He cuts himself off, shaking his head. "Don't make me feel that again."

I lift a hand, resting it over his. "Then stay with me. Here. Now."

His eyes soften, the storm in them easing. "I'm not going anywhere."

The words settle between us. They are quiet, certain, truer than any vow spoken aloud. I take his hand, though my fingers tremble as they curl around his. The movement pulls at the healing skin along my arms, a sharp reminder that victory does not erase the cost. Together we look out over the ruins, happy tears pouring down my face. The fortress is broken, the corruption gone, but the scars remain—on the land, on us. And that is how it should be. Scars are proof of survival, reminders of what was endured, and what we chose to face anyway.

I watch quietly as the light spreads across the land. We mourn what we must leave. But what rises from the grief... that's ours to shape.

The bloom pulses once more in my palm. Not as a weapon, not as a relic. Just a reminder. A reminder of what was lost and what will rise again.

25

EVANTHE

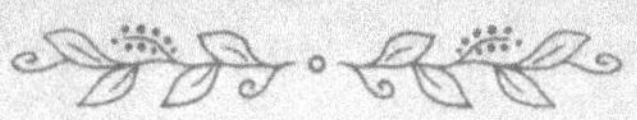

The fractured remnants of Murick's fortress still cling to the horizon behind us, jagged silhouettes against a sky that is finally beginning to breathe again. The dark veil has thinned, dissolving into pale light, mist rising in slow spirals as though the land exhales for the first time in generations. Yet, even as the air clears, my chest feels heavy, tangled in grief and dread. I walk a few paces ahead of the others, isolating myself, eyes trained on the horizon where Meraki lies beyond the veil's shoreline. My heart beats unevenly, each pulse carrying the weight of names I dare not speak too loudly.

"My father was taken. Then Sorrow fell. Only my aunts remain," I whisper to myself, the words tasting like ash. "If the vampyr left anything behind...let it not be death."

Memories come in flashes, unbidden. The scent of my aunts' herb cellar, fresh and comforting, the way dried lavender and sage clung to the air. Their laughter echoing through the library walls, warm and unrestrained, weaving safety into every corner. I see their hands guiding mine as a child, teaching me how to press roots into soil, how to listen to the hum beneath the earth even before they knew of my magic. Those memories feel fragile now, like glass held too tightly.

I close my eyes and whisper to the Great Divine, asking for mercy I am not sure I deserve. My voice trembles, the prayer thin, "If they still live, let them be spared. If they are gone, let them have gone gently. And if I must carry their silence, let me carry it without breaking."

The silence around me is heavier than before, and Aero notices. His footsteps slow until he is beside me, his presence steady but cautious. "You fear for them," he says gently, his voice low, careful not to intrude but unwilling to let me drown alone.

I nod, my throat tight. "They were the keepers of my family's stories. If I lose them...I lose them all again. Every tale, every song, every memory that survived the Omen. It will be as if none of it ever existed."

Aero's gaze is steady, his hand brushing mine briefly, grounding me. "Then let's move quickly," he says softly. "If they still live, they must know they weren't forgotten. That you fought for them. That you carried them here."

His words are quiet strength, but they do not erase the fear gnawing at me. I glance toward the horizon, imagining Meraki's people still unaware of what has happened here. It is still daylight. They do not yet know the omens have been defeated. My chest tightens with dread. What if the creatures reached my aunts before vanishing? What if victory means nothing because the last good things were taken with it?

"Victory means nothing," I murmur, "if the heart of home is already gone."

Behind us, Hera's voice cuts through the tension, practical and firm. "We should gather food. Enough to sustain us for the journey. Two days' travel through rough terrain will break us if we don't prepare."

Diaspor nods, already moving toward the edges of the ruins, his knowledge of the terrain guiding him to forageable roots and herbs. Feliks mutters something under his breath but obeys, scavenging the last of our dried meats, his hands quick and restless. Around the fire they build, Liri kneels, her fingers pressed into the soil. She murmurs a blessing for my family, her voice trembling but resolute. "May the soil remember your kin and guide you safely to them."

Her words pierce me, fragile and kind, and I clutch the bloom tighter against my chest. The crystal hums faintly, no longer as a weapon or a relic, but as a reminder.

We ready our packs, replenished and renewed, though the weight of what lies ahead presses heavier than any burden on our shoulders. Two days' travel, rough terrain. No shortcuts, no illusions—just grit.

I lead the way, the bloom pressed to my chest, the veil's shoreline beckoning. My voice is low, almost swallowed by the wind. "It's not homecoming I fear. It's returning to find the heart of home already gone."

Aero walks beside me, his silence steady, but I feel his eyes on me. I realize suddenly how much I have made this about myself. All too much about my grief, my dread, my family. And yet he is here too, carrying his own storms. He is probably a wreck inside, thinking about facing his father, about seeing his mother for the first time since he learned the truth of his blood.

I stop, turning to him, my voice breaking. "I keep speaking of my aunts, of what I might lose. But you... you're walking toward something just as heavy. Facing your father. Seeing your mother again. I've been drowning in my own fear and forgetting that you're carrying yours too."

Aero's eyes soften, though the pain flickers there. He exhales slowly. "I won't lie. I am afraid. Afraid of what I'll see in him. Afraid of what I'll see in her. I don't know if I can forgive either of them. I don't know if I want to. But I know I have to face them. And I know I don't want to do it alone."

I reach for his hand, gripping it tightly. "You won't. Not now. Not ever. We walk into this together. My grief, your fear...they're threads of the same cloth. We carry them side by side."

He nods, his jaw tight, but his hand squeezes mine back. "Then let's keep walking. Whatever waits for us in Meraki, we'll face it. Together."

The horizon stretches ahead, the veil's shoreline faintly shimmering in the distance. My chest aches, my heart tangled in grief and dread, but Aero's hand in mine steadies me. The bloom pulses faintly against my chest, a reminder not of what was lost, but of what remains.

We mourn what we must leave. But what rises from the grief is ours to shape.

Under the canopy of a sun-dappled grove, the light filters through in fractured beams, painting the moss and bark in shifting gold. The air is soft here, gentler than the jagged silence of Murick's fortress, and for the first time in what feels like lifetimes, the group breathes without the weight of shadow pressing against their lungs. My steps slow, and I turn to the companions who have walked beside us through ruin and fire.

"You should go home," I say, my voice quiet but firm, carrying the ache of both gratitude and worry. "Be with your people. You've carried enough of this burden. Let the soil of your own villages hold you now."

Liri smiles softly, the wind tugging at her braids, her eyes bright with a resilience that humbles me. "Not yet," she replies, her voice like a song carried on the breeze. "You returned us to freedom. We walk with you to the veil. We will not leave before the journey is whole."

Her words settle into me like roots, steady and unyielding. Aero glances between us, his gaze lingering on Liri before turning to me. He nods, his voice low but resonant. "Family isn't just blood. It's those who stay when it's easier to leave."

The truth of it hums through the grove. The group moves forward with steadier breath and looser shoulders, the tension that had bound us in the fortress unraveling in the light. The Mortia's shadow no longer clings to us. The light isn't a threat—it's a promise.

Birds return to the air, their wings slicing through the canopy with joyous abandon. Wildflowers bloom where ash once laid, their colors vivid against the muted soil. My steps no longer sink so heavily into the earth; instead, the ground feels alive beneath me, welcoming me again, humming faintly with recognition.

Liri walks ahead, her voice carrying softly. "There is a village just beyond this grove, nestled in the curve of the forest and stream. They are Fae, kin to mine. If there is anyone left there, they will receive us in peace."

The thought of peace feels fragile, almost too delicate to hold, but we follow her. The path winds gently, the stream's murmur growing louder, until the village comes into view.

Upon our arrival, laughter greets us. Children dart between the trees, their voices bright, unscarred by shadow. A child tugs at my hand, her eyes wide with wonder, her fingers small and warm against mine. Word spreads like wildfire, and soon the elders step forward, their faces lined with age but lit with recognition.

"You are the ones who fought the Mortia," one elder says, his voice trembling with awe. "You are the grove that grew, even in shadow."

He leans to bow, but I stop him. Placing my hand in his, I surprise myself as I begin jumping for joy. The elder surprises me too, jumping right along with me with child-like wonder.

The village prepares a feast, their joy spilling into

every gesture. Flowering wines shimmer in carved cups, roasted rootcakes steam on woven platters, emberfruit glows faintly, and honey petals glisten in bowls of carved stone. Music rises, the simple pipes and voices layered in joy, weaving through the air like threads of light.

I watch them all celebrate, my heart swelling, tears welling unbidden. "We were not meant for reverence," I whisper to Aero, my voice breaking. "And yet, here it is."

As the night softens, the Fae implore us to remain. "You've done your duty in saving the realms from the Mortia," one says, lifting a cup high. "Stay. Rest. Let the soil cradle you."

I swallow, my heart conflicted, the weight of truth pressing against me. "I was the one who struck the deal with Hale Mortia," I confess, my voice trembling. "I unleashed the Omen upon them. Their suffering began with my hand."

Bel steps forward, his eyes steady, his voice unshaken. "Maybe so...but it was only a matter of time before another unsuspecting human did the same. You ended what others would have perpetuated. That's no small thing."

His words do not absolve me, but they hold me. I bow my head, the bloom pressed against my chest, feeling the weight of both guilt and grace.

We rest on silken moss, the feast's warmth lingering in our bodies. Aero reaches for me, his hand steady, his eyes carrying both exhaustion and desire. The relief from the battle behind us overpowers any worry about what lies ahead. It courses through our bond, unspoken but undeniable. His touch is grounding, his presence over-whelming.

I feel his warmth for me, and I meet it with my own, not in the fever of battle but in the quiet of survival. His lips brush mine, tender at first, then deeper, carrying the weight of everything we endured. My hands trace the lines of his shoulders, the strength that held us through ruin. His breath catches, his fingers tightening against me, and the world narrows to the space between us.

We move together, not in haste but in reverence, each touch a promise, each kiss a release. The moss cradles us, the stars above witness us, and the earth hums beneath, steady and alive. Our bodies entwine, not as weapons, not as survivors, but as souls finding solace in each other.

When the storm of passion ebbs, I fall back onto the moss, my hair damp from the heat that consumed me. Aero, exhausted from the journey, falls asleep immedi-ately, his breath steady against my skin. I stare up at the stars, their light fractured but pure, and whisper to the Great Divine. "Let this peace be real. Let it not vanish when the veil closes."

The night holds me, the bloom pulses faintly in my palm, and for the first time since the Hollow, I believe peace might be possible.

26

AERO

The rhythm of our journey has changed. I notice it first in the way the air moves around us, slower, heavier, as though reluctant to let us pass. The trees stretch taller here, their trunks rising like pillars, their crowns brushing the sky with solemn grace. The vines that once tangled thick and wild now thin, curling back as if bowing to some unseen boundary. Every step carries us closer to the veil, and I feel it in my bones. The realm knows we are leaving. Even the wind feels reluctant, sighing through the branches with a mournful cadence, as though it, too, wishes to hold us here a little longer.

I glance at Eva. Her eyes are fixed on the horizon, scanning with the same intensity she carried through battle, through loss, through every shadow we endured. The weight of our mission is still carved into her brow, etched deep as if the land itself pressed it there. She doesn't speak, but I know her thoughts are heavy. She is already beyond this grove, already imagining what waits on the other side of the veil—her family, surely more grief, and perhaps silence.

I watch as Liri, Diaspor, Bel, and Phira pause at a clearing dappled with gold light. The sun filters through the canopy, scattering across their faces, painting them in warmth that feels almost ceremonial. They stand together, quiet, their breaths steady, their shoulders eased. For the first time since we began, there is no urgency in their movements. Only presence.

My heart tightens. These weren't just allies. They became family in ways the battlefield never promised. In the Hollow, in the fortress, in every step through shadow, they stood beside us. They carried us when we faltered, reminded us of songs when silence threatened to consume us. And now, as the veil looms near, I feel the ache of knowing they will not cross with us.

I speak first, my voice low but steady. "You should go. You're home. This place missed you."

Liri steps forward, her braids catching the light, her eyes soft but unyielding. She places her hand on my shoulder, grounding me with a touch that carries both strength and tenderness. "We came with you through every storm," she says. "Let us see you through the last swell."

Bel grins, his usual mischief tempered by sincerity. "Besides, we'll know if you don't return. The trees whisper, remember? They'll tell us if you falter."

Their words settle into me, heavy and comforting all at once. I watch as Eva kneels, her fingers deft and deliberate, weaving a small flower bracelet for Liri. "For you," she says, extending the gesture to the princess.

It says everything coursing through her. Gratitude, love, a friendship that will never be forsaken. Liri accepts it with reverence, slipping it onto her wrist as though it were a crown.

The rest of the group begins to exchange parting tokens. Diaspor presses a stone into my hand, etched with runes that shimmer faintly in the light. "For strength," he murmurs. Phira offers a feather kissed by morning dew, its edges glistening. "For flight, when the ground feels too heavy." Liri gives Eva a sprig of lavender, its scent sharp and soothing.

Eva's hands tremble as she accepts the sprig of lavender from Liri. The scent rises immediately, sharp and soothing, cutting through the heaviness in her chest. She holds it as though it is more than a gift, more than a token; it's a tether to everything they have endured together. Her eyes glisten, and though she tries to steady her breath, it comes uneven, caught between gratitude and grief.

Diaspor's stone still rests in my palm, its runes shimmering faintly, and Bel's feather gleams with dew, but it is Eva's reaction that stills the clearing. She presses the lavender to her lips, closing her eyes, and for a moment, she looks as though she might break.

"You've been more than companions," she whispers, her voice raw. "You became my family when the world tried to strip me of it. Every step through shadow, every breath in the Hollow...you carried me. And now I have to leave you."

Her words hang in the air, fragile and heavy. Liri reaches forward, brushing a tear from Eva's cheek with the back of her hand. "We are not gone," she says softly. "The soil remembers. The wind carries. You will find us in every grove, in every stream. Family does not vanish when paths divide."

Eva nods, but her tears fall freely now, streaking down her face. She tries to smile, tries to hold herself upright, but the weight of parting presses too hard. She turns to Bel, her voice breaking. "You made me laugh when I thought I'd forgotten how. You reminded me that joy can survive even in ruin. I don't know how to walk without that."

Bel's grin softens, his usual mischief tempered by sincerity. "Then don't walk without it. Carry it. Every time you smile, every time you find light in darkness, you'll know I'm with you. The trees will whisper it back to me."

Diaspor steps closer, his hand resting briefly on Eva's shoulder. "You gave us courage," he murmurs. "You reminded us that even broken soil can bloom again. That is not something that leaves with you. It stays, rooted here, rooted in us."

Eva's sob catches in her throat, and she presses the bloom against her chest, as though anchoring herself against the tide of emotion. "I don't want to go," she admits, her voice barely audible. "I know I must, but my heart...my heart wants to stay here, with you, with this soil that feels alive again."

Liri leans in, her forehead touching Eva's briefly. "Hearts are not bound by veils. Yours will walk here whenever it longs to. And when you return, we will be waiting."

The silence that follows is thick, but it is not empty.

It's filled with everything they could not say. Love, gratitude. The promise of tomorrow. No one speaks of goodbye, because goodbye feels too final, too sharp. Instead, they let the silence carry the weight, let it speak in ways words never could.

We walk together until the trees part, revealing the streaming boundary. The air shifts, charged with magic, rippling like water. It is a place where worlds thin, where memory clings to every breath. The stream itself glows faintly, its surface shimmering with colors that shift and dance, reflecting not just light but the essence of both realms.

Eva stops at the edge, her hand tightening around mine. Her eyes are wide, shimmering with tears, but her voice is steady. "This is harder than any battle," she whispers. "Leaving you all behind. Leaving this soil that healed me. I thought victory would feel lighter, but it feels like carrying another wound."

Liri rests her hand on the surface, her fingers trailing across the water. She turns to us one last time, her voice steady, carrying the weight of promise. "This place will wait for you. You are always welcome in the shade of our groves."

I nod, my chest tight. "If the veil stays open, then maybe the story doesn't end."

I glance back once more. The Fae figures stand in the clearing, backlit by blooming light, their silhouettes radiant, their hands raised in gentle farewell. They do not call out, do not weep. They simply stand, present, their silence carrying the weight of eternity.

The river is alive beneath me. I stand knee deep in its current, the water tugging gently around my legs, cool and insistent, as though reminding me that I am part of it, not separate. The wide, serpentine flow glows faintly with enchantment, a soft radiance that pulses like veins of light beneath the surface. It feels familiar, almost ancestral, as if every drop carries memory—of Fae songs, of tides that once spoke to my blood, of a rhythm older than any war.

Lush foliage overhangs the banks, heavy with dew, their leaves whispering in the breeze. Wisps of light flicker across the surface like fireflies, darting and weaving, reflections of magic that never truly left this place. Ahead, the veil hovers low and iridescent, stretched between tangled roots and mist-laced water. It shimmers like a curtain of breath, waiting, reluctant, but ready to part.

Behind me, Eva, Hera, and Feliks wait in a shallow canoe woven from reeds and silver thread. The craft is delicate but strong, its surface glinting faintly in the river's glow. Eva sits at the front, her posture tense, her eyes fixed on the veil. Hera is steady, her hands resting on the rim of the boat, her gaze sharp and protective. Feliks fidgets, muttering under his breath, half grumbling, half awed, his bow laid across his knees.

I raise my hand. The water responds instantly, bending into shimmering arcs around us. It coils upward, ribbons of liquid light, wrapping protectively around the canoe. The river knows me. It listens. It remembers.

With a breath, I release the spell. The current surges

forward, smooth and strong, pushing us toward the veil. The water coils tighter, braided ribbons guiding us, shielding us. The veil shudders as we approach, not torn but rippled open by the river's own will. It parts like a sigh, shimmering, reluctant but yielding.

I step onto the back of the craft, riding the wave with practiced balance. My feet grip the woven reeds, my body sways with the rhythm, and I feel the river's pulse beneath me. Beyond the veil, the river drops, spilling from a cliff into the sea.

But we do not fall. I command the flow, my hands outstretched, my will steady. The water curves, spirals, lowers itself like a great staircase, carrying us downward in sweeping arcs. Salt spray kisses our skin, cool and sharp, and stars flicker overhead, scattered across the night sky like shards of memory.

The water swells beneath us, lifting the canoe into a tide-wrought chariot. I stand tall, hands outstretched, guiding us past towering bluffs. The cliffs rise like guardians, their faces carved by centuries of waves, their shadows deep and solemn.

"This realm remembers her," I murmur, my voice carried by the wind. "It must."

Eva lifts her hand above her brow, shading her eyes from the sun as she looks into the distance. Her jaw drops, her breath catching. "Look!" she cries, pointing toward the open sea. In the distance, specks move across the horizon. Ships...Fae ships, their sails glinting faintly as they move away from Stillstar. She smiles, her eyes bright with wonder. "They are returning to their realm."

I turn to her, my voice lifting over the wind. "They get to return because of you, Eva."

Her smile falters, softens, and I see the weight of my words settle into her. She looks back at the ships, her eyes shimmering, and I know she carries both joy and sorrow.

The rocks beneath our passage smooth, the sharp edges dissolving into flat shore. The waves release us gently, carrying the canoe onto warm, moonlit sand. The tide ebbs, my magic fading with it, leaving only the quiet hum of the sea.

Eva steps forward first, barefoot now, her feet sinking into the sand. The land hums softly beneath her, welcoming her, recognizing her. Hera exhales in disbelief, her shoulders loosening, her eyes scanning the horizon. "Finally, we are home," she gasps.

Feliks is already moving, scouring the shore, muttering half grumbles, half praises, his awe poorly hidden. I watch silently. My magic ebbs like the tide, my purpose fulfilled in quiet grace. The river's pulse fades from my skin, but its memory lingers. I feel the weight of what we carried, the battles fought, the shadows endured. And I feel the release. The quiet, steady release of knowing we have crossed over into the next leg of our journey and that the realm has remembered.

Eva turns back to me, her eyes bright, her smile trembling. "We made it," she whispers.

I nod, my voice low, steady. "We did."

The sea stretches before us, vast and endless, its surface shimmering beneath the forming stars. The ships move steadily across the horizon as the sun sets. Their sails catching the wind, their forms fading into the distance. The land hums beneath us, and the sand is so warm.

We stand together, uncertain of what we will find inland.

But we are home.

Mama says to keep the candle low, but the dark feels heavier when I do.
It flickers against the windows, a watchful dance. The elders say the
vampyr don't cross the salt lines, but the salt keeps disappearing by
morning, as if the sea itself is swallowing it whole.

Tonight the air changed again. The gulls stopped crying all at once,
like someone pinched the sound out of the sky. Even the waves went
quiet. That's how we know they're near—when the island forgets
how to make noise.

I saw something at dusk, just before we barred the door. A figure
standing at the edge of the treeline, too still to be human, too tall to be
anything I've ever known. It didn't move, but I felt it looking at me. If
they knock tonight, I will not answer.

- Journal entry of Twelve-year-old
Merakian girl, Jaela Akis

27
EVANTHE

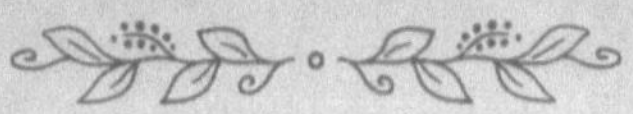

The soft shorelines of Meraki stretch wide before us, windswept and sun warmed, familiar in a way that makes my chest ache. The cliffside veil behind us is dissolved, replaced by the scent of herbs, salt, and the promise of coming rain. I stand at the edge of the tide, my toes sinking into the sand, and for a moment, I can't not move. The horizon is the same as it had always been, but I am not.

The town of Parea lays inland, three days walk through foothills and old farmlands now touched by shadow and silence. I know the path well. I walked it as a child, chasing after my aunts' laughter, carrying baskets of herbs, listening to the hum of the soil beneath my feet. Now, the thought of returning fills me with both longing and dread.

I kneel briefly, pressing my fingers into the sand. The grains cling to my skin, warm and alive. "This is the place that shaped me," I whisper, my voice trembling. "Where every echo feels like it carries my name."

The earth hums faintly in response, subtle but sure. My magic flows again, not in torrents as it has done in the Fae Realm, but in quiet streams. It's as though the land recognizes me, welcoming me back.

I breathe deeply, the air tasting like memory. Like my aunts' tea, steeped with herbs and honey. Like Sorrow's laughter, sharp and bright, echoing through the thicket paths. I close my eyes, and for a moment, I can almost hear Skira's insistent voice in my ear, nagging, frustrating, relentless. I had cursed her persistence then, but now I miss it. The silence feels heavier without her.

Through the bond, I feel Aero's tension like a storm building at his center. His thoughts are guarded, but I see past them. King Phineas Vouvali. The man who once held the illusion of fatherhood. Iason. The snake hiding behind princely decorum. Aero's mind is a tempest, his fear and anger coiled tight. That man, Phineas, would bleed this land for vanity. That cannot happen.

I turn to him, watching the way his shoulders stiffen, the way his gaze lingers on the horizon. "You're thinking of him," I say softly.

Aero's eyes flick to mine, sharp but weary. "I cannot help it. Every step closer to Parea feels like walking into his shadow."

I reach for his hand, hoping to offer some piece of solace. "You are not his shadow. You are the tide that will wash him away."

He exhales, the storm within him easing slightly,

though it does not vanish. "And you? What do you feel, standing here again?"

I looked back at the shoreline, at the waves curling against the sand. "I feel everything. Joy. Grief. A little fear too, if I'm being honest. This land remembers me, but I don't know if I am strong enough to remember it without breaking."

Hera steps closer, her eyes scanning the horizon. "You are stronger than you think. This land does not ask for perfection. And the people of Meraki sure as Hades won't either. You're here. That's what matters."

Feliks mutters behind her, half grumbling, half awed. "Three days' walk through shadowed farmland. I suppose it's better than another fortress full of Mortia soldiers."

His words draw a faint smile from me. Even in ruin, he finds humor.

We begin to move inland, the sand giving way to grass, the shoreline fading behind us. The path is familiar, but the silence isn't. Fields that once sang with birds and laughter now lay quiet, touched by the darkness left behind in the Omen's wake. The soil hums faintly beneath my feet, but it is weaker, strained.

I press my hand to the ground as we walk, whispering softly, "I am here. I remember you. Do you remember me?"

The earth responds, faint but present. My magic flows again, subtle but sure, weaving through the soil, reminding it of life.

Aero walks beside me, his storm still simmering. I feel it through the bond. "Phineas will not win," I say quietly. "Iason will not bleed this land. We will not let them."

He nods, his jaw tight. "Then we must be ready. Parea is not just a town. It is a stage. And they will use it to play their illusions."

I look ahead, the foothills rising in the distance. "Then we will break their illusions. We will show them truth."

———

The ridgeline stretches before us, rolling in gentle waves of grass and stone, the kind of landscape that seems to breathe with its own rhythm. Each step carries us closer to Parea, closer to the hearths and shadows of my childhood, and though the air is soft and the wind forgiving, my chest feels heavy. Aero walks just behind me, his hand hovering close to my back, never quite touching, but near enough that I can feel the warmth of his presence. I resist the urge to reach for him, to comfort him, because I know what weighs on him. He feels responsible. For me, for us, for the land itself. I have to remind myself that his silence is not distance; it's merely burden.

We push forward together, the group settling into a steady rhythm over the grassy ridgelines. The path is old, marked with faded stones that jut from the soil like forgotten teeth. I remember them from long ago, when children ran barefoot here, reckless and laughing, chasing each other through the fields with no thought of war or omens. Those stones guided us then, and they guide us now, though their edges are worn and their stories muted.

Hera moves with quiet grit, her steps deliberate, her shoulders squared. Feliks hovers near her, his eyes flicking often to her belly, then to her boots, as though he expects the ground itself to betray her. "Maybe slow down just a little," he mutters, his voice low but insistent.

Hera shoots him a wry look, her lips curling into something between amusement and irritation. "Pregnant doesn't mean fragile," she said. "I'm not made of glass."

I chuckle under my breath, the sound escaping before I can stop it. "They're already parenting," I murmur, "and the baby hasn't even seen sunlight."

Feliks flushes and mutters something incoherent, but Hera's grin lingers. Their bickering is a strange comfort, a reminder that life presses forward even in the shadow of war.

My thoughts drift ahead, to Parea. To the possibility that my aunts had survived the omen. I picture them at the hearth, stirring tea, mumbling mantras under their breath, their voices weaving together like threads of memory. "Please," I whisper to myself, "let them be stirring tea and mumbling mantras at the hearth." The thought is fragile, but it keeps me moving.

As the sun begins to dip, the hills ahead darken softly, shadows stretching long across the ridges. The air cools, the scent of earth deepening, and I feel the weight of history pressing closer. I slow, placing a hand on Aero's arm.

"Do you think it's still standing? Parea?" I ask.

Aero hesitates. "I want to say yes."

"But you're not sure."

"No," he admits. "Not after everything the realm has endured."

I draw a breath, the air sharp in my lungs. "If the city survived, will they welcome me back? After all this death?"

His gaze flicks to me, steady and earnest. "You're their monarch, Eva."

"That doesn't guarantee anything."

"No," he agrees softly. "But I'm sure they've been waiting for someone to believe in again."

I swallow, the truth of that settling heavy in my chest. "And you? Will they accept you?"

Aero's jaw tightens, but his voice stays even. "Some will. Some won't. I'm prepared for both."

I squeeze his arm, grounding him the way he grounds me. "You stood with me through all of this. You saved lives. That matters."

"Maybe," he says. "But I'm not worried about them accepting me."

I blink up at him. "Then what are you worried about?"

"That they won't accept you," he says. "And that it will hurt you more than any battle ever could."

The wind shifts, carrying the faint scent of stone and memory.

"We'll face it together," I say.

Aero nods, the tension in his shoulders easing just a little. "Together."

And we keep walking, the last light fading. The city, our future, waiting in the dark ahead.

28

EVANTHE

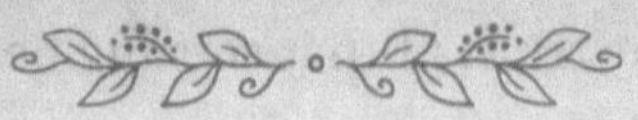

The air of Meraki is different. Softer, warmer, carrying with it the familiar scents of salt and soil, of herbs drying in the sun, of rain waiting just beyond the horizon. Relief washes through me as my boots press into the earth of my island again. A part of me will always miss the Fae Realm, even though I have only known it in its war-ravaged state. The fractured forests, the haunted rivers, the endless shadow. There is beauty there, even in ruin, and I carry it with me. But this...this island of Meraki is my home. The land that shapes me, the soil that whispers to me as it did when I was a child.

The countryside flattens as we press forward, brush giving way to tilled soil and old stone fences. The ridge-lines soften into fields, their boundaries marked by walls built generations ago, stones stacked by hands that believed in permanence. My heart tightens at the sight. These fences have stood through storms, through so much loss and many new dawns. They are scarred, but they endure.

Ahead, a cluster of cottages appears, their rooftops sagging slightly from time and hardship. The sight makes my breath catch. These homes have weathered the omens, the Mortia. I can almost taste the fear that spread like rot. They still stand, weary but unbroken.

The group's pace quickens at the sight. Boots click against stone and soil with renewed hope. Hera's stride lengthens, Feliks mutters something under his breath that sounds almost like a prayer, and Aero's hand brushes close to my back, steadying me without touching. We move as one, drawn forward by the promise of life.

As we enter the village center, quiet ripples into frantic whispers. Children stare, their wide eyes unblinking. Mothers drop baskets, herbs scattering across the ground, roots rolling into the dust. Old men rise from benches with trembling eyes, their hands shaking as they lean on canes.

Villagers gather, drawn by the sight of us. Some kneel, their knees pressing into the earth. Others bow deeply, their foreheads nearly touching the ground. The air thickens with reverence, with desperation, with expectation.

A wave of emotion swells around me. I feel all their adoration. There's also a desperation, hoping that my being here will make things better. It presses against my chest, heavy and overwhelming. They think I've come to save them. That I bring safety on my shoulders.

I swallow, steadying myself. My voice rises softly, but loud enough to carry across the square. "The Omen is no more," I say. "The Mortia with it. You are safe now, not just while I'm here."

Gasps ripple through the crowd. Tears follow. A few fall to their knees, pressing their foreheads to the earth. Some whisper prayers, their voices trembling, their words carried by the wind.

I step forward, my hands open, my voice steady. "Share this truth with your neighbors. Tell them the shadow has lifted. Let hope ripple outward, beyond this village, beyond these fields. Let it spread like fire, like song."

The villagers weep openly now, their tears mingling with laughter, with disbelief, with relief. A mother clutches her child to her chest, whispering blessings. An old man presses his hand to the soil, murmuring, "Thank you, Great Divine." Children dart forward, their eyes wide, their voices rising in questions.

"Is it true?" one asks, her voice high and trembling. "The monsters are gone?"

I kneel, meeting her gaze. "It is true," I say softly. "The monsters are gone. You are safe."

Her eyes widen, tears spilling down her cheeks, and she runs back to her mother, her laughter breaking through the silence.

Behind me, Aero stands tall, his gaze scanning the crowd. Hera's hand rests on her belly, her mouth curling into a grin at the sight of the happy families. Feliks wraps his arm around her, pulling her close.

The square fills with voices, with prayers, with laughter. Even the cottages seem brighter, the fences stronger, the soil richer. Hope returns, fragile but alive.

I stand in the center, the bloom pressed against my chest. Aero's hand finds mine, and I whisper to him, "This is the place that shaped me. Where every echo carries my name. It's not fair, what they've been through. Despite the hardship, being back here feels right. It feels good, but I'm afraid I don't deserve their kindness."

He leans over, letting his lips brush my forehead. "Of course you do. You are their monarch. You are my queen. There's no one more deserving. Don't forget that."

The earth hums faintly beneath my feet, subtle but sure. My magic flows again, weaving through the soil, reminding it of life. The land remembers me, and I remember it.

The villagers press closer, their voices rising, their hands reaching. I raise mine, steadying them, calming them. "It's true. You are safe," I repeat. "Not because of me, but because of you. Because you endured. Because you stood strong. Every horde of vampyr is gone."

Their voices quiet, and their eyes fix on me. I feel the weight of their exhaustion. But I also feel their resilience. This war has shed them just as much as it has shaped me. None of us will be the same, but maybe that's okay. Maybe we are better for it.

I stand in the center of them, closing my eyes, and for a moment, I can almost hear Skira's voice. I had cursed her persistence so many times before, but now I miss it desperately. But then I see her among the clouds, no longer chained to this place, and I smile. Opening my eyes,

I find Aero stepping toward me. He places his hand on my back, and I let my body melt into his.

Meraki is alive again.

The villagers gather what they can, their hands moving with a kind of reverent urgency. Root vegetables pulled from cellars, dried meats wrapped in cloth, rough bread baked from last season's barley. All of it carried to the square as though each offering is a prayer. The air smells of earth and smoke, of salt carried inland from the sea, of barley crusts and herbs dried too long but still clinging to their fragrance.

A fire crackles gently at the center of the village square, its light spilling across the worn stones. Lanterns swing overhead, catching the night breeze, their glow swaying in rhythm with the laughter that begins to rise. The villagers sit shoulder to shoulder, elbows brushing, bowls balanced in their hands. They eat simply, but the act itself is sacred. Every bite is a declaration: we are still here.

At first, the laughter is tentative, fragile, like a bird testing its wings after a storm. But it grows, weaving through the square, carried by voices that have been silent too long. Children giggle, their mouths full of bread. Old men chuckle, their eyes wet with tears. Even the mothers, weary from months of fear, allow themselves to smile.

One villager, a man with hair silvered by age, leans forward, his voice deep. "There was a boy," he begins, "taken by the vampyr. He was small, no older than ten. We searched for him for days, but the shadows swallowed him whole. We never found him. But we remember him. His laughter, his mischief. He is not gone...not while we speak his name."

The square falls silent, listening. The fire pops, sending sparks into the air. The man's eyes glisten, but his voice does not falter. He speaks in honor, not pity.

Another villager, a woman with hands callused from years of tending herbs, lifts her chin. "My grandmother," she says, "would not leave her garden. The vampyr came, and we begged her to run, but she stayed. She said the soil needed her, that the herbs would die without her. She vanished that night. But I still see her in the lavender, in the sage, in the thyme. She is not gone...not while the garden grows."

Each tale is spoken with heart, a way to honor them, each voice carrying memories that no doubt will live on. The villagers do not weep for what is lost; they remember, fiercely, defiantly.

I listen, my fingers absentmindedly trailing the rim of my empty cup. The stories press against me, heavy and familiar. I see Sorrow in their stories, I think. My father's silence in their pauses. The weight of memory is everywhere, woven into every word, every breath.

Aero shifts closer, his presence steady, the bond glowing between us. He places his hand on my thigh, reminding me that I am not alone. Hera leans into Feliks, her voice low as she scolds him softly for fussing too much. He mutters under his breath, his eyes darting to her belly, his worry obvious. Hera rolls her eyes, but her smile lingers.

I smile, the warmth of it breaking through the heaviness. "I still have them," I whisper. "Through it all, I still have them."

The fire dims slowly, its crackle softening into embers. A villager begins to sing, her voice low and trembling at first but steadying as the melody carries. It is an old lullaby, one I remember from my childhood, sung by mothers at hearths, by sisters in fields, by grandmothers in gardens. The words are simple, but they carry the weight of generations.

Children curl beneath makeshift blankets, their eyes heavy, their breaths slowing. The song wraps around them, soothing, steady, carrying them into dreams free of shadow.

I lift my gaze to the stars, their light fractured but pure, scattered across the sky like shards of our ancestors. I whisper thanks to the ones I have lost. Sorrow, Skira, my father, my mother. Their names press against my lips, carried into the night.

And fiercely, I promise. Promise that I will protect the ones still here. Promise that I will carry them, guard them, remember them. I will not let the soil forget. I will not let the stars fade.

The fire dims as the song lingers beneath the stars. And I let the night carry me to sleep.

29
EVANTHE

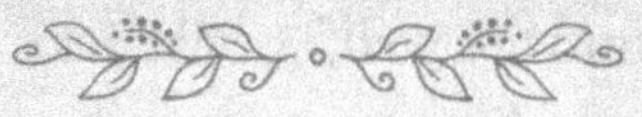

The sun dips low as we crest the final hill, its light spilling across the horizon in long, fractured beams. The sky is painted in hues of violet and gold, but the beauty of it cannot soften the ache in my chest. Below us stretches Parea. My town, my childhood, the place where laughter once rose like birdsong. Now, rooftops sag and crack, walls are streaked with ash, silence pressing down where voices once filled the air.

I stop at the ridge, my breath catching. "It smells like sage and citrus," I whisper, "but only in my memory." The air is heavy, carrying faint traces of smoke and damp stone, but none of the scents that defined this place for me. No herbs drying in the windows, no citrus peel tossed into the hearth. It is all thinner now, quieter. Like chest ghosts holding their breath.

Aero stands just behind me, his hand hovering close to my back. He knows better than to break the fragile thread of my thoughts. Hera and Feliks move ahead, their pace quickening as they break off toward the city square. Hera's eyes are sharp, desperate, fixed on the streets that will lead her to her mother. Feliks clasps her hand tightly, his knuckles white, as though he might lose her in the rubble if he lets go. Before she gets too far ahead, she looks back at us. "We'll come find you at the High Tower once I've had the chance to speak with my mother."

"I hope you find her well," I call back.

I watch them disappear into the shadows of the district, their figures swallowed by the silence. My own path lies elsewhere. Aero and I turn toward the narrow lane where my aunts lived, the place that was my anchor, my sanctuary.

My pace wavers. My legs want to sprint, to tear through the streets until I reach their door. But my heart demands caution. Every step feels heavy, each breath a prayer. If they're gone, I will feel hollow in a way no magic can fill.

The lane is narrower than I remember, the cobblestones uneven, weeds pushing through cracks. The cottages lean against each other like weary companions, their shutters closed, their gardens overgrown. My chest tightens as I reach the door of my aunts' cottage. The wood is worn, the paint peeling off in little flakes, the handle cold beneath my hand.

I turn the knob sand push it open. The cottage is dark. Still. The air smells faintly of earth and dust, of herbs long since dried. My breath catches, my throat tight. Tears burn behind my eyes.

And then—

"Evanthe?"

The voice cracks with disbelief, fragile but unmistakable. Aunt Maria.

I stumble forward, my tears spilling freely now. "Aunt Maria!" I cry, rushing to her. She stands in the doorway of the kitchen, her hair streaked with silver, her eyes wide and wet. I throw myself into her arms, the embrace hard, trembling, desperate. She holds me tightly, her hands clutching at my shoulders, her body shaking with sobs.

Aero steps outside, his presence steady but wanting to give us space.

Moments later, footsteps echo on the cobbled path outside. Another voice, sharp with shock. "Eva?"

I turn just as Aunt Cybele appears, a basket of potatoes balanced in her arms. She gasps, the basket toppling onto the stones, potatoes scattering across the ground. She drops everything and runs, her arms outstretched, her voice breaking.

"Eva!"

I meet her halfway, the reunion loud, messy, wonderful. She clutches me tightly, her sobs mingling with laughter, her hands trembling as they press against my face, my shoulders, my hair. "You're here," she whispers. "You're alive."

We collapse together in the doorway, the three of us tangled in tears and laughter, our voices rising into the silence of the lane. The cottage breathes again, the air filled with memory, with life.

I press my forehead against theirs, my tears falling

freely. "I thought I'd lost you," I whisper. "I thought the vampyr had taken you before we could end the Mortia."

Maria shakes her head, her voice trembling. "We hide. We pray. We wait. And now you're here."

Cybele's hands cup my face, her eyes shining. "You came back. You came home."

A creaking from the floorboards draws our attention to the doorway, where we find Aero standing, a smile plastered across his handsome face. Aunt Cybele waves him over to us. "Well, get in here, sailor. This celebration isn't complete without you."

Aero steps forward, posture straightening as though he's preparing for battle. "I, uh...didn't want to intrude."

Maria snorts, wiping her cheeks with the back of her hand. "Intrude? Boy, you helped bring our girl home. That earns you a seat at our table for the rest of your life."

Aero blinks, caught between gratitude and mild panic. "That's...very generous."

Cybele reaches out and grabs his wrist, tugging him closer with surprising strength. "Generous? Please. You think we're letting the man who kept our Evanthe alive just stand in the doorway like a stranger?"

Maria nods firmly. "You're family now—whether you like it or not."

Aero glances at me, as if silently asking whether this is safe. I laugh, wiping my own tears. "You might as well surrender. They don't take no for an answer."

Cybele pats his cheek—gently, but with the authority of someone who has raised half a village. "Good. He looks like he needs feeding. Has anyone fed you? You're all bone and storm."

Aero's ears redden. "I...eat."

"Not enough," Maria declares. "Sit. We'll fix that."

Cybele leans in, lowering her voice conspiratorially. "And don't you worry, dear. We'll teach you how to handle our Eva. She's a handful."

Aero's mouth curves into a small, helpless smile. "I'm aware."

Maria laughs, delighted. "Oh, he's perfect."

I shake my head, warmth blooming in my chest as Aero finally lets himself be pulled into the circle of their affection.

The cottage fills with our voices, our laughter. No matter what lies ahead, it feels so good to be home.

The cottage smells faintly of earth and smoke, the kind of scent that clings to stone walls after years of hardship. My aunts move with quiet purpose, their hands steady even though I can see the tremor of emotion in their fingers. They brew tea with what herbs remain. A little lavender, some clove, and anise. The lavender is brittle, and the clove a bit too sharp, but together they make something warm and comforting.

Steam swirls upward from the clay cups, curling into the air like ghosts. I sit at the table, my hands wrapped around the cup, the warmth seeping into my skin. My voice cracks at first but steadies as I begin to recount everything.

"The veil," I say softly, my eyes fixed on the steam. "The Fae have been through so much. Then the bloom cracked. The rift wouldn't close." I look at Aero. "In fact, I'm not sure if it ever did close. Then there was battle after battle. And now we're here, but...Sorrow. She's gone."

The words spill out, heavy and relentless. I tell them of the fractured forests, of the river that glows with enchantment, of the bloom that remembered me when I thought I was lost. I tell them of Sorrow, her sacrifice, the way her laughter still echoes in my chest. I tell them of Skira, of her insistent voice. How I had cursed her persistence but now miss it with every breath.

Aunt Maria presses a hand to her lips. "Oh, child..."

"She was relentless," I continue, staring into the steam of my tea. "Always pushing. Always reminding me of what I didn't want to face. But she kept me alive, even when I didn't want to hear her."

Aunt Cybele leans forward, her eyes soft. "Some voices stay with us long after they're gone."

I nod, breath shaking. "Hers does."

I draw in a slow breath, steadying myself. "And then... the Mortia."

Both aunts stiffen, their fingers tightening around their cups.

"It wasn't just a creature," I say. "It was a hunger. A shadow that remembered every wound the realm ever suffered. It fed on fear, on grief." My hands tremble around the cup. "It wanted to unmake everything."

Maria's voice cracks. "How did you stop something like that?"

I lift my gaze to them, the memory sharp and bright. "We didn't fight it with strength. Not really. We fought it with what it couldn't understand."

"Which was?" Cybele whispers.

"Love," I say. "Sacrifice. The kind of power it thought was weakness." I exhale shakily. "We gave it everything we had. Aero stood with me even when the darkness tried to tear him apart. And the bloom…it stayed with me. It showed me what the Mortia feared most."

Maria's eyes widen. "And what was that?"

"Hope," I say softly. "The kind that refuses to die."

Cybele reaches across the table, her hand covering mine. "You faced a nightmare, Evanthe."

"And you didn't let it win," Maria adds, tears slipping down her cheeks.

I close my eyes, letting their warmth steady me. "We ended it," I whisper. "All of us. Together."

My aunts nod, their eyes glossy. Maria clears her throat. "We feared for your life the whole time. I would wake in a cold sweat from nightmares of the Mortia swallowing you whole."

Her hands tremble against her cup.

"And now the wretches are gone?" Aunt Cybele whispers, her voice fragile.

"All of them." I nod, my voice soft. "You can sleep through the night again."

Tears spill down their cheeks, silent but steady. They

press their hands to their lips, their shoulders shaking. The silence of the cottage fills with memory, with relief.

I swallow, my voice breaking. "Can I stay? Just for tonight. Curled up beside your hearth, like I used to."

They look at me, their eyes soft but firm. Aunt Cybele reaches across the table, her hand pressing against mine. "You are monarch now, girl," she says gently, lovingly. "You know we want you with us all of the time, but your people need to see your light standing tall. It's time you return to the High Tower."

My heart buckles slightly, disappointed I can't go on pretending things are the way they used to be.

"Why should one eat more, sleep softer, live higher just for bearing the title?" I whisper, my voice trembling. "That tower was built to separate a crown from its people. I don't want to live above them. I want to live among them. Down here, beside you."

My aunts smile, their tears still falling. "Then reshape it," Aunt Maria said softly. "Reshape it from the inside. Make it what it should have been."

I press a kiss to each of their cheeks, my tears mingling with theirs. "I will," I whispered. "I promise."

Stepping into the night with Aero, the air feels heavier, colder. The tower glows faintly above Parea, distant and cold, its light fractured but steady. I stare at it, my chest tight, my breath shallow.

"If I must claim that place," I whisper, my voice sharp with resolve, "I will reshape it from the inside."

Aero's hand brushes mine, comforting me, steadying me. The night stretches wide, the stars scattered across the sky, the glow of the tower above, a beacon that seems to watch without warmth. My aunts' words still echo in my chest, their insistence that I stand tall, that I claim the mantle of monarch. I promised them I would reshape it, and I meant it.

But as the silence of the lane presses in, my thoughts turn to what lay ahead. Meraki will not remain quiet for long. Aero's people will be arriving soon, fleeing the land that has been devastated by famine, looking to us for refuge. Their return will bring unique voices, new faces, but also their own shadows. With them will come their king.

The thought makes my stomach twist. The man who put Aero through so much pain as a child. The man who forced him, a boy barely old enough to understand cruelty, into a cage with a bear. I have seen the scars that torment left on him, the way his silence sometimes carries the weight of that moment. The treacherous king will walk these shores, cloaked in authority, his presence a poison.

I clench my fists, the bloom pressed tight against my chest. The thought of it makes me want to tear him to pieces, to strip away the illusions of power he wears like armor. He has hurt Aero, and for that alone I can never forgive him.

But I am tired. The journey has stretched long, the battles have carved deep into me, and my body aches with exhaustion. My heart burns with fury, but my limbs beg for rest. I look at Aero, his profile sharp against the lantern light, his eyes fixed on the horizon. He carries his storm quietly, but I feel it through the bond.

"We will face him," I whisper. "Not tonight. But soon."

Aero's jaw tightens, his silence speaking louder than words. He knows. He remembers even if he doesn't want to. He has carried it all these years.

I lift my gaze to the tower again, its glow fractured against the night sky. "I will reshape it from the inside. And when his shadow falls across Meraki, I will not let it linger."

The stars scatter above us, as if my words have rearranged fate itself. The earth hums faintly beneath our feet, and the night stretches wide with promise and threat. Aero's people will indeed return. The king will come. And I will be ready. Tired, yes, but ready.

30
AERO

The marble steps of the High Tower rise before us, gleaming faintly in the last light of day. Each one carries the weight of centuries, carved to impress, polished to intimidate. My boots strike against them with a rhythm that feels too loud in the silence of Parea's scarred streets. Eva walks beside me, her shoulders squared, her eyes fixed on the doors above.

When we reach the summit, the massive doors groan as they open, their hinges protesting against years of disuse. The sound echoes through the chamber beyond, a hollow reminder that this place is built to last even when the city around it bleeds. Inside, polished floors stretch wide, untouched tapestries hang in perfect order, and golden sconces flicker with enchanted flames that have never gone out.

Eva's voice breaks the silence. "The city bleeds, and yet this place remains untouched. It feels wrong."

I watch her face as she speaks. Her jaw is tight, and her

eyes scan every corner like she is seeing it for the first time. She has walked these halls before, but tonight they seem foreign to her, alien. Outside, the streets are scarred. Their walls scorched, windows shattered, blood dried in alleyways. Inside, the chambers gleam, perfumed faintly with lavender and cedar. The contrast is staggering. This was built to elevate. But it feels like isolation.

The throne room stretches before us, silent, its air heavy with the faint perfume. The tapestries depict victories long past, battles fought during many Noonsnights by monarchs who believed themselves divine. The marble gleams beneath our feet, reflecting the flicker of enchanted flame. It is beautiful, but it is hollow.

A knock breaks the silence. The sound is sharp, urgent, cutting through the stillness. Hera stands at the threshold, her face pale but steady. Feliks is beside her, his hand resting protectively on her back, his eyes darting between us and the hall behind him.

Hera's voice is urgent. "Your aunts, are they alright?"

Eva steps forward, her voice trembling slightly but steady. "Yes. Thank the Great Divine." She pauses, her eyes softening, her breath catching. "Your mother?"

Hera's eyes soften, her lips trembling into a faint smile. "Alive. She's frail, but stubborn as ever."

Feliks adds, his voice tinged with humor and sorrow, "She tried to make soup with nothing but salt and a prayer."

I smile faintly, the tension easing between us for a moment. "Even in ruin, the roots hold."

But the moment does not last. Hera's gaze shifts, her

voice hesitant. "I told her about our relationship...and that he's from Baros."

Eva's reaction is immediate, sharp. Her eyes widen, her voice rises. "Hera! We can't go telling people about this—not until the time is right."

Hera nods quickly, her eyes downcast, her voice trembling. "I know, I know. I made her swear to keep it between us."

Her hand drifts to her midsection, a gesture that does not go unnoticed. Her fingers press lightly against her belly, her eyes flickering with fear and hope. "It's just... I wasn't ready to tell her about this. And I needed to tell her one honest thing. After everything she's been through, and without me here through the worst of it, I couldn't keep everything from her."

I shift my gaze to Feliks. His face is tight with guilt, his eyes heavy. He looks like he's the one who broke something, even though all he did was love her. I suppose I would feel the same if it were Eva.

Feliks steps forward, his voice steady but tinged with worry. "Eva, we have to tell them all soon anyway. It would be so much worse if they arrive and take everyone by surprise."

Eva hesitates, her breath shallow, her eyes darting between us. Then she nods slowly, her voice soft but firm. "You're right. But we do it carefully. On our terms."

The silence presses in again, heavy and suffocating. I feel the weight of what is coming, the storm building around us. They will all know soon. If this goes wrong, her people will never trust me. If they don't accept me, I can't make her choose between me and her place among them. It's who she is meant to be.

I look at Eva, her wild mahogany hair spilling around her shoulders, her eyes fixed on the throne that looms above us. She is monarch now, whether she wants it or not. The people will look to her, will demand her light, her strength. And with my people arriving soon, with their treacherous king walking these shores, all Hades could break loose.

This is the man who made my childhood a nightmare and then let me believe I should be grateful for it. The man who forced me into a cage with a bear, who watched with cold eyes as I fought for survival. The scars of that moment have never left me. They live in my silence, in the weight I carry. That darkness didn't end with me.

He watched as my brother Iason tortured innocent creatures in the forest. He knew the vile thing he was becoming and did nothing. The thought of him makes Eva's jaw tighten, her eyes burn. She wants to tear him to pieces, to strip away the illusions of power he wears like armor. I feel her fury through the bond, sharp and relentless. But I also feel her exhaustion. She is tired from the journey, from the battles, from the weight of memory.

We stand together in the High Tower, the marble gleaming beneath our feet, the tapestries watching with silent eyes. The moment is approaching, and we are caught at its center.

She wraps her arm around mine, and I lean in. "The truth is a force. And soon we will be standing in the heart of it."

Without pause, she replies, "There's no one I'd rather be standing beside."

———

The chamber is quiet when we enter, the heavy stone walls muffling the chaos of the city outside. Candlelight flickers across the room, casting long shadows that dance against the tapestries, softening the edges of the world. For the first time since we crossed through the veil, since the Mortia fell, there is silence. But it is not peace. The Mortia threat has passed, yes, but the tension of King Phineas's impending arrival looms like a shadow, pressing against my chest, whispering of old wounds and ghosts that refuse to stay buried.

Eva moves slowly, her steps deliberate, her eyes distant. She begins to undress, her fingers working at the ties of her tunic with a kind of absent grace. I watch her, the way her movements carry weight, the way her mind is clearly elsewhere. She is here, in this chamber, but her thoughts are already on tomorrow, on the people, but mostly on the king who will soon walk these streets.

I step behind her, my hands steady, my breath soft against her hair. I wrap my arms around her waist, pulling her gently against me. "Just one night," I whisper, my voice deep, pleading. "Let's forget the world."

She turns, her hands finding my chest, her fingers splaying over the steady rhythm of my heart. Leaning in, she presses her forehead against mine, our breath mingling in the candlelit quiet. Her eyes close, her lashes brush against her cheeks, and for a moment, the weight of tomorrow eases.

I kiss her, slow at first, melting into her. Then deeper, more urgent, as though the world itself might vanish if I don't hold her close enough. My hands move to her back, tracing the lines of old scars and new strength, memorizing the map of her survival.

Her tunic slips from her shoulders, the fabric falling away like a sigh. I help her out of it gently, reverently, my fingers lingering against her skin. She undresses me in turn, her touch lingering at my collarbone, then my ribs, as if memorizing me all over again, as if reminding herself that I am here, alive, hers.

We fall into the bed together, limbs tangling, skin warm against skin. The linens are cool, the air heavy with candle smoke and sea salt. I trail kisses down her shoulder, her collarbone, the dip of her waist, each touch a vow, each breath a promise.

Eva arches into me, her fingers threading through my hair, her breath growing heavier with each touch. Our movements are slow, deliberate, not about urgency or escape, but claiming each other in the quiet. Reminding ourselves that we are more than guardians or deities, more than battles and scars.

I call out her name like a vow, my voice breaking against her skin. She answers with a soft gasp, her body responding to every shift of mine, every press, every breath.

We move together, rhythm building like a tide, gentle, then cresting at the top, and crashing into oblivion. We lie here, hearts still hammering inside our chests. Then a welcome stillness. The world outside fades, the chaos silenced. The shadow of King Phineas is pushed back for just a moment. There is only us, only the quiet claim of our bond in the dark.

The tide ebbs, the rhythm stills, and we lie together, our breaths mingling, our bodies pressed close. I trace circles on her bare shoulder, my fingers gliding along her skin. Her head rests against my chest, her hair spilling across me.

Outside, the wind shifts, the scent of sea salt and storm rolling in, pressing against the stone walls, whispering of what's to come.

I close my eyes, my hand steady against her shoulder, my breath slow. Tomorrow, we face kings and ghosts. But tonight, she is mine. And I am hers.

31
EVANTHE

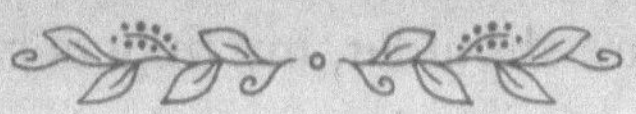

Morning light filters through the tall, narrow windows of the High Tower, spilling across the stone floor in fractured beams. Dust motes drift lazily in the air, catching the glow, turning it into something almost sacred. I stand at the base of the spiral staircase, staring upward. The marble steps curve along the outer wall, winding higher and higher until they vanish into shadow. My chest tightens at the sight.

I know what waits at the top. The place where monarchs once stood, looking down on their people as though they were distant figures, as though their voices could only be heard from above. That place was built to separate, to elevate, to remind the people of their smallness. I refuse it.

"I will not speak from above," I say, my voice steady. "I will speak among."

The words echo faintly against the stone, swallowed by the silence of the chamber. A reassuring warmth extends from Aero through our bond, and my tight shoulders ease a bit. Hera and Feliks stand nearby, their faces solemn, their bodies tense with purpose. Hera's hand rests lightly on her belly, and her eyes find mine. "This is good. They will respect you more for it. And if they don't right away, they will have to learn how."

Feliks hovers close, his hand brushing against her arm, his gaze flicking toward me with quiet concern. No one else argues or questions. They simply nod, their steps purposeful and quiet as they leave to gather the townspeople. Their figures vanish through the heavy doors, their footsteps fading into the distance.

I turn back to the staircase, my breath shallow. I place my hand against the cool stone of the wall, grounding myself. Then I begin to climb.

The steps are worn, their edges smoothed by centuries of monarchs who believed themselves divine. My feet press against them, steady, deliberate. I climb halfway, no farther. From this height, I can see the square beyond the tower's gates. The crowd is gathering. Their faces are worn, eyes wide, children clinging to their parents.

I pause, my hand gripping the railing, my chest tight. The sight of them fills me with both grief and resolve. They have endured so much. And now they look to me.

I draw a breath, steadying myself. My voice rises, carrying across the square.

"The Mortia is gone," I say, my words sharp, deliberate. "The Omen with it. You do not need to fear the night anymore."

The crowd stirs, their murmurs rising, their eyes

widening. Children clutch tighter to their parents, old men press their hands to their hearts, women cover their mouths with trembling fingers.

"You are safe," I continue, my voice steady despite the ache in my chest. "You may return to your homes. You may rebuild."

The words hang in the air, heavy but hopeful. The crowd shifts, their murmurs growing louder, their breaths quickening.

"And I will give you everything I can to help you do it," I say, my voice breaking slightly, my eyes burning.

The square erupts. Murmurs ripple through the crowd. Then sobs. Some fall to their knees, their foreheads pressing against the earth, grief and gratitude colliding in a wave that presses against me, heavy and overwhelming.

I grip the railing tighter, my breath shallow. I want to tell them I understand. That I have lost Sorrow, my sister, my laughter. That I have lost my father, his silence pressing against me even now. That I have lost pieces of myself, fragments of who I was before the veil, before the battle, before the crown.

But I do not.

"They need strength," I whisper to myself, my voice low, steady. "Not sorrow. I will be that for them."

The crowd continues to weep, their voices rising, their bodies trembling. I stand halfway up the staircase, my hand steady against the railing, my voice carrying across the square. I do not speak of loss. I do not speak of grief. I speak of safety, of rebuilding, of hope.

"Look at one another," I call out, my voice firm but

warm. "You stand here today. You have endured what no one should ever have faced. And still...you are here."

The sobs soften, shifting into quiet, desperate listening.

"You have survived the darkest nights our realm has ever known," I continue. "And now, at last, dawn belongs to you again."

A woman near the front lifts her trembling hands to her mouth. A child clings to her skirts, staring up at me with wide, wet eyes.

"You will plant gardens again," I say. "You will open your windows without fear. You will walk your streets without looking over your shoulder. The shadows that hunted you are gone."

A murmur ripples through the crowd—disbelief, hope, something fragile and bright.

"You will rebuild," I promise. "Not because I command it, but because it is who you are. Because this city remembers how to rise."

An older man steps forward, voice shaking. "And...and will it last, my lady? Will the peace hold?"

I meet his gaze, letting the certainty settle in my chest before I speak.

"Yes," I say. "Because we will protect it together. Because the realm stands with you. Because you are not alone anymore."

A chorus of soft cries answers me—relief, gratitude, release.

"You have given enough to fear," I say, my voice rising.

"Now give yourselves to tomorrow. To rebuilding. To laughter. To life."

A young boy lifts his voice, small but clear. "Are we really safe?"

I smile, the warmth of it spreading through me. "Yes," I say. "You are safe. And you will stay safe. I swear it."

The crowd exhales as one, like a single breath held for years finally released.

"Hope is not a whisper anymore," I say. "It is yours. Take it. Carry it. Let it grow."

The morning light filters through the tower's windows, spilling across the square, catching the tears on their faces, turning them into something almost holy. The air hums with memory, with promise.

I stand among them, not above. And I will be their strength.

Later that day, the air around the High Tower feels heavier, as though the stone itself is bracing for what is to come. I stand near the gates, the faint hum of the city drifting upward. Hammer strikes against broken beams, voices calling across ruined streets, the sound of life trying to stitch itself back together. The tower looms behind me, its marble walls gleaming in the fading light, its silence pressing against my back.

Three warriors of Parea approach, their steps measured, their faces solemn. They are broad-shouldered, scarred, their armor dented from battles fought not just against the Mortia-born vampyr. When they reach the gates, they kneel before me, their heads bowed.

"We want to serve you, Monarch," one says, his voice carrying the weight of conviction. "Let us help rebuild."

The words strike me harder than I expect. I hesitate. I have never wanted servants. I have never wanted people to kneel before me, but I know the desire to do something when your world has fallen apart, even if it's mostly simple tasks. My heart tightens.

"I don't want to be waited on," I say, my voice firm, my eyes scanning their bowed heads. "I want to walk beside you."

The silence that follows is thick but not empty. They lift their eyes, their gazes steady, their expressions softened by hope. They are not asking to serve out of duty. They are asking to serve out of belief. They believe in what we can build together.

I think of Princess Liri, her grace, her strength, the way she led not from a distance but from the heart of her people. She never stood above them. She stood among them, her hands steady, her voice carrying like song. That's certain. This is a new day for Meraki. This is a chance to make things different. What would Liri do?

I draw a breath, my voice softening. "You may have chambers within the High Tower," I say. "Not as servants, but as guardians, as companions in rebuilding."

Their eyes shine with purpose, their shoulders straightening. One bows his head again, his voice trembling with gratitude. "Thank you, Monarch."

They ask what they can do for me, their voices eager,

their bodies leaning forward as though ready to leap into action.

"Settle in," I reply, my voice steady. "Then go help the townspeople clean up the shambles. They need hands, not crowns."

Their eyes glisten, their faces breaking into faint smiles. They bow once more then rise, their steps purposeful as they leave to begin their work. The air feels lighter as they go, their presence a promise, their loyalty a gift.

I turn back into the tower, the silence pressing against me again. Aero waits near the council chamber, his eyes shadowed. Hera and Feliks stand at the window, their eyes fixed on the horizon as though it might betray us.

We gather in the council chamber, the air heavy with expectation. The marble walls gleam behind the tapestries that hang silently. The candles flicker faintly, casting a warm light upon them. I turn to Aero.

"The ships from Baros...they'll be here soon. We need to be ready."

His jaw tightens, eyes fixed on the horizon. "Yes, they won't just bring supplies or soldiers. They'll bring claims. They'll try to take what isn't theirs."

Hera presses her hand protectively against her belly, her voice low but steady. "And who will they try to claim first? You, Eva. Or you, Aero. They'll want to bind you both to their will."

Feliks shifts uneasily, gaze hard on the window. "I don't trust their timing. They'll arrive with smiles, but behind them will be chains. We've seen their deceitful ways."

I shake my head, refusing the idea of being bound by their chains. "We'll meet them with truth. No illusions, no crowns raised above the people. If they come with war, they'll find we've already survived one."

"And if they come with lies, we'll cut through them. I won't let Phineas twist this land as the men did before him," Aero vows.

Hera's eyes soften, welcoming the battle before us. "Then we stand together. Whatever they bring, whatever they demand, we answer as one."

Feliks exhales, letting his shoulders fall. "Good. Because if they think they can break us apart, they'll learn quickly we're stronger bound."

The words hang in the chamber, heavy but resolute. The silence that follows is not empty. It is filled with promise. We can do this. We are family now. Nothing can tear that apart.

32
EVANTHE

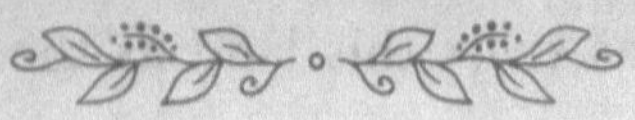

The knock comes before the sun has fully cleared the eastern cliffs. Two men stand in the doorway, thin as reeds, clothes torn from salt and wind, their skin sallow with hunger. They smell of brine and desperation, and when they bow, it is with the slow, trembling bend of men who have not rested in days.

Aero stiffens beside me. Feliks straightens from where he'd been sharpening a blade, his eyes narrowing.

"State your purpose," Aero says.

The older of the two messengers lifts his head. His lips are cracked, his breath shallow. "Your Highness...we come from Baros."

Aero's eyes widen. Overhearing the commotion, Feliks steps forward. "You crossed the sea in that condition?"

"In a fishing boat," the younger man answers, his voice barely more than a rasp. "The only vessel we could take without drawing the king's supply."

I recall the treacherous sea serpent we faced in the sea

on our way to Stillstar. The way the waves rose like walls and crashed like thunder during that storm.

Aero's steel-colored gaze sharpens. "Why risk such a journey?"

The older messenger swallows, his throat bobbing. "To warn you, my prince. The first fleet...it is coming. Within the next week or two."

A chill moves through the chamber, subtle but unmistakable. Feliks mutters a curse under his breath.

Aero's jaw clenches. "And what did King Phineas promise you in return for taking such a risk?"

The men exchange a glance of fear, resignation, something hollow.

"We get to live, Your Highness," the older one says. "We get the honor of taking part in Baros's return to our homeland."

The words land like stones in the room. Aero's expression doesn't change, but something in him goes still. Feliks looks away, jaw working, as if the words scrape against old wounds.

I step forward to address the weary men. "You will be given food, water, and rest. You are safe here."

Relief floods their faces so quickly it hurts to witness.

They bow again, deeper this time, as if their spines remember how to bend under something other than fear. I lead the guards to escort them away to the stables where they can clean up and find a plate of food.

Silence settles behind them, thick and heavy.

Aero exhales slowly. "He's moving faster than I expected."

Feliks nods once, grim. "He's desperate. That must mean the famine has gotten worse."

"I'd say that's a fair assumption, given his messengers have been reduced to nothing more than skin and bone," Aero replies, his voice somber.

I feel it too. The shift in the air, the tightening of something inevitable. What kind of leader sends two men so fragile into a raging sea to do his bidding with only the hope of a safe place to land and makes them believe that it is an honor to do so?

After closing the door behind them, the High Tower hums with a silence that feels heavier than stone. I stand near the council chamber window, watching the fractured light spill across the floor, when another messenger arrives. What now? His steps are hurried, his breath uneven, and he bows low before speaking.

"The elders request your presence in the throne room," he says, voice trembling. "Only two remain, but they ask for you directly, Monarch."

The words strike me like a bell. My chest tightens, my breath catches. I know what this means. The time has come to speak of Aero and Feliks's lineage, the truth that has lingered unspoken, waiting like a shadow at the edge of every conversation.

I dismiss the messenger gently then turn back to the chamber. Aero is already watching me, his stormy eyes fixed on mine. Feliks leans against the wall, his arms crossed, his eyes flicking toward the horizon as though betrayal might come crashing through the windows at any moment.

Hera sits nearby, her hand resting protectively on her belly. "What did they want?"

"They've called for me," I say, my voice low but steady. "The elders. Only two remain."

Aero's jaw tightens further. "They'll want answers," he says. "They'll want to know what you intend to do with Baros. With me. With Feliks."

Hera shifts, her brow furrowed. "They'll expect you to sit on the throne," she says softly. "To rule from above, as monarchs always have."

Feliks snorts, his voice sharp. "And they'll expect us to bow. To vanish into the background. They'll see Aero and me as reminders of everything they banished."

I draw a breath. "Then we must be ready. We must walk into that chamber knowing what they expect and knowing what we will give them instead."

Aero steps closer, his presence steady, his silence heavy. "They'll look at me and see the man they tried to erase, Eva," he says, his voice low, his eyes burning. "They'll see Baros in my blood. They'll see the cage, the bear, the cruelty. And they'll wonder why you stand beside me."

I reach for his hand, "Because you are not their shadow," I say firmly. "You are my sword. My strength. That means you are the strength of Meraki too."

Shaking his head, he crouches down, letting his head fall into his hands. Hera exhales, her voice trembling. "They'll look at me and see a woman carrying a child into uncertainty. They'll wonder if I'm reckless, if I'm selfish. Yes, I stepped down from my stone on Noonsnight, but I was once your enemy. They'll wonder if I can stand beside you, Evanthe, without faltering."

Feliks shakes his head, his voice sharp. "They'll look at me and see nothing but betrayal. A man tied to Baros by blood, standing in their sacred chamber. They'll wonder why you allow me to breathe their air."

His words cut deeper than he knows. I feel the sting of them in my chest, not because I believe them, but because I know the elders might. They will see his lineage as a stain, a reminder of exile and cruelty. Yet, when I look at Feliks, I don't see betrayal. I see loyalty carved into every scar, devotion in every glance he casts toward Hera, courage in the way he stands here despite knowing how they'll judge him. The elders will never understand the nights he kept watch while we slept, the way he fought with desperation not for glory but for survival. They will not see the man who has already given everything to protect us.

And Aero, his silence is heavy beside me. He carries the same blood, the same exile. If they condemn Feliks, they condemn him too. My heart twists at the thought. How many times must they be punished for the sins of men long dead? How many times must they prove themselves worthy of breathing the same air?

I know the elders will look at me differently as well. They will wonder why I stand beside them, why I let their presence stain the sacred chamber. It wasn't all that long ago that I thought they were nothing more than thieves coming to steal our throne. I was wrong, and I can't abandon them now. The thought of losing Aero is unbearable. They are mine. My people.

I step forward, my voice rising, steady, clear. "Then let them wonder," I say. "Let them question. Let them doubt. We will show them what I see in you. What you mean to the future of this island. That, without you, Meraki has no future."

The silence presses in, heavy, suffocating. The air hums with memory, with promise, with fear.

Aero breaks it. "And what of everyone else arriving?"

I pause, my breath shallow. "I will tell them the people of Baros are coming," I say. "I will tell them we must meet them with clarity, not fear. I will tell them we will hold a feast, a celebration of survival and restoration. And when their bellies are full and their homes are mending, I will tell them—not all of it, but enough."

Hera's eyes widen, her voice trembling. "Enough to make them see Aero and Feliks as more than shadows?"

I nod. "Enough to make them see us as one. Enough to make them see that we are not asking them to fight a war. But that I must be honest with them."

Feliks exhales sharply, his voice tinged with bitterness. "Honesty is a blade, Eva. It cuts both ways. They may not forgive us for carrying Baros in our blood."

I meet his gaze, my voice firm. "Then let them see the blade. Let them see the edge. Let them see that we are not afraid to carry it."

The silence lingers, heavy, pressing against us like stone. Then Hera rises, her steps slow but steady, her hand still pressed against her belly. "Then let us go," she says softly. "Let us walk into the chamber together. Let us show them we are not shadows, but we are light."

We move as one, our steps echoing against the stone floor. The corridor stretches endlessly before us, its walls lined with faded banners, its torches flickering weakly. Each step carries the weight of centuries, the weight of expectation.

When we enter the throne room, the air is heavy, solemn. The throne looms at the far end, adorned with sconces and spear tips, a relic of dominance, of separation. Its marble gleams faintly in the candlelight, its presence oppressive.

The two elders sit at a table beside it, their robes faded, their faces gaunt from grief and survival. I recognize them. They were once vibrant, their voices strong, their laughter carrying across the square. Now, they are hollowed by war, their eyes sunken, their hands trembling.

I move to sit with them, my steps steady. One elder, his voice cracked but firm, gestures to the throne. "No, Your Highness. You must sit upon the throne. We are here as your advisors, nothing more."

I stare at the chair, my stomach twisting. The marble gleams, the spear tips glint, the weight of centuries presses against me. "That throne is everything I hated about Noonsnight," I say, my voice sharp, my jaw tight. "I won't rule from above."

I ignore the request and sit directly across from them at the table. Aero stands behind me, his presence steady and his silence heavy. Hera and Feliks flank him, their eyes fixed on the elders, their bodies tense.

I draw a breath, my voice rising, "The people of Baros are coming here."

The elders' faces pale, their eyes widening. Their gazes flick to Aero and Feliks, thinly veiled disgust and confusion pressing against their expressions.

"This can't be true. Baros was built by the men we banished," one says, his voice sharp, his eyes burning. "They were cruel. They were the reason we created Noonsnight."

I nod, my voice soft but firm. "I know. But they're coming. And we must meet them with clarity, not fear."

The silence presses in, suffocating. The elders exchange glances, their eyes wary. One taps her fingers on the table. "And how exactly will this be accomplished?"

I lean forward, my hands steady against the table. "We will hold a feast," I say. "A celebration of survival and restoration. When their bellies are full and their homes are mending, I'll tell them only what they need to know as not to overwhelm them."

The elders shift, their robes rustling, their eyes flicking between me and Aero, between me and Feliks. Their faces are pale, their breaths shallow.

"We're not asking them to fight a war," I continue, my voice sharp, my eyes burning. "But I have to be honest with them."

The silence lingers, heavy, pressing against us like stone. The throne looms behind the elders, its spear tips glinting as if mocking my silly plans. An unshakable relic of the wars we fought against one another to sit upon it. I watch them, waiting. *Just say something, damnit.*

Finally, one of them unfolds her hands to address me. "As you wish, Your Highness. But do not be surprised if the people of Parea do not take kindly to such strategies. Their hatred of this...lineage is deep rooted."

———

The square is alive in a way I have not seen in weeks. The air hums with voices, laughter, and the faint strains of music played on old instruments that have survived war. Tables stretch across the cobblestones, overflowing with roasted vegetables, fresh bread, and wild herbs. The scents of rosemary and thyme mingle with the sweetness of baked barley loaves, and for the first time in what feels like forever, the air is light. Children dart between benches, their laughter ringing like bells, their hands sticky with honey. Mothers smile, and fathers clap along to the beat. The people of Parea breathe as though they have remembered how.

I stand at the edge of the square, beside Aero, Hera, and Feliks. My heart pounds, each beat echoing louder than the music, louder than the laughter. Aero's hand hovers near mine, steady but not grasping, his storm-colored eyes scanning the crowd. Hera leans lightly against Feliks, her hand pressed protectively to her belly, her gaze sharp but softened by the sight of children running free. Feliks watches the horizon even here, his jaw tight, his eyes flicking toward the edges of the square as though he's expecting shadows to creep back in.

Across the tables, I catch sight of Maria and Cybele. My aunts stand together, their hands folded, their faces lined with exhaustion but softened by pride. Maria's eyes glisten as she meets mine, and Cybele inclines her head in a slow, deliberate nod. It is not just approval. It is encouragement, a silent reminder that I am not alone, that the blood of my family runs steady in me, even now, their quiet strength pressing against my back like a hand guiding me forward.

I draw a breath, steadying myself. The words I carry are heavy, but they must be spoken.

"As I've said before," I begin, my chest tight, "you are safe now. The Mortia is gone. The vampyr defeated. And we will continue to rebuild."

The crowd quiets, their eyes turning toward me, their breaths shallow. The music falters, the laughter softens, the air shifts. I feel the weight of their attention pressing against me.

Then comes the harder truth.

"That said," I continue, my voice firm, "soon, ships will arrive. From Baros. From the lineage of those we once banished."

Murmurs ripple through the crowd, sharp and restless. Faces pale, eyes widen, and hands tighten around cups and plates.

"Aero and Feliks are of that lineage," I say, my voice steady despite the ache in my chest. "But they are not our enemies. They are our allies. My bond with Aero is strong.

He has stood beside me through every battle and will remain."

I do not mention my Fae blood. I do not mention Aero's divinity. Some truths must wait. Not out of shame, but out of care. There's only so much change these people can handle right now. The murmurs grow louder, concern rising. A few voices break through, sharp and questioning.

"How can we trust them?" one man calls, his voice trembling with fear.

"What if they come to claim what we've rebuilt?" a woman asks, her eyes burning with suspicion.

I stand firm, my voice rising above the crowd. "We meet them with strength. With unity. The people of Baros have faced a grave famine. They are tired, weak. Their younglings are all wasting away to skin and bone. We can't let ancient grievances get in the way of basic decency."

The words hang in the air, heavy but resolute. The murmurs soften, though they do not vanish. The crowd shifts, their eyes flicking between me and Aero, between me and Feliks. Aero watches me, pride and worry mingling in his eyes. His jaw tightens, his storm still simmering beneath the surface.

The feast continues, the music rising again, the laughter returning in fragments. I walk among the people, doing my best to listen and reassure them. A woman with soot-stained hands reaches for me first, her voice trembling. "Evanthe...will they treat us kindly? These people from Baros?"

I take her hands gently, hoping to steady her. "They

will come as allies," I say. "Not conquerors. They come because they must, because we are their only hope. And I will be here with you every step of the way."

Her breath shudders out, relief softening her shoulders.

An older man steps forward next, leaning heavily on a cane. "We've rebuilt before," he mutters, though fear flickers in his eyes. "But never with outsiders watching."

I meet his gaze, firm but warm. "You rebuilt after storms. After famine. After shadow. You will rebuild again. And no one, Barosian or otherwise, will take that strength from you."

He nods slowly, gripping my hand as though anchoring himself. A young boy tugs at my sleeve, his voice small. "Will they be scary?"

I kneel so we're eye to eye. "Some might look different. Some might sound different. But different doesn't mean dangerous." I smile softly. "And you are braver than you think."

He beams, the fear melting from his face. Two sisters approach next, their arms linked tightly. "Will they stay long?" one asks. "Will they change things?" the other adds.

"I can't be certain how long they will stay," I say. "But the only changes that will come are the ones we choose together." Their shoulders ease, their grip loosening.

A fisherman with salt-crusted hair bows his head. "You speak of hope, my lady. But hope has been hard to hold." I place a hand over his. "Then let me hold it with you," I say. "Let us carry it together until it grows strong again." His eyes shine, and he nods, swallowing hard.

A mother with a baby on her hip steps close to Aero, her voice barely a whisper. "Are we truly safe now?"

His eyes widen then soften with relief that someone trusts him enough to look to him for answers. "Yes," he says. "You are safe. Your children are safe. The vampyr are gone, and they won't be returning."

I smile as she exhales shakily, pressing her forehead to her child's.

As I move through the crowd, hands reach for mine, some callused, some trembling. I meet every gaze and question with all the grace I can muster.

"You are not alone," I tell them. "You are stronger than you know. And I am here. With you."

And slowly, like dawn breaking over the sea, their fear begins to lift. I know trust will take time. I know suspicion will linger, fear will fester, doubt will grow. But I have planted the seed.

"Let them eat," I whisper to myself, my voice low, steady. "Let them grieve. Let them question. We will still be here tomorrow."

33
EVANTHE

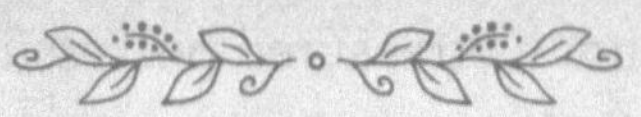

The feast is behind us now. The laughter, the music, the scent of roasted vegetables and fresh bread still linger faintly in the air, but the square has emptied. The tables have been cleared, the torches extinguished, and the people have returned to their homes with bellies full and hearts heavy with questions. The truth has been spoken, and now the waiting begins.

I wake before dawn, the tower walls cold against my skin, the silence pressing in. My body aches with exhaustion, my mind heavy with the weight of yesterday. I want to sleep, to let the quiet hold me for just a little longer, but footsteps approach. Aero's presence fills the chamber before he speaks.

"We need eyes on the western shores," he says, his tone carrying no room for argument. "I know it's all happening so quickly, but the ships will come soon. We should be ready."

I close my eyes, my breath shallow. He is right. Of

course he is right. But I am so tired. The people are still reeling from the feast, from the truths I laid bare. They looked at me with hope, yes, but also with fear.

I meet his gaze. "I cannot shake the memory of the elders' words, the stories they told us when we were children. I recall their voices, cracked with age but sharp with memory. They spoke of the men they banished, men who treated women not as treasured possessions but as property, as tools, as bodies to be broken. They spoke of violent hands and cruel tongues, of nights filled with fear and days filled with silence. They spoke of Skira's intervention, of the hope it gave them, of the relief they felt when the shadow of those men was lifted.

And now, I cannot help but fear I am taking all of that hope away. Just when they think the worst is behind them, I tell them the ships are coming. I tell them Baros will arrive. I tell them you and Feliks carry that blood."

Before I can go on, he leans in, wrapping his arms around my trembling frame. I cling to him as if the embrace will keep me from falling apart. Then he lifts my chin. "I want to take back everything those men did to your people. It torments me that I'm powerless to fix this for you. But we cannot wait blindly. We must be ready."

I step closer, the weight of his words settling into me like a stone dropped into deep water. "Aerb...you're not powerless," I say softly. "You're standing here. You're choosing differently than they ever did. That matters more than you think."

His jaw tightens, but I don't let him look away.

"What was done to my people can't be undone," I

continue. "Not by you, not by anyone. But we're not defined by what they suffered. And you're not defined by the position you were born in."

I draw a breath, steadying the tremor in my chest before I go on. "You're right. We can't wait blindly. We have to be ready. But don't carry their sins as if they're yours. I don't want you fighting ghosts that don't belong to you."

My hand finds his, fingers brushing his knuckles.

"Fight with me for what comes next. That's what we can change."

Nodding, he rises to his feet. I join him, moving toward the square, and we gather the volunteers. They are few, but they are eager. Pareans who stepped forward after the feast, their eyes shining with purpose. They are farmers, hunters, healers...ordinary people who have survived extraordinary shadows. They stand before me now, waiting for instruction.

I divide them into three groups.

"North," I say, my voice clear. "You are skilled scouts. You know the land, the cliffs, the hidden paths. You will watch the northern shores. Report immediately if ships are spotted. Do not engage. Do not linger. Return with speed."

They nod, their faces solemn. Everybody is tense with readiness.

"West," I continue, my gaze shifting to Hera and Feliks. "You will take this path. Your strength, your intuition will serve us well. Watch the western shores. Stay together. Trust each other."

Hera ties her last satchel upon her saddle and places her hand on my shoulder. "Let's save some starving babies and show King Phineas how it's done."

I smile brightly. "Be careful." She and Feliks nod in unison.

"South," I say finally, my voice softening. "Aero and I will take this path. Together."

Horses are procured, their hooves striking against the stone, their breath steaming in the cold morning air. Supplies are packed. We have bread, dried herbs, water skins, and blankets. Enough to last us a couple weeks if it takes that long. The groups prepare, their movements purposeful, their voices hushed.

I mount my horse, the leather reins rough against my palms, the saddle creaking beneath me. I turn back, my eyes scanning the city. The towers rise, the walls gleam, the streets stretch silent. The people sleep, their breaths steady but their dreams fragile.

"Let it hold," I whisper, my voice low but steady. "Let them rest. Let them have faith in me."

The horse shifts beneath me, its muscles tense, its breath sharp. Aero mounts beside me. I watch Hera and Feliks ride west, their figures strong against the horizon. The scouts riding north, their movements swift, their voices hushed.

Each group of us sets off in different directions, the city fading behind us. The air hums with promise, with fear. A shiver runs down the nape of my neck. I shake it off. With each step away, I carry the weight of their trust.

The southern shoreline is only a day's ride, but the journey feels longer. The terrain shifts beneath us as we travel through dense forest giving way to open stretches of scrub, then to soft sand that clings to the hooves of our horses. The air grows salty, the tang of the sea sharp against my tongue, and the sound of waves becomes a lullaby that follows us even before we see the water.

Aero rides beside me, his posture rigid as he scans the horizon. He doesn't speak much, but his silence is not empty. It is watchful, protective, filled with the storm he carries inside. I find comfort in it, even as my own thoughts churn.

When the trees finally break, the shoreline stretches before us. It's vast and endless, the sea rolling in shades of silver and blue beneath the fading light. The sand glows faintly, soft beneath our boots as we dismount. The horses snort, shaking their manes, grateful for rest.

We lead them to a clearing just beyond the beach, where the forest bends back enough to give us shelter but still leaves the sea in view. Aero moves with practiced ease, his hands steady as he begins to gather wood. I watch him for a moment, the way he crouches low, the way his movements are efficient, purposeful. He has done this countless times before, and the familiarity of it comforts me.

The fire catches quickly under his care. Flames crackle, casting warm light across my face, chasing away the chill of the evening. The glow paints his features in gold and shadow, his storm-colored eyes reflecting the flicker.

He prepares a simple meal—roasted root vegetables and dried fish, the scent earthy and comforting. He works quietly, his hands steady, his movements deliberate. I sit beside him, watching the smoke rise, curling into the night air. The stars begin to appear overhead, faint at first, then brighter, scattering across the sky like fragments of old yarns the elders would tell.

The fire burns low, its crackle soft, its glow steady. I tilt my head to the sky, my breath catching.

There it is, an outline in the constellations, the shape unmistakable. Skira, my chaotic guardian. The stars form her figure, wild and untamed, her presence etched into the heavens. One star twinkles brighter than the rest, sharp and insistent. My chest tightens, and my breath catches.

"You're watching me, aren't you?" I whisper, my voice soft, trembling.

Aero notices my gaze, his eyes following mine. "Skira?" he asks softly, his voice low, steady.

I nod, my eyes burning. "She's here. I can feel it."

We sit in silence, the fire between us, the stars above. The waves crash gently in the distance, the forest hums, the air filled with memory. Aero reaches for my hand, his touch steady, grounding. I let him hold it, my fingers curling into his, my breath steadying.

"Whatever comes," I say, my voice firm, my eyes fixed on the stars, "we face it together." The words hang in the air, carried on the rhythm of the waves that crash gently beyond the trees. The stars scatter, and for the first time in days, I feel peace. It's fragile, fleeting, a thin veil stretched over the unrest that still stirs in my mind. But it's peace.

The feast lingers in my memory. The laughter that tried to rise but tangled itself in questions and suspicion. The elders' words echo still, their faces pale with the weight of history. The people's eyes haunt me most: wide, uncertain, breaths shallow as they clung to hope even while doubt gnawed at them. And beyond all of this looms Baros, its ships, its lineage, and the storm it threatens to bring to our shores.

Skira's presence is etched into the stars above, chaotic and untamed, yet protective. Her guardianship feels close, a reminder of the forces that have carried me this far. Beside me, Aero is the embodiment of storm and silence, strength woven into every breath. Feliks stands as loyalty itself, devotion carved into his scars, courage unbroken even when suspicion cuts at him. Hera, with her belly carrying the future, radiates resolve, steady even when fear presses close.

And then there is me. My throne and the secret lingering in my blood. I wonder if my mother or father would be proud of me now. Would they see a daughter strong enough to bridge this divide, to stand at the cusp of history and hold two fractured peoples together? Or would they see only the cracks, the risk of failure?

The fire crackles, and the smoke rises. Aero's hand is steady in mine, his silence no longer heavy but soothing. Through the bond between us, I feel him pressing calm into my chest, reminding me that I am not alone. He leans closer, his shoulder brushing mine, and the warmth of his presence steadies me more than any crown ever could.

"This moment matters," I whisper, half to him, half to the stars. "If we falter now, the story will be written without us. And I want our story to be on the right side of history."

Aero squeezes my hand, his storm quieting into something tender. "It will be," he says softly. "Because you're the one writing it."

The sea hums, the waves crash. Above us, Skira's constellation burns brighter, as if listening. And for the first time, I don't just feel peace. I feel purpose. Fragile, yes, but alive.

34
AERO

The forest rustles and creaks around us, like it knows what's coming. I sit on a flat stone near the shore, the sea stretching out before me in a sheet of pale silver. The sun hangs low, casting long shadows through the trees, and the wind carries the scent of salt and pine. It's quiet...too quiet. The kind of quiet that presses against your ribs and makes you feel like you're being watched.

Eva crouches a few feet away, her fingers trailing through the sand like she's trying to read it. She hasn't spoken in a while. Neither have I. There's nothing left to say that doesn't taste like fear.

Two days we've waited here. Just the two of us. Watching. Listening.

I picture the ships. The sleek, dark vessels with sails stitched in gold thread, bearing the crest of King Phineas Vouvali. They'll be full of soldiers, trained to kill without hesitation. Full of wives, veiled and silent, including my mother. And children. The ones I grew up beside. The ones I still call siblings, even though I know now we share no blood.

One of them, I dread most.

Iason.

He's the kind of person who makes shadows feel safe. He is the embodiment of cold, calculating cruelty. I remember him as a boy. His lifeless eyes, sharp smile, always watching. He once drowned a servant for spilling wine. I tried to stop him, but I was too late. He found humor in my efforts. I can still hear his voice. "Weakness is contagious. I'm curing it." And then he laughed.

He's pure darkness. And I know, without a doubt, he'll be on one of those ships. Phineas will want him by his side. There's a reason he let Iason's darkness grow all these years. Why he never lifted a finger to put a stop to it. It's because Iason is a weapon to be used against anyone who might question his authority.

I clench my fists, and the tide responds. Waves lap harder against the shore, stirred by something deeper than wind. I breathe slowly, trying to calm the storm inside me.

If Phineas finds out the truth that my mother bore a child not of his blood, but of a sea god, he'll take her head. And then he'll come for mine and Eva's.

I glance at her. She's watching the horizon now, her eyes narrowed, her jaw set. She's trying to be strong. For Meraki. For me. She doesn't truly know how much danger we are in. I rise and walk to her, kneeling beside her in the sand. "You should rest," I say.

She shakes her head. "Not until I see them."

I nod. I understand. The waiting is worse than the battle.

"I keep hoping," she says quietly, "that maybe they'll come in peace."

I look out at the sea. "Phineas doesn't come in peace. He comes with a ledger. He'll weigh what he's lost against what he can still take."

She turns to me. "And what do we do when he tries?"

"We protect what's ours," I say. "We protect you. This island. I won't let him hurt you or your people."

"You mean our people."

"Yes, of course. I mean our people, Eva."

She studies me, her eyes searching. "Even if it means facing your family?"

I hesitate. "They were never truly mine."

"But they were," she says. "You loved them once."

I swallow hard. "I did. And some of them...I still do. Even if I shouldn't."

She reaches out and takes my hand. Her touch is grounding. Warm. "You don't have to carry all of this alone."

"I do," I say. "Because if I don't, they'll burn this place to the ground. And you'll be the first they try to break. He will go after you in an effort to get to me."

She doesn't flinch. "Then let him try."

I almost smile. Almost.

We sit together in silence, the wind picking up, rustling the leaves above. A gull cries overhead. The tide shifts.

And then I hear it. Hoofbeats. I'm on my feet in an instant, pulling Eva up with me. We turn toward the forest path just as two horses burst through the trees, kicking up sand and pine needles.

Feliks and Hera.

Feliks reins in hard, his horse skidding slightly. "They're coming," he says, breathless. "First wave. Five ships, maybe more behind."

Hera's face is flushed, her braid loose, her eyes wide. "They'll be here by nightfall."

Eva doesn't hesitate. "We ride."

I nod, already moving toward the horses. The waiting is over.

The tide has turned.

And I will meet it head-on.

The forest hugs the shoreline like a secret, and we hide within it.

I crouch low behind a tangle of sea pine, the needles brushing my arms as I peer through the branches. Eva is beside me, silent, her breath steady but shallow. Feliks and Hera flank us, their horses tied farther back, out of sight. The air is thick with salt and anticipation.

The ships have arrived.

Five of them, just as Feliks said. Sleek, dark vessels with hulls carved from ironwood and sails that ripple like black silk. They anchor just offshore, and already the smaller boats are ferrying soldiers to land.

The first boots hit Meraki's sand.

Baros soldiers. They are gaunt, sunburnt, their armor dulled and dented. They move like men who haven't eaten properly in weeks. I count them as they unload crates, barrels, and bundles wrapped in cloth. Supplies...or what's left of them.

Then I see him.

King Phineas.

He steps off the boat with the grace of someone who's never had to earn it. His raven-black hair is tied back, not a strand out of place. His eyes are ice blue, sharp as broken glass, scanning the shore like he owns it. His cheeks are fuller than his men's, his robes clean and embroidered. He's taken the lion's share of provisions, no doubt. Let his people starve while he dines on dried figs and salted meat.

My blood surges.

I feel the adrenaline spike, my pulse thudding in my ears. Eva places a hand on my arm, grounding me. I nod once then turn to the others.

"Let me take the lead," I say.

Feliks frowns. "You sure?"

"He'll expect it," I reply. "He'll assume I've made good with Meraki's monarch to benefit Baros. Let him believe it."

Eva's eyes meet mine. "And if he doesn't?"

"Then I persuade him," I say. "Or I stall him long enough to protect what matters."

She nods, but I see the tension in her jaw. She hates this. So do I.

We step from the trees, slow and deliberate. The

soldiers notice us first, their hands on hilts, eyes narrowing. But they don't move. Not yet.

Phineas turns.

His gaze lands on me, and for a moment, there's recognition. Not warmth. Just calculation. Then another figure steps into view.

Iason.

He looks exactly as I remember. Stringy pale hair hanging in his face, skin like parchment, and those same ice-blue eyes, so light they're almost white. He's thinner than the others, but his posture is straight, his hand resting casually on the hilt of his sword. Not a care in the world.

He isn't the strongest. But in a fit of rage, he's dangerous. I've seen him break a man's ribs with a single blow. And he wields a blade like it's part of him.

His eyes flick to me, and a slow smile spreads across his face. It's not friendly.

We keep walking.

I feel Eva beside me, her presence steady, regal. She doesn't shrink. She doesn't falter. She walks like the sea itself—calm on the surface but capable of swallowing kingdoms.

We stop a few paces from Phineas.

He looks me over, expression unreadable. Then his gaze slides past me, landing on Eva. And something shifts. His eyes widen slightly. His lips part. And then he speaks.

"Who is this stunning creature?"

Every instinct in me lashes out. I want to rip him

apart, to bury him in the sand and let the tide take what's left. But I don't move. I don't blink.

"This is Evanthe Siderus," I say, voice steady. "The monarch of Meraki. And my bonded."

Phineas raises an eyebrow, intrigued. "Monarch?" he repeats, tasting the word. "A woman?"

Eva doesn't flinch. "A leader," she says. "Regardless of gender."

Phineas chuckles, low and dry. "How...progressive."

Iason steps closer, his eyes never leaving me. "Bonded, you say?" he murmurs. "How quaint."

I ignore him.

Phineas studies Eva then me. "Well, Aero. It seems you've been busy."

I meet his gaze. "I've been building something worth protecting."

He smiles, but it doesn't reach his eyes. "Let's see if it's worth sharing."

The tide has brought them.

Now we see what they intend to take.

35
EVANTHE

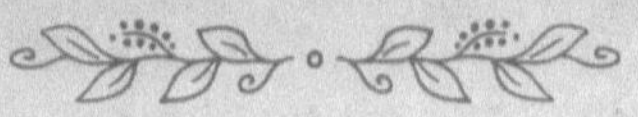

The sand shifts beneath my boots as I stand beside Aero, watching the tide deliver the people of Baros to our shore.

King Phineas has agreed, reluctantly, to come with us to Parea. He doesn't hide his disdain for the idea of following rather than leading, but he masks it behind a thin smile and a tone too smooth to trust. Aero stands tall beside me, his jaw tight. I feel his tension through our bond like a taut string pulled between us.

Then, from the largest ship, more figures emerge.

A woman steps down first. She's tall, graceful, her movements clearly practiced. Her hair is lighter than Aero's, a soft ash-blonde braided down her back. Her gown, though elegant, is dulled by salt and travel, the hem stained with sea spray. She carries herself like someone who's learned to survive by appearing composed.

This is his mother.

The woman who bore him. Who raised him. Who

stood beside Phineas while he tore Aero down, year after year. A rush of emotion hits me—conflict, curiosity, but mostly an urge to protect my bonded. I want to hate her. I want to understand her. I want to ask her why she didn't stop it. Why she didn't shield him.

She pauses at the bottom of the ramp, her eyes scanning the shore until they land on Aero. Her face softens. And then she smiles. It's a quiet smile, unsure, but unmistakable. I see the resemblance. The curve of her lips, the way her eyes crease. That's where he gets it.

Aero doesn't move. But through our bond, I feel the storm inside him. He's not angry—not exactly. He's remembering. He's unraveling. He's standing in front of the woman who gave him life and watched it be bruised.

Behind her, more figures descend. Children, young adults, all dressed in fine garments dulled by the journey. They carry satchels and bundles, their eyes wide as they take in the forest, the sand, the unfamiliar air. These are Aero's half-siblings. The ones who grew up in the palace while he was cast aside.

Feliks stiffens beside Hera as another woman steps down. It has to be his mother. She's shorter than Aero's, with sharp features and a gaze that flickers with recognition the moment she sees her son. Her hand flies to her mouth. Tears spring instantly to her eyes.

Feliks doesn't wait. He walks toward her, slow at first then faster. She meets him halfway, arms wrapping around him tightly, sobs muffled against his shoulder. Hera watches quietly, her hand resting on her belly, her expression unreadable.

The siblings gather around them, tentative, unsure. One of the younger girls reaches for Feliks's hand. He squeezes it gently.

I turn back to Aero. He hasn't moved. His mother is still watching him, her hands clasped in front of her, waiting.

I step closer, my shoulder brushing his. "You don't have to speak to her," I whisper.

"I know," he replies. "But I want to."

He walks forward, slow and deliberate. His mother straightens, her eyes shining. When he stops in front of her, she reaches out but doesn't touch him.

"Aero," she says softly.

He nods. "Mother."

She smiles again, but it's sadder this time. "You look strong."

"I had to be."

She flinches, just slightly. "I've had so much time to think about everything while you've been away...while so many have perished. I wanted to protect you. I just... I didn't know how."

"I know," he says. "I know now."

They don't embrace. But something passes between them—a thread of understanding, frayed but intact.

I give them space, turning to Phineas, who's watching the reunion with mild disinterest. He's already calculating, already deciding how to use this.

"We'll welcome you," I say, stepping forward. "You, your wives, and your children. The High Tower has room."

Phineas raises an eyebrow. "And my soldiers?"

"They'll set up camp outside the city walls," I reply. "We'll provide what we can. But Parea has only just begun to heal from our own battles."

He doesn't like it. I see it in the way his jaw tightens, the way his fingers twitch at his side. But he doesn't argue.

"Very well," he says. "For now."

I nod. "For now."

Aero rejoins me, his expression unreadable. I take his hand, and he lets me. The bond between us hums quietly, steadying us both.

The people of Baros begin to move, gathering their things, organizing their groups. The soldiers speak in low tones, already scouting the perimeter. The wives and children look tired, worn thin by the sea and the silence.

They need rest. They need food. They need safety.

And we need time.

As we lead them toward Parea, I glance at Aero. His eyes are on the horizon, but his thoughts are with the past.

We walk together, into the unknown, into the fragile peace.

And I swear to the Great Divine, I will not let them break what we've built.

***

We walk through the gates of Parea just as the sun begins to dip behind the mountains, casting long shadows across the cobbled streets. The air is thick with dust and the scent of ash that still clings to the city like a memory. The people of Baros trail behind us. They are tired, quiet, their fine garments dulled by travel and salt. King Phineas walks near the front, his chin lifted, eyes scanning every corner like he's already cataloging what he'll change.

The townspeople gather as we pass. They don't speak, but their eyes say enough. Curiosity. Distrust. I don't blame them. We've fought too hard to rebuild this place. To reclaim it from the Omen's ruin. And now we're bringing in the very people who once turned their backs on us. Who watched from across the sea as we burned.

Aero walks beside me, his hand brushing mine. He's silent, but I feel the tension in him through our bond. He's watching everything. His people, not all of them but many, his past walking behind him. The children of Parea peek out from behind doorways. Elders stand with arms crossed. No one cheers. No one welcomes.

I catch a glimpse of the broken fountain in the square, still cracked down the center. The market stalls are half-empty, the stone walls scorched in places where fire once raged. The High Tower looms ahead, proud but weathered. Its windows are dark, its banners faded.

Surely, the Barosians are wondering if this is what Parea always looks like. I want to tell them it's not. That once, it was vibrant. That once, music echoed through these streets, and laughter spilled from every corner. But I don't. Because right now, this is what it is. And they need to see it.

We reach the High Tower, and the guards open the gates. I nod to them, and they step aside, letting the Barosian nobles and their families enter. Phineas's soldiers peel off, heading toward the outer fields where they'll set up camp. Their king doesn't look pleased, but he says nothing.

Inside, the halls are cool and quiet. The stone walls bear the marks of battle—scratches, burns, places where darkness once collided with steel. I lead them up the winding staircase, past the council chamber, past the library, to the guest quarters.

"These rooms will be yours," I say, turning to Phineas. "There's enough space for your wives and children. You'll have privacy and guards posted nearby."

He nods, inspecting the space like a merchant appraising goods. "Adequate," he says.

I bite back the urge to snap at him, *You're lucky we're offering anything at all.* Aero says nothing. His face is unreadable, but I feel the storm beneath it.

Phineas turns to his family. "Rest. We'll speak more in the morning."

They begin to settle in, murmuring among themselves, grateful for the chance to lie down on solid ground. Aero's mother lingers near the doorway, her eyes flicking toward us, but she doesn't speak.

We leave them there, climbing the final flight of stairs to our own chambers. The moment the door closes behind us, I exhale. The silence is heavy. My nerves are frayed, my body aching. I sink onto the edge of the bed, pulling off my boots with slow, tired hands.

Aero stands near the window, staring out at the city below. The moonlight catches the edge of his jaw, the curve of his shoulder. He's beautiful. But he looks so far away.

"You okay?" I ask softly.

He nods, but it's not convincing. "I don't know what I expected," he says. "Seeing her again. Seeing all of them."

"She looked at you like she wanted to say more."

"She always did," he murmurs. "But she never has."

I cross the room, wrapping my arms around his waist from behind. He leans into me, just slightly. The bond between us hums, warm and steady.

"I'm proud of you," I whisper.

He turns, pressing a kiss to my forehead. "I'm proud of you too."

We're just beginning to relax when there's a knock at the door. Aero stiffens. I glance at him then move to open it. It's her. His mother stands in the hallway, her hands clasped in front of her, her eyes uncertain.

"I'm sorry to disturb you," she says. "I just...I wanted to speak with Aero, if that's alright."

He looks surprised. Not angry. Just surprised. I step back. "Of course. I'll give you privacy."

He reaches for my hand. "You don't have to go."

But I know better. He needs this moment. Without me. Without the bond humming between us. Just him and her. Mother and son.

"I'll be just outside," I say gently.

He nods, and I slip out, closing the door behind me.

I sit on the bench in the hallway, listening to the quiet murmur of their voices through the stone. I don't try to hear the words. I just let them speak. Let them begin to unravel the years between them. Let him ask the questions he's carried for so long. Let her try to answer.

The moon rises higher, casting silver light across the tower. The gaunt faces of Aero's family haunt my mind. If that is the condition the king's wives and younglings are in, I can only imagine what state the common people of Baros will be in by the time they arrive. The risk of taking them in is great, but what we are doing is good. I can hear my yia-yia's voice reminding me, *The path you pave for others is the one you'll walk tomorrow.*

This is the beginning of something new and fragile... but worth fighting for.

36

AERO

I step out into the corridor, the door to my chamber closing softly behind me. The stone walls feel colder out here, quieter. Evanthe is somewhere nearby. I know she's giving me space, even though I didn't ask for it. She always knows when I need it. It's hard to believe only months ago we were at each other's throats. Now, I'd tear anyone to shreds for even looking at her the wrong way. The Fae weren't wrong when they said a bonding between two souls is much greater than the hold any marriage could carry.

My mother stands at the far end of the hallway, her hands folded in front of her, eyes cast down. She looks smaller than I remember. Not physically—she's still tall, still graceful—but something in her posture has changed. Like she's finally let herself feel the weight of everything she's carried.

I walk toward her slowly. She lifts her gaze when I'm close, and I see the shimmer of tears already forming.

"I didn't expect you to come right away," I say.

"I wasn't sure I should," she replies. "But I needed to."

I nod then gesture toward the empty sitting room across the hall. We step inside, and I close the door behind us. The room is dim, lit only by the moonlight spilling through the high windows. Dust lingers in the corners. It hasn't been used in a long time.

We sit across from each other, the silence stretching between us like a thread waiting to snap.

"I know," I say finally. "I know Phineas isn't my father."

Her breath catches. She doesn't speak right away. Her fingers tighten around the edge of her gown.

"How long have you known?" she asks.

"Not long. But I've suspected for years. He never looked at me like I was his son. Not once."

She nods slowly, her eyes glistening. "You're right. He's not, and he didn't."

"Then who is?"

She hesitates. "A soldier. From the northern provinces. I was told he died before you were born. I loved him. But Phineas...he found out about our relationship. He threatened to kill me. To kill you. I had no choice. I was surprised he didn't execute me on the spot without question. I think my only saving grace was the humiliation he would face if all the people of Baros found out."

I lean back, the words settling into my chest like stones. I feel them through my ribs, through my spine. I've always known I didn't belong to Phineas. But hearing it, hearing her say it aloud makes it real. Even if she didn't truly know that man…that deity, who fathered me.

"You kept it from me," I say. "All these years."

"I did it to protect you," she says, her voice trembling. "Phineas is cruel, yes. But he's also powerful. If he knew you weren't his blood, he would have had you executed—or worse."

I laugh bitterly. "Worse than throwing me into a cage with a starving bear?"

She flinches.

"I was ten," I say. "Ten years old. And he locked me in with that beast to 'test my strength.' I still have the scars. I still remember the sound of its growl. The way it lunged. The way I screamed."

Tears spill down her cheeks now, silent and steady. She doesn't try to wipe them away.

"I'm so sorry," she whispers. "I should have stopped him. I should have done more."

"You should have done anything."

She nods. "You're right. I'd give anything to go back in time and stop him from hurting you. I was so weak. I don't deserve your mercy."

I stand, pacing the room, my hands shaking with fury. Not just at Phineas, but at the years I lost. The years I spent trying to earn love from a man who saw me as a threat.

"I'm not afraid of him anymore," I say. "He can't defeat me. Not now."

She looks up, her eyes wide. "Please don't underestimate him, Aero. Or Iason. I beg you."

"Iason?" I scoff. "He's a coward. A shadow."

She wipes the tears from her wild eyes and grips my shoulders, pulling me closer.

"He's ambitious. And Phineas feeds that ambition. I've heard them, behind the palace walls, talking about how easy it would be to replace you, to crown Iason instead, if you don't do what they want."

I stop pacing.

"They said that?"

She nods. "They said you were too chaotic. Too unpredictable. That Baros needs someone obedient. Someone controllable."

I feel the heat rise in my chest. I reach out a hand, pressing my palm against the wall to steady myself as the wave of anger washes over me.

"They'll never control me," I say. "Not again."

She stands, crossing the room to me. Her hands reach for mine, tentative.

"I know I failed you," she says. "I let fear guide me. I let him hurt you. And I'll never forgive myself for that. But I'm asking you, please don't let your power blind you. Don't let your strength make you reckless. You're more than what they tried to make you."

I look into her eyes. I see the pain there. The regret. The love she buried for so long.

"I don't know if I can forgive you," I say. "Not yet."

She nods. "I understand."

"But I'm glad you told me."

She squeezes my hand. "You deserve the truth. You always did."

We stand there in silence, the moonlight casting long shadows across the floor. Outside, the city sleeps. But inside me, something has awakened. After all the years of deception, there's finally clarity.

I am not Phineas's son. I am not his heir. I am something else.

Something stronger.

And I will not be replaced.

The morning light filters through the High Tower's windows, casting long golden streaks across the stone floor. I stand beside Evanthe at the entrance to the dining hall, waiting for the Barosian nobles to arrive. The air smells of roasted root vegetables, fresh bread, and sea salt carried in from the open windows. It's a comforting scent, but my stomach is tight.

They're late. Not surprising. Phineas never arrives anywhere without making people wait. It's a tactic. A reminder that he believes time bends for him. Finally, the doors open.

He enters first, flanked by two of his wives and a handful of his children. Their garments are fine but stale, wrinkled from travel, their faces drawn. They look around the hall with a mix of curiosity and judgment. Iason trails behind, his pale hair hanging in his face, eyes scanning the room like he's already measuring it for conquest.

Evanthe greets them with a nod. "Welcome. I hope you rested well."

Phineas offers a thin smile. "Well enough."

We lead them to the long table set near the hearth. The chairs are carved from Meraki oak, the cushions faded but clean. They sit slowly, surveying the room like it's beneath them. I take my seat beside Eva, across from Phineas. Iason sits to his right, his fingers drumming lightly on the table. The others settle in, murmuring among themselves.

Evanthe begins.

"We wanted to speak with you about what Meraki has endured. Before we discuss where your people might settle, you should understand the weight this island has carried."

Phineas raises an eyebrow. "Go on."

Eva doesn't flinch. "For too long, we were hunted. The vampyr plagued our nights, feeding on our people, tearing through villages. We lost families. Friends. Entire towns."

One of the younger wives gasps softly. A child beside her clutches her hand.

Eva continues. "We fought back. We survived. But the scars remain. The people of Meraki are cautious. Protective. They've only just begun to rebuild."

Phineas laughs. "Vampyr? Really? Are you certain? Such things belong in silly tales told to scare younglings into good behavior."

I move forward, but Eva places her hand on my chest, keeping my temper from getting the better of me.

"Yes, we are absolutely certain. They were blood-drinking fiends. I faced them myself, watched them drain the life of far too many."

Phineas leans back, fingers steepled. "And you think the people of Meraki will welcome us?"

Eva meets his gaze. "Not immediately. But I've done my best to assure them your presence won't harm what they've rebuilt."

I feel the tension rise in the room. Phineas doesn't like being told what to do—especially not by a woman. I know that look in his eyes. The flicker of disdain. The quiet calculation. So I speak.

"You will have all the plentiful land you need," I say, keeping my voice calm. "And enough distance from the other people of Meraki to give them time to get used to the idea. It is a wise strategy."

Phineas scoffs. The sound is sharp, dismissive. He doesn't even try to hide it.

"Wisdom," he says, "is earned through leadership. Not through exile."

I bite down on the inside of my cheek. Hard.

He still sees me as the boy he used to punish. The one he threw into cages. The one he humiliated in front of courtiers. He hasn't changed. Not really.

But I have.

Evanthe places a hand on my arm, grounding me. I nod once, then turn back to Phineas.

"You're not being exiled," I say. "You're being given a chance. A new beginning. But it has to be done with care."

Phineas studies me, his eyes cold. "I'll think about the offer."

The words hang in the air like smoke. I glance at Iason. He's watching me with that same smirk he wore as a child.

The one that says he's already planning something, already imagining how he'll twist this to his advantage. My stomach turns. This isn't over. Not even close.

We finish the meal in silence. The nobles eat slowly, their movements delicate, their eyes flicking between Eva and me. They're trying to understand us, trying to decide if we're threats or tools.

Afterward, we escort them back to their quarters. Phineas walks ahead, his robes trailing behind him like a shadow. Iason lingers, his gaze resting on me a moment too long before he turns away.

Once they're gone, I exhale, the sound sharp in the silence.

"You did well," Eva says.

"Make no mistake, he doesn't respect me. He never will."

"He doesn't have to," she replies. "He just has to listen."

I nod, but the sick feeling in my stomach doesn't fade. I can feel Eva watching me, worried. Still, I can't stop my eyes from flicking toward the door as if Phineas will return, his sword drawn.

"Phineas is thinking," I mutter to myself. "And when he thinks, people bleed. I won't let him bleed Meraki. Not while I still draw breath."

Before I can answer, the door bursts open. One of our guards rushes in, his breath uneven, his face pale.

"Monarch," he says, bowing quickly, "there's a confrontation in the city street. A Parean citizen and one of the Barosian men. It's escalating."

My chest tightens. Of course. It was only a matter of time.

"Where?" I demand.

"Near the market square," the guard replies. "Crowds are gathering."

I rise immediately, my steps steady despite the twist in my stomach.

"Take us there."

We move quickly through the tower, down the marble steps, into the streets. The air is heavy, the silence pressing, broken only by the distant sound of raised voices. As we near the market square, the noise grows louder, shouts and curses erupting.

The crowd parts as we arrive, their eyes wide, their breaths shallow. In the center, a Parean woman stands, her face flushed, her hands clenched into fists. Opposite her, a Barosian soldier looms, his armor gleaming, his jaw tight. Between them lies a broken basket, its contents spilled. Apples roll across the cobblestones, herbs scattered, bread torn.

"You think you can take whatever you want?" the woman shouts, her voice trembling with fury. "This is my stall, my food, my work!"

The Barosian soldier sneers, his voice sharp. "Your stall is in our way. We need space for our men. Move it."

The crowd murmurs, their voices rising, their eyes burning with suspicion. Pareans press closer, their faces pale, their breaths shallow. Barosians stand firm, their hands on their weapons, their eyes sharp. The air hums with tension, with fear, with anger.

Eva steps forward, her voice rising above the crowd, clear and strong.

"Enough."

The voices falter, the murmurs soften, the air shifts. All eyes turn toward her, waiting to see how their new leader will react.

The Parean woman's eyes burn, her voice trembling. "Monarch, he tried to take my stall. He said it was his right."

The Barosian soldier's jaw tightens. "We need space. We are soldiers. We have orders."

I step beside her. "Your orders do not include stealing from citizens."

The soldier sneers. "We are here at the king's command. We take what we need."

The crowd murmurs again, shocked to hear such rebellion. Fear presses in, suspicion rises, offense clearly taken.

Eva draws a breath, her voice steady, her eyes burning. "No. You are guests in this city. You will not take from its people. You will not treat them as property."

The soldier draws in a deep breath, his fists clenched. "We are soldiers. We are Baros."

I step closer. "And we are Parea. You will respect our people."

The silence presses in, heavy, suffocating. The crowd watches, their eyes wide, their hearts in their throats. The Parean woman trembles, her hands clenched now too. But the infuriating Barosian soldier stands firm. I need to diffuse this.

Eva moves closer, her voice softening. "Look at her," she says, gesturing to the woman. "She has survived war, shadow, hunger. She has rebuilt with her hands, her strength, her resolve. And you would take that from her? You would strip her of what little she has left?"

The soldier's eyes flick to the woman, seeming to search her for signs of such strength. The women of Baros did not carry themselves with such high heads. They would never slap the hand of a soldier for taking their apples. They would curtsy and offer them another. But they have to learn that isn't how we do things here.

"She is not your enemy," she continues, her voice rising. "She is your ally. She is the reason you have food to eat, a city to walk in, a place to rest. Without her, without them, you have nothing."

The silence is deafening. The soldier's jaw tightens, but his breath begins to soften.

I step forward, lifting my hand to the square before us. "You want space? You ask. You want food? You trade. You want respect? You give it."

The soldier exhales, his shoulders lowering, his jaw unclenching. He looks at the woman, his brow furrowing in confusion. "I...did not mean..." he mutters, his voice low.

The woman's eyes burn, her voice trembling. "You did. But you can choose differently now."

The silence lingers, heavy but shifting. The crowd watches, their breaths shallow, their eyes wide. Eva steps forward. "Let it be known, this city will not bleed for Phineas's pride. It will not break for Baros's arrogance. We will stand together, or we will fall apart. Choose."

The soldier exhales again, his shoulders lowering farther. He bends, gathering the spilled apples, the torn bread, the scattered herbs. He places them back into the basket, his movements slow but steady. He looks at the woman, his voice low. "Forgive me."

The woman's eyes glisten. She hesitates then nods slowly. "Do not take from me again."

The soldier nods, his jaw tight, but his eyes softened. "I will not."

The crowd exhales, their breaths steadying as the tension eases. I move beside Eva, placing my hand on her lower back. "One conflict resolved. Many more to come."

She nods. "Then we will resolve them. One by one. Until peace is not just spoken but lived."

The fire in the crowd softens, their voices quiet. The Parean woman gathers her basket, her hair wild and frazzled from the confrontation. The Barosian soldier steps back, his shoulders lowered.

As the crowd disperses, whispers linger. Pareans murmur of predictions for the future, both good and bad. Barosians mutter of caution, of change. The air hums with the unknown.

The Parean woman lingers, her basket steady in her hands. She looks at me. "Thank you," she whispers.

I nod, my voice soft. "You are strong. Do not forget it."

The Barosian soldier lingers too. He peers up at me, his voice low. "I will remember."

I nod confidently. "See that you do."

We return to the tower, happy to be within its walls for a moment. I exhale. "It will not be easy."

"No," Eva replies, "but nothing worth keeping ever is."

I nod. "Then we will keep it."

She looks at me. "Yes. We will."

Peace is fragile, but alive. And we will hold it.

37
EVANTHE

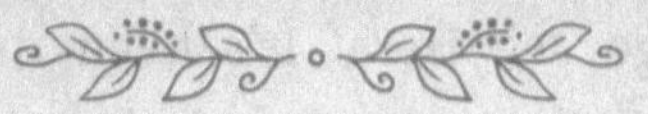

Aero's voice drifts through the stone corridor as I pass by the open archway to the garden terrace. Feliks sits across from him, legs stretched out, arms folded tight across his chest. The air between them is heavy like the sea before a storm.

"I didn't think he'd come," Feliks says, his voice low and bitter. "Not after everything."

"He came for power," Aero replies. "Not for you."

Feliks scoffs. "He never came for me. Not once. Not when I was starving in the barracks. Not when I was chained in the pit. He only comes when there's something to take."

I pause, hidden just beyond the arch. I shouldn't eavesdrop, but their words are raw, unguarded. I can't help myself. Aero leans forward, elbows on his knees.

"I'm sorry, Feliks. I didn't know it was that bad between you. I thought maybe he had stored up all his rage for me. He's your father," Aero says gently.

Feliks's eyes flash. "He's a tyrant. And I'm his mistake. A son he would never really want to claim as his own even if we share the same blood."

Aero doesn't argue. He just nods, the silence between them saying more than words could. I feel the ache in Aero's chest through our bond, the way he carries Feliks's pain like it's his own. I step away, giving them space.

I need to go see Hera. It's been days since we've spoken, and I miss her calm, her clarity. She always knows how to untangle the knots in my mind. I make my way through the west wing, past the old library and the sunlit corridor that leads to her chambers.

But something feels wrong. The air shifts subtly, like the scent of iron before blood. I slow my steps, senses flaring. My fingers twitch toward my mother's dagger at my hip.

Then I see them. Phineas and Iason step from the shadows near the tapestry alcove. Their smiles are too smooth, too rehearsed.

"Evanthe," Phineas says, voice like silk over thorns. "A word, if you please."

Caught off guard, I stop abruptly. "King Phineas, I'm on my way to see Hera."

"This won't take long," Iason adds, his hand resting casually on the hilt of his blade.

I take a step back. "I'm sure whatever it is can wait. Probably best if we discuss when Aero can be present."

Phineas moves forward. "You've been quite the influence on Aero. I wonder what he'd be without your...guidance."

A chill crawls up my spine, but I keep my expression still. "He'd be exactly who he is," I say, voice low. "With or without me."

Phineas hums, amused. "You give yourself too little credit. Or perhaps...too much."

Iason steps closer, blocking the light from the corridor. "Aero was always impressionable," he says softly, almost kindly. "Eager to please. Eager to belong. You've taken advantage of that."

My pulse kicks, but I don't step back farther. "I've done nothing but stand beside him."

"Stand beside him?" Phineas repeats, laughter sharp as glass. "No, child. You've steered him. Molded him. Turned him against his own blood."

I meet his gaze, refusing to look away. "If you believe that, then you never knew him at all."

Iason's smile doesn't reach his eyes. "We know him better than you think. And we know what happens when someone like you gets too close to someone like him."

My fingers curl at my sides. "Someone like me?"

"A monarch clinging to fading power," Phineas says. "A girl who thinks she can hold a kingdom together with sentiment and stubbornness."

Iason leans in, voice dropping to a whisper meant only for me. "Aero will have to choose eventually. And when he does...I wonder if you'll still be standing."

My breath tightens, but I force steel into my spine. "I'm not afraid of your threats."

Phineas smiles. Slow, cold, certain. "Oh, Evanthe. You should be."

I reach for my dagger, but Iason is faster. He lunges, blade flashing.

I twist, barely dodging the strike, but Phineas grabs my arm, yanking me toward him. His knife glints in the light, aimed for my throat.

I cry out. Not loud, more like a silent scream. A pulse of fear shoots through me. And then the air shifts again. This time, it's not subtle.

It's tidal.

A roar echoes down the corridor, and suddenly, Aero is there. Faster than thought, faster than breath. His eyes are wild, glowing with sealight, his body charging toward them.

He slams into Phineas, knocking him to the ground with a force that cracks the stone beneath them. Water surges from the walls, from the very air, wrapping around Aero's arms like living armor. Their eyes widen at the sight, their faces draining of all color as the water answers his call, his power on full display.

Iason tries to strike him from behind, but Aero turns, a wave crashing from his palm and sending the prince flying into the wall. Iason crumples, groaning. Phineas struggles beneath Aero's grip, but the water binds him, pressing him down like the weight of the ocean itself.

Aero's voice is thunder.

"What was your plan?" he demands. "You think the people of Meraki would follow you?"

Phineas laughs casually, even pinned. "Follow? No. They'll kneel."

"You're delusional."

"They've been weakened," Phineas sneers. "This vampyr you speak of...what a gift. It softened them. It broke their spirit. It wouldn't take long to send my soldiers to each town, to take back the island that was once ours."

I step forward, blood pounding in my ears.

Phineas turns his head toward me, eyes full of venom. "It's too bad you've fallen for the wench's spells," he spits. "She's poisoned you. I warned you of this witchcraft, but you are too rebellious. Just like your mother."

Aero goes still. Deadly still. The water around him begins to boil. I feel it through our bond. The fury, the betrayal, the heartbreak. He's held back for so long. For diplomacy. For peace.

But this...this is the line.

Aero lifts his hand, and the water rises with it, swirling into a vortex above Phineas's chest. The king's eyes widen, but he doesn't beg. He just smiles.

"You'll regret this," he says.

"No," Aero replies. "I'll finally be free."

The water crashes down. It's not loud. It's quiet, like the sea reclaiming a drowned man. Phineas's body goes limp, the light in his eyes extinguished. The water recedes, leaving only silence and the scent of salt.

Aero stands over him, chest heaving, eyes dimming. I move to him, placing a hand on his arm. He doesn't speak. I don't need him to.

Iason groans from the wall, clutching his ribs. Guards rush in moments later, drawn by the commotion. They freeze at the sight of the king's body. Then look to Aero, exchanging bewildered expressions. They murmur among themselves as they try to grasp how so much water has appeared from nowhere.

Aero straightens, his voice calm and collected. "Phineas attempted to assassinate the monarch of Meraki. He failed."

The guards nod, dragging Iason away. No one questions him. Not after what they've seen. We walk back to the garden terrace in silence. Feliks is still there, staring at the horizon. He turns as we approach, eyes flicking to Aero then to me.

"It's done," Aero says.

Feliks tilts his head. "Done, done? Why? I mean, I can think of a million reasons why, but what happened?"

"They tried to kill Eva," Aero growls.

Feliks's eyes widen as he turns to face me.

"I'm alright," I reassure him. "We're going to be alright."

No one mourns. Not today. Certainly not for a man who brought only pain. As the sun dips below the sea, casting gold across the waves, I feel something shift in Aero.

A release.

And the promise of a future no longer haunted by the past.

38
AERO

The air feels different now. I stand in the courtyard beneath the High Tower, the stone warm beneath my boots, the scent of sea salt and scorched magic lingering in the breeze. The body of King Phineas has already been taken away, wrapped in cloth, carried by guards who didn't ask questions. No one weeps. No one protests.

Except Iason.

He watched me kill the man he called father with eyes like ice and venom. But even he didn't cry. He just stared, calculating. I should've ended him too, but Evanthe needed me. And I needed her.

She stands beside me now, her hand in mine, her presence anchoring me to the moment. Her skin is warm, her breath steady. She's alive. That's all that matters.

I glance at her, and she meets my gaze. "Eva…" My voice comes out rougher than I expect. "Are you hurt?"

She exhales slowly, the sound trembling at the edges. "I'm alright," she murmurs. "Shaken. But alright."

I step closer, unable to stop myself. "He shouldn't have touched you. I shouldn't have let him so close to you."

Her eyes soften, but there's steel beneath it. "Aero—"

"I know," I say, cutting her off gently. "I know what you're going to say. That we have bigger things to worry about. That the people need us focused." I swallow hard. "But I need to hear you say you're safe."

She reaches out, her fingers brushing my wrist. "I'm safe," she says quietly. "Because you were here."

The words hit me harder than any blow. I look down at her hand then back at her face. "I thought I was going to lose you," I admit. "For a moment, I—" My breath stutters. "I couldn't breathe."

Her thumb strokes once along my skin. "You didn't lose me. Even if you had been out of reach, I would have fought like Hades."

I nod, but the knot in my chest doesn't loosen. "I know what this means," I say. "What comes next. The Barosians...my people...they'll need answers. They'll need leadership." I pause, searching her face. "But right now, all I can think about is you."

She steps closer, her forehead nearly touching mine. She's safe.

Phineas is gone.

The man who haunted my childhood. Who carved fear into my bones. Who taught me pain before I understood love.

Gone.

I thought I'd feel triumphant. I thought I'd feel free, but all I feel is hollow. But a rush of footsteps breaks the silence. I turn just as my mother rounds the corner, her gown trailing behind her, her face pale and stricken.

"Aero," she breathes.

I brace myself, but she doesn't hesitate. She runs to me, arms wrapping around my shoulders, her body trembling against mine.

"I heard," she says. "I heard what happened."

I nod, unsure what to say. Her tears soak into my tunic, and I let her cry. Let her mourn the man she once feared, once obeyed, maybe even loved in some twisted way.

"I'm sorry," she whispers. "For everything. For not protecting you. For letting him hurt you."

"I know," I say. "It's done now."

She pulls back, eyes searching mine. "You did what I couldn't."

"I did what had to be done."

She nods, and I see it in her face. The grief, the guilt, and strange relief. She doesn't ask for forgiveness again. She knows it's not hers to claim.

Behind her, Phineas's other children gather. They're quiet, solemn, but not broken. One of the younger girls clutches her brother's hand, eyes wide with uncertainty. Another boy stares at the tower, as if trying to understand what it means to live in a world without their father.

None of them cry. None of them mourn.

Hera arrives next, her steps quick, her face flushed. She rushes to Feliks, wrapping him in a fierce embrace.

"I thought—" she starts, but he cuts her off with a kiss to her forehead.

"We're alright," he says. "Eva's alright."

Hera turns to me, tears in her eyes. "Thank you."

I nod. "We protect each other."

Feliks steps forward, his expression grim. "What do we do about Iason?"

I glance toward the prison that contains the prince.

"He's the worst of them," Feliks says. "Phineas was cruel, but Iason...he enjoys it."

I know he's right. Iason doesn't want power. He wants destruction. He wants chaos. He wants to see people break. I open my mouth to respond, but a shout cuts through the courtyard. Two guards sprint toward us, breathless, eyes wide.

"My lord," one pants. "Iason, he's gone."

"What?" I snap.

"He escaped. Somehow. The cell was empty. No signs of struggle."

A hot, pulsing fury builds inside me. "How could you let this happen? He couldn't just vanish."

"There was hole dug beside the cell wall. We didn't see it before. Perhaps it was a secret passage someone dug up while hiding from the vampyr," the guard replies, his voice hushed.

Letting my head fall into my hands, I feel the blood drain from my face. The air thickens. The bond between me and Evanthe pulses with alarm. Iason is loose.

I turn to the guards, voice sharp. "Then we hunt him down."

They nod and rush off, already shouting orders to the others. I look at Feliks. "He won't get far."

Feliks nod. "He's smart. But he's arrogant."

"He's dangerous," Hera adds. "And he knows his life is on the line. No man is more dangerous than one with something to lose."

Evanthe steps beside me, her hand finding mine again. "We'll find him."

I nod, but my mind is already racing. Iason is out there. And this time, he's not latched to Phineas's leash.

This time, he's hunting on his own. I have to stop him.

The thicket tears at my arms like it knows I'm chasing a ghost.

Branches claw my skin, roots twist beneath my boots, and the sun mocks me with its slow descent. Iason's trail is everywhere. There are broken twigs, smeared footprints, scraps of cloth. But none of it leads anywhere. He's clever. Too clever. He's laid false paths like a spider spinning webs in every direction, and we've followed each one like fools.

Feliks curses behind me, breath ragged. "He's buying time."

"I know," I growl.

Evanthe doesn't speak. She moves beside me, silent and sharp-eyed, her presence the only thing keeping me from unraveling. I feel her worry through our bond, but she doesn't try to stop me. Not yet.

We break through the last of the trees and stumble onto the shore. The sea stretches out before us, vast and silver under the fading light. Waves crash against the rocks, and gulls cry overhead. It's quiet...too quiet.

Three Barsonian ships were moored here when they arrived. Now there are two.

Iason is gone.

I sprint down the worn planks, scanning the water, searching for a sail, a shadow, a sign. Nothing. Just the endless churn of the tide and the mocking horizon.

"He took the Virelia," Feliks says, pointing to the empty berth. "Fastest of the fleet."

"He planned this," I mutter. "Every step."

Evanthe touches my arm. "Aero..."

But I'm already moving. I leap onto the nearest ship—the Thessan—and shout to the crew. "We sail. Now." Feliks hesitates, eyes wide. "Aero, the winds—"

"Iason is out there," I snap. "And we're going after him."

Feliks climbs aboard behind me, sword still drawn. "Then we'll need every hand."

Eva follows, her expression unreadable. She doesn't try to stop me. Not yet. The sails unfurl, and the ship groans as it pulls away from the dock. The sea welcomes us with a slap of salt and spray. I stand at the bow, eyes fixed on the horizon, heart pounding with fury. Iason had a head start, but I have rage. Rage burns longer than wind.

But hours pass. Maybe more. The sun sinks, and the stars blink awake. The sea stretches in every direction, indifferent to our hunt. The group works in silence, sensing the tension that coils around me like a storm.

Iason could be anywhere. He could be nowhere. He could be laughing.

Evanthe joins me at the bow, her cloak whipping in the wind. She doesn't speak at first. Just stands beside me, watching the waves. Then, softly, she speaks, "He's gone."

I don't answer.

"You know it," she says. "You feel it. Wherever he has gone, he is out of reach."

"I feel nothing but fury."

She turns to me, eyes shining. "You feel betrayal. You feel the weight of every wound he's ever carved into your soul."

I clench my fists. "He deserves to pay."

"He will," she says. "But maybe not by your hand."

I look at her, and the ache in my chest deepens. "You want me to let him go?"

"I want you to live."

The words hit harder than any blade. She steps closer, her hand finding mine. "If the treacherous seas don't swallow him, the Great Divine will. You know that. You've seen what justice looks like. It doesn't always wear your face."

I close my eyes.

I see Phineas falling.

I see Iason laughing.

I see myself, lost in a storm of vengeance, chasing shadows across an ocean that doesn't care.

"We have each other," she whispers. "That is all that matters."

I open my eyes. She's right. Iason may escape the blade, but he'll never escape the reckoning. And I won't lose myself chasing him into oblivion. I turn from the bow, the wind still biting, the sea still vast. And for the first time in days, I feel something close to peace. I've finally stopped letting them define the battle. Evanthe squeezes my hand, and I hold on. We sail into the night, and the sea, vast and unknowable, carries us forward.

39
EVANTHE

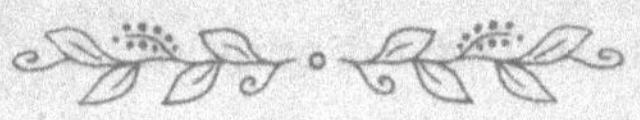

Three weeks go by in a hurry. The last of the ships from Baros crest the horizon just after dawn, their sails limp from the long journey, hulls weathered and groaning. I stand at the edge of the bluff with Aero, watching them crawl toward the shore like wounded animals seeking sanctuary. The sea glitters beneath them, soft and forgiving, as if it knows what they've endured.

Aero doesn't speak, but I feel the ache in him through our bond. It pulses low and steady, like a bruise that never quite fades. These are his people...what's left of them.

And there are so few.

I count the heads as they disembark. The children cling to their mothers. The elders lean on their makeshift crutches. Young men lift their hollow eyes, dragging their feet to shore, their skin red and mottled from the relentless sun. They move slowly, cautiously, as if unsure the land will hold them. The famine has carved them thin. The sea has stripped them raw.

Still, it is a good feeling to help them. To offer them food, shelter, safety. To give them a place to begin again.

My heart feels full watching the townspeople of Parea greet them with baskets of bread, pots of stew, and quiet nods of welcome. No one cheers. No one celebrates. But there is kindness. And that is enough.

We don't waste time. The kitchens have been preparing for days. The courtyard fills with the scent of roasted vegetables, fresh herbs, and warm grain. Children eat with both hands, eyes wide with disbelief. Some cry. Some laugh. Some simply sit and breathe.

Aero moves among them like a shadow, offering water, lifting crates. He is even speaking softly to the elders. But I see the tension in his shoulders. The way his eyes flick to every face, searching.

Still no sign of Iason.

None of the new arrivals have seen him. None know where he went. Some don't even know who he is. The unease coils in Aero's chest, and I feel it through our bond. It's not panic. Not fear. Just a quiet readiness. A knowing. If the day comes, we'll have to face it.

Later, as the sun dips low and the sky turns lavender, I walk through the streets of Parea. The city hums with life again. The broken walls have been mended. The scorched rooftops replaced. The market stalls brim with fruit and cloth and laughter. The Omen of Vampyr left scars. But the people have stitched them closed.

I find Hera in the garden behind the tower, sitting

beneath the old olive tree with her hands resting on her belly. She looks peaceful but tired.

I sit beside her, brushing a leaf from her shoulder. "You look like a goddess."

She snorts. "I look like a melon."

"You look like hope."

She smiles, eyes soft. "It's strange. For so long, I couldn't think about the future. Not really. Every day was survival. Every night was fear. But now…"

"Now you can dream."

She nods. "I think about names. About lullabies. About what kind of world this child will grow up in."

"A world you helped save."

She leans her head on my shoulder. "We all did."

We sit in silence for a while, the breeze rustling the leaves above us. Then I speak.

"I want you to stay."

She lifts her head. "What? I'm not leaving Parea. We only just got back here."

"No, in the tower. With me. With Aero. You and Feliks. You're more than friends now. You're family."

Her eyes fill with tears. "Eva…"

"You're my sister," I say. "Not by blood, but by everything that matters. And besides all that, it's too quiet there without the two of you bickering."

She laughs, hugging me tightly, and I hold her close, feeling the warmth of her and the promise of new life.

Then I hear the familiar creak of the garden gate and the soft shuffle of footsteps on stone. Aunt Maria and Aunt

Cybele appear, baskets in hand, their faces lit with surprise and delight.

"Well, look at this," Aunt Maria says, setting her basket down. "Two queens in the garden."

"Three," Hera corrects gently, patting her belly.

Aunt Cybele chuckles and leans down to kiss my forehead. "We thought you'd be buried in scrolls and council meetings."

"I escaped," I say. "Just for a little while."

They settle onto the bench across from us, the baskets between us spilling with dried lavender, fresh bread, and bundles of herbs. The scent of clove and lemon balm wraps around us like a blanket.

"I was actually hoping to talk to you," I say, brushing a leaf from Hera's shoulder. "About something important."

Aunt Maria raises an eyebrow. "You're not pregnant too, are you?"

Hera snorts. I shake my head. "No. But I've been thinking a lot about family. About what it means now."

Aunt Maria's eyes soften. "Go on."

"I want Hera and Feliks to stay in the tower with me and Aero."

Hera squeezes my hand, her eyes glistening.

"And I want you both to come too," I say, turning to my aunts. "You've always been my home. I want that home close."

They exchange a glance, the kind that carries decades of shared thoughts.

"Oh, Evanthe," Aunt Maria says gently. "That's a beautiful offer."

"But we couldn't leave the cottage," Aunt Cybele adds. "It's where your father grew up. Where you took your first steps. Where we buried our memories in the garden."

"I understand," I say, though a small ache blooms in my chest.

Aunt Maria reaches across the basket and takes my hand. "Just promise us one thing."

"Anything."

"Don't let that tower keep you too busy to visit."

I smile, tears prickling at the corners of my eyes. "I could never stay away."

Hera leans her head on my shoulder, and my aunts begin unpacking the basket, laying out bread and herbs like an offering. The sun dips lower, casting long shadows across the garden, but the warmth remains.

We eat together, laugh softly, and talk about baby names and old recipes. A lifetime of tragedy has made it impossible to imagine what this would feel like, but here I am. I guess I wasn't starless after all.

***

The moon hangs low over Parea, casting silver light across the rooftops and the quiet streets below. The city breathes gently now. No longer gasping, no longer bracing for the next blow. It's strange, this stillness. Beautiful...but unfamiliar.

I sit on the balcony of the High Tower, wrapped in a shawl, my fingers curled around a cup of warm tea. Aero joins me, barefoot, his hair damp from a late wash, his eyes soft with exhaustion. He settles beside me, and for a long moment, we just listen to the wind.

"It almost feels wrong," I say quietly.

He glances at me. "What does?"

"This peace. This quiet. Existing in a world where we're not under constant threat. I'm not quite sure how to exist in such stillness."

He nods slowly. "It feels like holding your breath after you've already surfaced."

I smile at the image. "Exactly."

We sit in silence again, the kind that doesn't need filling. But my thoughts are loud tonight. They press against my ribs, asking to be spoken.

"There's work to be done," I say. "Even now. Especially now."

Aero leans back, arms folded behind his head. "You're thinking about the island."

"I'm always thinking about the island."

He chuckles. "Of course you are."

I sip my tea, letting the warmth settle in my chest. "I keep thinking about Skira. About what she said to me before the vampyr came. About the violence we've allowed to fester among our own people. The rivalries. The grudges. The way we've let fear shape our laws."

Aero's expression darkens slightly. "She wasn't wrong."

"No," I say. "She wasn't. And I promised her I'd make it right."

He turns to me, fully now. "How?"

"I want to go south," I say. "To see if Petre and his

friends were able to set up their carved throne. Their Agape."

Each hopeful face of the group of travelers back in Meraki floods my mind. The four of them gathering around us. Then the woman Kallisto, who introduced us to their visionary...

This is Petre. Two moons ago, he had a dream that we would build a throne made of a single oak tree. This throne would be placed upon the highest hill along the southwestern shore of Meraki, and we would call it Agape.

Aero's eyes widen slightly. "You think they did?"

"I don't know," I admit. "But I want to believe they tried. That somewhere, in the quiet corners of Meraki, people are building something better."

He nods, thoughtful. "Unconditional love. Duty to their people. That was their vision. You know I'm not one for superstition, but I can't shake the feeling that we met them for a reason. That it was fate."

"I think you're right. And it might just be the way forward," I say. "Not just for them. For all of us."

Aero reaches for my hand, lacing his fingers through mine. "You want to bring that vision north."

"I want to learn from it," I say. "I want to see what it looks like when people choose compassion over control. When they build something not because they're afraid, but because they believe in each other."

He's quiet for a moment then says, "You've always believed in people."

"Even when they didn't believe in themselves."

He kisses the back of my hand. "Then let's go."

I blink. "You mean it?"

"Of course," he says. "You're not going alone. And besides, I want to see it too. I want to see what hope looks like when it's carved of devotion and honor. Their Agape."

I laugh softly, tears pricking at the corners of my eyes. "You always know what to say."

He shrugs. "I just know you."

We sit together, watching the moon drift higher. I know it's only been months, but it seems so long ago. So much has happened since we met the wanderers. We can only hope they survived.

Below us, the city sleeps. But tomorrow, it will wake. And we will begin again.

Not with swords or fear. But with love.

And the promise of something better.

EPILOGUE

Evanthe

It's been a little over a year since the last scream of the vampyr echoed through our streets.

A year since the fires died down, since the blood dried on the stones, since the people of Meraki looked up from the ashes and asked, *What now?*

And somehow, impossibly, we answered.

Parea is whole again.

The city hums with life—not the frantic pulse of survival, but the steady rhythm of renewal. The walls are no longer scorched. The rooftops no longer sag. The market vendors call over one another in a cheerful din, their stalls crowded with curious hands and quick bargaining. Children run barefoot through the square, their giggles rising like birdsong. The scent of rosemary and fresh bread drifts from open windows. Music plays again, its soft, joyful melody echoing through the corridors.

There is no trace of the Omen here. Not in the stone. Not in the sky.

Only in memory.

Today marks the anniversary of our Agape. The day we chose a new way forward. Not with crowns or conquest, but with compassion. With service to one another.

The people gather in the olive grove just beyond the city gates, where the sun filters through the leaves like gold dust and the wind carries the scent of salt and soil. At the center of the grove stands the new throne. It's carved from wood, tall and simple, its surface etched with symbols of unity and love without condition.

It is not a seat of power. It is a promise to the people.

Beside it, beneath the shadow of its grace, sits the old throne. The one that once stood in the High Tower, adorned with sconces and spears, polished to gleam like a warning. We placed it here not to honor it, but to remember. To remind ourselves what happens when we turn on one another. When we mistake fear for strength. When we forget that leadership is not dominion. It is devotion.

I stand before both thrones now, the people gathered around me in a wide circle. Aero is at my side, his hand warm in mine, his gaze steady. Feliks and Hera sit nearby, their baby cradled in Hera's arms, her cheeks flushed with joy and exhaustion. The child, little Thaleia, is the first born into this new Meraki. She is the future, wrapped in linen and love.

I take a breath, letting the moment settle into my bones.

"We gather today," I say, my voice rising through the grove, "not to celebrate victory, but to honor transformation."

The crowd is silent, listening.

"A year ago, we stood in ruins. We had lost homes, loved ones, hope. We were fractured. But we chose to rebuild. Not just our walls...but our ways. We chose Agape."

I gesture to the wooden throne. "This is not a symbol of rule. It is a symbol of responsibility. It belongs to all of us. It reminds us that leadership is not about being above—it is about being among."

Murmurs of agreement ripple through the crowd. I see elders nodding, children watching with wide eyes, young couples holding hands.

I continue. "We have rebuilt Parea. We have restored our villages. We have welcomed the people of Baros, fed them, housed them, and even healed some of them. We have not forgotten the pain their ancestors brought, but we have chosen not to repeat it."

I glance at Aero, and he meets my gaze. He smiles, pride beaming radiantly from behind his eyes.

"No sign of Iason has reached our shores," I say. "But if he dares to return, he will find a people not weakened by mercy but fortified by unity."

I welcome Feliks. He clears his throat. "We will protect what we've built. Not with vengeance. But with vigilance."

Hera smiles, rocking Thaleia gently. "And we will raise

our children in a world where love is not a luxury, it is a law."

The crowd cheers softly, a wave of warmth passing through the grove.

I step down from the stone platform, walking among the people. They touch my hands, my shoulders, my arms. Not as subjects, but as kin. I see the faces of those who once feared me, now filled with trust. I see the eyes of those who once doubted me, now filled with light.

Later, as the sun begins to set, we gather for a meal beneath the olive trees. Long tables stretch across the grove, covered in linen and lanterns. Bowls of figs and olives, platters of roasted fish, loaves of honey bread. Laughter rises like music, and so many stories are shared.

I sit beside Hera, watching her feed Thaleia mashed sweetroot from a wooden spoon. The baby gurgles, her tiny fingers grasping at the air.

"She's strong," I say.

"She's stubborn," Hera replies. "Just like her aunt."

I laugh. "She'll need to be."

Hera turns to me, her eyes soft. "Thank you. For asking us to stay. For making us family."

"You were always family," I say. "We just needed the world to catch up."

Aunt Maria and Aunt Cybele arrive with baskets of herbs and jars of lemon preserves. They kiss my cheeks, and fuss over my hair, then settle beside me with warm smiles.

"We're proud of you," Aunt Maria says. "Not for surviving. But for choosing to live."

Aunt Cybele nods. "And for helping others do the same."

I lean my head on their shoulders, letting the moment wrap around me like a quilt. As the stars blink awake above us, Aero finds me again. He pulls me into a slow dance beneath the trees, his arms around my waist, his forehead resting against mine.

"What's next?" he whispers.

I smile. "Everything. But we can start by packing our things for the journey back to the Fae Realm. Elder Thorne will be expecting us. I'm sure he has much to tell us, and I can't wait to see Liri, Diaspor, Bel, and Phira again."

"If 'everything' starts with packing, then I suppose I can manage that. And...going back to the Fae Realm with you? That part doesn't scare me anymore."

I laugh. "It feels good to think of going somewhere not because we need to save the realms but because we want to. Because there's more to learn. More to build."

His smile softens, the tension he's carried for so long gone. "Then let's build it," he murmurs, brushing his fingers against mine. "Whatever comes next...let's shape it together."

We sway together in silence, the wooden throne watching over us like a sentinel of hope. Around us, the people laugh and feast, unaware of the deeper truths we carry.

Neither Aero nor I speak of the gifts that live beneath our skin. The power that surged through him when he brought down Phineas, the quiet force I've felt stirring in me since the vampyr fell. These abilities are not for spectacle. Not for fear. Not for politics.

They are sacred.

And they will remain a secret, held close by our circle: Feliks, Hera, my aunts, and a few others who understand the weight of such knowledge. If the day comes when Meraki needs more than words, more than diplomacy, we will be ready.

But until then, we choose peace. We choose love. And beneath the shadow of the wooden throne, surrounded by laughter and lanterns, I believe it.

We are no longer waiting for the end.

We are writing the beginning.

AUTHOR'S NOTE

Thank you so much for reading *A Fate of Night and Nettle*, the final book in the Blood and Bloom Trilogy. Reaching the end of this journey has been an incredible experience, and I am deeply grateful that you chose to walk these pages with me.

If you enjoyed this story, I would truly appreciate it if you took a moment to leave a review on Amazon or Goodreads. Your words help other readers discover these books, and they make a tremendous difference to authors like me.

For those who are curious about what became of Iason after the events of this book, I have written a special bonus scene that explores his fate. You can receive it by visiting my website and navigating to the Bonus Content section.

If you would like updates on future projects, exclusive content, giveaways, and upcoming releases, you are welcome to join my newsletter. You can sign up through the Newsletter page on my website www.santanasaunders.com

ACKNOWLEDGMENTS

This story took months to bring to life, and even longer to shape into what it is now. I never could have reached the end without the unwavering support of my family and my team.

To my husband, my sounding board, my anchor, my closest friend—thank you. Your steadiness and belief in me carried this book through its hardest moments. I can't imagine walking this path without you. And to my girls, my three wild, brilliant spirits—thank you for letting me disappear into these fictional worlds and welcoming me back every time. You hold my whole heart.

My beta team, thank you so much for not holding back. Your honest feedback and random text messages made this story what it is today. You gave me the confidence I needed to take the next step. I'd be lost without you.

Jenn, my editor, thank you for guiding this story with such care and clarity. Your insight, patience, and sharp eye helped shape these pages into their best form. I'm grateful for every note, every conversation, and every moment you spent helping make this book its best.

Stef, your work continues to astonish me. Every cover you create feels like you reached straight into the heart of the story and pulled out its truest image. I'm always amazed by how you take my scattered notes and turn them into something breathtaking.

To every ARC reader who dove in early and cheered loudly, I'm endlessly grateful for your fierce love of this world.

And finally, thank **you**— for your readership, messages, reviews, and enthusiasm. You are the lifeblood of my writing journey. It's all for you and it's all because of you. I'm forever grateful.

9 798990 166325